IN THE
CLEAR LIGHT

IN THE
CLEAR LIGHT

———— • ————

A novel by

Fiona Kidman

W · W · NORTON & COMPANY · NEW YORK · LONDON

'Show Me the Way to Go Home,' Words and Music — Irving King,
Copyright © 1925 for all countries by Campbell Connelly & Co. Ltd, for
New Zealand: Chappell & Co. (N.Z.) Ltd, 77 Grafton Rd, Auckland

'Mairzy Doats' by Milton Drake/Al Hoffman/Jerry Livinston.
Copyright © 1943 Miller Music Corporation for Australasia. J. Albert &
Son Pty. Ltd. Used by Permission. All rights reserved.

Author's Note: For help with research the following are thanked: Ian
Kidman; my parents, Flora and the late Hugh Eakin; Jean Dickinson;
Robert and Mary Small; Tom Tague; staff at the Nestle's Factory in
Parnell; Wynne Colgan and Peter Harcourt.

This book was written during the author's tenure of the 1981 Scholarship
in Letters. The assistance of the New Zealand Literary Fund and its
Advisory Committee is greatly appreciated.

Library of Congress Cataloging in Publication Data
Kidman, Fiona, 1940-
In the clear light.
I. Title.
PR9639.3.K5P3   1985   823   84-22673

ISBN 0-393-01987-X

W. W. Norton & Company, Inc., 500 Fifth Avenue, New York, N.Y. 10110
W. W. Norton & Company Ltd., 37 Great Russell Street, London WC1B 3NU

1 2 3 4 5 6 7 8 9 0

For Ian Kidman, who was there,
and
Carol Noble, 1942 - 1979

Part One
CLARA

CHAPTER ONE

Clara has been waiting for Ambrose all day, without really believing that he will come. Sometimes it seems like a dream that he has ever been there at all, that he even exists. Yet the evidence of his dark presence is in the room, a vase of fat thick-petalled roses, the colours like clotted cream and red wine mixed together; milk and some eggs.

How those Americans live, she thinks. They seem to have so much of everything. Clara has asked Ambrose where he gets things from, but he only laughs at her; and the warehouses, where all the supplies for the Americans stationed in Auckland are kept, are so close at hand that she supposes it is a silly question.

Still, she said to him once, childishly, 'I won't eat what you've brought me if you don't tell me.'

He had looked at her lazily then and said, 'Oh yes you will.' But his eyes, protruding slightly against the blue-black skin, had studied her with care, as if to reassure himself that he was right. She knows that her illness is a weapon and is ashamed when she uses it, and knows at the same time, that she will continue to do so. Her contrariness frightens her. She thinks of herself sometimes as a wayward child and is angry at what she sees. She spends whole days practising self-discipline, of being, as she sees it, older and more sensible.

So that she has reconciled herself to his not coming by the time evening approaches. As on other days she listens to the tap dripping and wonders whether it is worth the effort of getting up to turn it off, until at last, as if by magic, or the innate workings of the curious plumbing system in Paddy's Puzzle, it turns itself off, justifying what she has chosen to describe as her laziness. Nobody's perfect. She listens to the sound of her own breathing and wonders if it will turn itself off in the end, like the tap.

But although the tap has been driving her mad, when it stops she does not hear it. It might have stopped for a minute or an hour before she notices. She wonders whether she will know when her own breath is simply going to stop functioning. A part of her hopes that she will not, because to know would be frightening; another part of her thinks that she would like to know so that she could give warning of the event. She would like to have her one last scene. She will want Ambrose to know, to have him summoned to her side.

Who else? Janice perhaps. She will weep a lot. Mumma? No, not Mumma. She might weep too, and Clara does not want to see her crying, for Mumma's tears are of the unshed and most painful variety. Ma Hollis from across the passage? Well so long as she doesn't bring Billy. None of it will matter much though, as long as they bring Ambrose.

She is dozing when he comes. There has hardly been time to detect his footstep outside before the key is slipped into the lock and the door opens. She is shocked at the suddenness of his coming when she least expects it, and overjoyed, and at the same time apprehensive. Until he walks in, she hasn't realised just how apprehensive. Worried, yes; and more than that, scared. When he walks into the room, her fear overwhelms her.

He stands looking at her, his green soldier's uniform a shadow on the wall of Paddy's Puzzle. Outside, the children of Cleveland Road scream 'Choc-lit, Choc-lit' beneath the windows of the chocolate factory.

She wants to put it off, now that he has come, to play some little game with him. Soon she must tell him about the letter. In just a minute more she will tell him that her sister Winnie has written to say that tomorrow she will be coming there to stay. But it is so momentous, and although she has prepared herself all day, when it comes to the point she is still not ready to tell him.

Part Two

HAMILTON TOWN

CHAPTER TWO

Winnie was shocked when the child tried to suckle her. She was lying in bed with a stack of pillows behind her with her own baby at her breast and Clara tried to take her other breast in her mouth. She smacked the child with the side of her hand catching her a blow on her face.

Clara slid off the bed whimpering and backed away from the bed. A red mark was starting to stain her pale skin.

Winnie was shocked at herself then. The child was only three, and it wasn't all that long, maybe a year, since Mumma had stopped breastfeeding her. Mumma always kept the babies on as long as she could; she believed that she wouldn't have another baby as long as she was producing milk, she seemed to keep on believing it even though it had failed her more than once. But she'd been all right for three years now, maybe she'd kept Clara on her even longer than Winnie thought. Mumma didn't tell her things like that, even though Winnie was grown up and had a baby of her own.

'Clara,' Winnie called to her sister. 'I'm sorry. Come here.'

Clara crouched down on the floor near the wall, still whimpering in the back of her throat. 'It's all right,' Winnie said. Her milk had stopped flowing, and the baby was grizzling. She felt a fresh flash of anger. Why wasn't Mumma looking after the child, now she had her hands full? She'd been looking after Clara on and off ever since the child was born. So maybe Mumma hadn't fed her after all. She'd never really thought about it until then. It was disgusting the kid trying to nibble at her, it was like an animal, having your own sister trying to chew away at you. Jeanna, the baby, started to wail. Clara looked as if she was going to flee, and Winnie remembered that the front door was open and tried to remember if she had latched the gate.

7

'Clara, it's all right,' she said again, only more urgently. 'Look, it's just that you're such a big girl now, and Jeanna such a little baby. I was afraid you might squash her. Come on, you can come back and sit on the bed if you're careful. There's a good girl.'

Clara inched towards the bed, and climbed back on to the edge. Winnie watched her, wondering if she would try anything with her again, but the child only looked back with thoughtful eyes. Or so it seemed to Winnie, though she dismissed the idea then as fanciful. Clara was too young to think about anything yet. And she would soon forget. Her breast filled with a painful but delightful tingling, the milk coming back and flooding down towards the nipple. She settled Jeanna back to her suckling and the room was peaceful again. Clara put her thumb in her mouth and remained, watching.

As Winnie had expected, Clara did forget. Yet she supposed that there was some time in her life when being with Winnie had changed. It was strange, because she spent more time with Winnie, yet Mumma loved her more. She never understood it when she was small, and she often wondered who she really belonged to.

She even had her name to thank Winnie for, though as she grew older, it seemed increasingly unlikely that the story she was told when she was small could really have been true. It was hard to reconcile with the Winnie she knew as she grew older. But Mumma had told her and she supposed it must be so, even though Mumma was strange and wild in a way that the world beyond their small railway house could not see. Her story was that when she was born Winnie was just nineteen and every Saturday night until she met Reg she went to the movies with her girlfriends, and the film star that everyone loved was Clara Bow, the 'It' girl, the mad flapper of the twenties; and the 'It' that she had, so the older ones said in shocked tones, was supposed to be s-e-x — Mumma could never bring herself to say the whole word, she always had to spell it. Winnie was crazy about her, just like all the other girls, and she begged Mumma to call the new baby Clara. She argued that whatever 'It' was suppose to stand for, it didn't really matter because everyone knew Clara Bow was really well behaved, because it was written into her contract that she would get more money if she was good.

The trouble was, that by the time Clara heard the story, Winnie had changed a lot, and Clara Bow had broken her contract and it was said that she'd lost a lot of money. That meant she was badly behaved after all, and Winnie flatly denied that she had had anything to do with the naming of Clara at all. 'It was a funny story we told you when you were little to amuse you,' she would say. 'Nobody really meant it.'

Not that Clara believed her. She went to see 'It' and 'No Limit', years later, sitting in the back seat of the Embassy with Robin who she believed she loved in those days, when they were having a revival of Clara Bow's old films. It gave her goose pimples sitting there and watching this blonde woman flapping around and making the audience laugh, and cry a bit too, and thinking that Winnie had had a vision of her becoming like the woman on the screen. She wondered then, what it was that had made Winnie so want to call her Clara, as if, in understanding that, she might somehow know more about Winnie herself. Some dream of a life which, even then, she knew was impossible for her, but which she still imagined might be possible for Clara? But she didn't really think so. Just the sort of madness that takes people over when they get an idol. For herself, she would rather be one.

Whatever it was, Winnie got over it quicky. Three years after Clara was born, Winnie was a respectable married lady and she had Jeanna who came to be called Jeannie, and later Caroline, and Clara supposed that they were her idols. And after a while, the story about her name had changed completely. Winnie said it was 'a good solid old name' and dug out that Mumma had a great aunt called Clara, and said that that was who she had been named after. Clara didn't really believe her and she didn't really care.

If she cared about anything, she supposed that it was the way people change, that people who laughed and had fun and once had dreams, could change so much that they had to cover up who they really were. Or had been. It was to do with Hamilton she guessed, and being stifled. It was about having two faces, one for your real self and one for the rest of the world, and in the end not knowing which one to believe. It was the reason for escape.

Winnie standing in light.

Clara remembered things which happened to her very early in her life, even if she didn't remember exactly that first time that Winnie hit her. But there was a starting point, maybe it was that event, from which time onwards she began to remember things very clearly. Robin would tell her that this was not true, that people only believe they remember things, when in fact they have been told them so often that they come to believe that it is they who recall the event. Because he was right about so many things, she examined this idea carefully, and decided that this was not true of her. Nobody would have told her the things she recalled. They were small things, tiny details, that the people to whom they had happened would be less likely to remember than the person watching, or things so intimate that, in Winnie's case at any rate, they would not have been repeated.

The kitchen of Winnie's house was at the back, with windows looking over a small patch of lawn. There was little to see for it is flat land round Hamilton, miles and miles of plains, first houses, then paddocks and cows. It might be said that Winnie's house had a view, by comparison with much of the town, for in the distance there was the blue line of Mount Pirongia. Closer to hand there was a struggling peach tree and a small plot of cultivated vegetables. Magpies, rude and incessant in their clamour, landed regularly amongst the rhubarb, and Clara was sent to chase them. She never knew whether it was intended as a diversion to occupy her, for she was a restless child always unloading pot cupboards and filling baths that nobody wanted and doing all the active annoying things that drove Mumma and Winnie to distraction; or whether she was actually being useful by chasing the birds.

Once when she was visiting, Mumma stood at the bench beside Winnie, her eldest daughter, swaying slightly on her knotted veiny legs and recited:

'One for sorrow
Two for joy
Three for a girl
and four for a boy.'

It impressed Clara and she thought that it was intended that the rhyming lines must go together and boys be a joy and girls be sorrow, and it worried her that their houses seemed to have more women in them than men, so that she was always relieved by the sight of men, and vaguely ashamed that she was not a boy, and sorry for Winnie that Jeannie had not been one either. She knew that Mumma had had boys and hoped for Winnie's sake that she would have them too. She was always meaning to be especially good for them because she was a sorrowful girl. In the end she gave up.

Winnie's bench was very white. She had scrubbed the wood every

10

day for as long as Clara could remember. There was a day in autumn that Clara remembered particularly. The sun made bright patches on the bench and the linoleum but it would not last for long. There were nasturtiums in a jam jar on the window sill. Winnie stood at the sink, her feet planted squarely in flat sensible shoes on the floor. Her clothes were all plain and sensible, and the first cold that bites the plains there must have already begun for Winnie was wearing a grey hand-knitted cardigan which made her twenty-four-year-old shoulders look more square and solid than they might otherwise have done. Her brown hair was cut in a neat blunt line around the nape of her neck and her clear skin looked as if it had been lightly polished along the cheekbones. On the open-faced shelves of the kitchen stood jars filled with ripe tomatoes and Golden Queen peaches in syrup, relishes and chutney. Today she had added crab-apple jelly and mint preserve. She had been storing up for winter. In the next room her baby slept. Clara had been very still all afternoon, unusually still for her, for the room was full of colour and pleasant smells, and she wanted to stay there with Winnie and not be sent home to Mumma who mostly sat and sighed in the little house at Frankton Junction, the suburb of Hamilton where the trains went, and which was not considered such a nice place to live, because of the soot and the railwaymen, who were working men, and not as prosperous as the people who lived on this side of the town. Mumma had resigned herself to Life but found it difficult to live it. Sometimes it seemed to have passed her by, and yet at other times she seemed determined to endure it in some strange and secret way which she demanded that Clara should share, and then the child would be afraid.

Mumma had tried though, in years gone by, to be that other person she would have liked to be. It had been her idea that the children called her Mama, and it was Clara, more than any of the others, who had corrupted it to Mumma. As over most things, she had stopped protesting, and Winnie and the older members of the family, of whom there were several, still called her Mama, especially in front of other people, but in conversation between themselves it had become Mumma. She was always neat and spent endless time ironing her clothes and rubbing at tiny spots, sewing incongruous little bows at the necklines of her blouses, peering at her needles through her thick glasses with her half-blind batty eyes. Mumma was careful of herself and she could pass for all right if you didn't know the truth about the Bentleys. She was proud of Winnie who had done well. Winnie had left Frankton Junction and moved to Hamilton. It didn't seem to matter that it was as far as she would ever go.

Not only that, Winnie was useful, particularly in the matter of looking after Clara. It meant that Mumma could still convince herself that her youngest and best-loved child was well cared for, while at the same time she could attend to the great passion in her life which was to grow potted cyclamen in a little glasshouse and sell them to people who had nice houses to keep them in. She had half a dozen orchids as well which were not for sale, except maybe very occasionally she would part with a flower for a special bridal bouquet. It made her sought after by the good (meaning rich) people of Hamilton. It was her stake in the world.

Winnie didn't really want to know why Mumma courted her so much. She liked to believe that it was still because she was the first-born, the best. Perhaps Mumma had encouraged her to believe that, for there was a certain wiliness about her. As for the other children, they had made their own way, those that were left. Two had died, both before Clara was born. It was hard for Clara to believe, when she grew older, that they had inhabited the same territory inside Mumma as she had, that that was as near as she would ever come to them. After Winnie there was Rita, who Mumma tolerated but regretted; she had married into the Junction. Then there were the two boys on farms, both hoping to be sharemilkers; Brian, and Frank, the younger and the next one up from Clara, and that still made him twelve years older than her.

What Clara particularly remembered that afternoon, was Reg coming in. It had been so warm and close in the kitchen and Winnie had sung a little to herself as she set by her provisions and she hadn't been cross or sent Clara outside to chase the birds once that afternoon. She didn't talk to her much, but occasionally she would pop something into her mouth, some morsel of food which conveyed approval, acceptance of her. Considering that they could have been mother and daughter, and would certainly have appeared that way to the casual onlooker, but were in fact two sisters sharing a kitchen, it seemed important to both of them that they like being together.

The door opened, letting in a gust of cold air. The sun had slipped quite suddenly and Clara knew instinctively that their afternoon was over. Reg usually bustled, he was that kind of man, slightly overweight and not very tall, barely the same height as Winnie. The Hoggards tended to portliness in middle-age though

Reg had a long way to go to that. They all had very fair hair which thinned early in the men, but there was something bluff and good-looking about them too. Clara had seen them all together at family gatherings, not Winnie's wedding, even she didn't pretend to remember back that far, and anyway there hadn't been many of the Bentleys at it. Mumma and Father had been there, but not all the brothers and sisters, because the Hoggards were all for small family weddings they said.

'We don't believe in big flashy affairs,' Mrs Hoggard had been heard to say, about that time.

What she really meant was that Reg hadn't made a very good marriage, and the Frankton Junction Bentleys were something of an embarrassment to the Hamilton Hoggards, and they couldn't think of any other way around introducing them to each other.

But Winnie had had a wedding dress, Mumma saw to that, and the best flowers of any bride in Hamilton that year. Maybe the Hoggards appreciated that, and Clara was sure that they were very nice to the Bentleys at the wedding. If they were patronising Mumma never said, and she kept the photos on the mantelpiece and tidied them as religiously as the contents of her glasshouse.

Whatever the arrangements they probably suited Winnie too because she only had eyes for Reg. Clara came round to understanding that she didn't know how to cope with the Hoggards any better than they did with her, at least not at the beginning, though she worked so hard to be a good wife and to live up to them that they soon appeared to forget. It might even have been, that in some mysterious way, they began to think of her as having been born a Hoggard herself. Whatever it was, it added up to sensible shoes, and lots of preserves and fishing up great-aunt Clara and pretending that the 'It' girl never happened.

On that autumn afternoon when she was five, Clara hadn't started trying to work out what made Winnie tick. She just felt the cold air as the door opened and waited for Reg to bounce in. But it bothered her straight away that he walked slowly.

She had been on the point of offering to go in and play with Jeannie who was crying in the next room. She was two by then and if Clara made funny faces and tickled her gently, she laughed and squirmed and turned off her tears. Sometimes Clara thought she would rather pinch the baby but she knew that she could win over Winnie by entertaining her, and that meant she would probably be allowed to stay the night. She did not know why she stayed on

13

in the kitchen but in the next room Jeannie quietened as suddenly as she had started her noise, and there was a tension in the room that held her.

Winnie raised her face, flushed and happy. Although she was tired, she was satisfied with her afternoon's work. She waited expectantly for Reg to kiss her.

Instead he stood behind her and put his hands around her waist and rested his chin on her shoulder. He didn't want to look at her.

'Look at what I've done,' she said.

'Nice,' he said.

'You're not looking,' she said pulling away from him so that he could see her jars.

'I said it was nice.' He answered sharply.

'What's the matter?' said Winnie, suddenly aware that there was something wrong.

'Nothing. Why should anything be the matter?'

'Reg?'

'Nothing. I told you. God, can't a man come in and touch his wife without being nagged?'

'I wasn't. Please Reg, I don't know what the matter is.' Beginning to shake and her face puckering. They hadn't had rows before. Other people had rows, all her life Winnie had heard other people having rows round Frankton, but here, in Winnie's town house, they didn't. The Hoggards weren't like that and now she was a Hoggard. They were polite and ate afternoon tea out of little fine cups and balanced plates on their knees and they didn't go out on Sundays; Mrs Hoggard always wore gloves and a hat when she went up town on a Friday and stopped to talk to other ladies in hats and gloves, and Mr Hoggard wore a gold watch chain across his waistcoat every day to the office of the stock-and-station place where he was managing director, and they never quarrelled; of that Winnie was positive, particularly as Mrs Hoggard had every single thing that anybody could ever want in their whole lives, including an electric stove, and a musical box that played 'The Blue Danube', and polished brass holders for the matchboxes, and a whole bedroom decorated in pink organdie, all to herself. Though this last item confused Winnie somewhat.

She and Reg were not angry people, and she stood there taken by surprise at what was happening to them. They glared at each other across the kitchen. Winnie wiped her hands carefully on her floral apron, and Reg backed off, looking awkward and silly in his blue serge suit, a good serviceable one which, with careful brushing, did for the insurance office he worked in, and walking out as well. His father wanted him to come into the stock and station with him but Reg had said he wanted to stand on his own feet first. Just lately his suit had been getting a bit thin and he was thinking about joining his father. As he put it to Winnie, he was 'just about ready'.

Winnie picked up a couple of jars and wiped them down, replacing them carefully on the bench as she did each one, not saying anything.

In the next room, Jeannie whimpered again, and at the sound of her cries, Winnie began to cry too.

Reg stood by, looking sullen and helpless. He had never seen her cry before, or not like this, heavy fat tears rolling noiselessly down her face, and her body heaving.

'I try to do things right,' said Winnie.

'Stop crying will you.' His voice was still irritable, but he didn't want her to keep on, and his face was chalky and strained.

Winnie flopped onto a chair at the table. 'I'm sorry, I've really been hard at it this afternoon, and I've been telling myself I feel really well all day, and I believed it but now I know it's not true, I'm getting it.'

Reg stared at her, as if she was demented.

'Getting what?'

'My period. I thought it wasn't coming but it is and I know you'll be disappointed and I don't know why we can't get it right but I know it'll happen soon. It took ages with Jeannie, didn't it love, but we got her in the end. And it's nice trying.' She searched his face to see if she had offended him saying this, being so forward.

He sat down beside her then and stroked her hand. Clara was very still and quiet and they had forgotten that she was there, and their baby had quietened again too. It was unreal in the room, like Hamilton itself. There are wide streets and long bridges over the river which divides the town, and over it all there is a sensation of slowness.

In all the years that Clara lived there, she felt that if only she could have speeded things up somehow it would have been all right. Each morning she would wonder how to make her day go faster, not that the days were necessarily unhappy or bad or that she was waiting for something special to happen the next day, because she made quite sure her life wasn't like that as she went along, giving it a momentum all of its own, but she couldn't help wondering what it would be like if somehow it all went by

15

a lot faster. It was especially bad on summer days when there was a build-up of clouds but no respite from the heat and the sky would appear to come down to meet the earth. Then all the space in the world, which is what they seemed to have on the wide Waikato plains, could not give them enough room to move.

It was like that, then, in this room. There was width and space and bridges too, if you liked, but there was nowhere for either Winnie or Reg to go, in the long silence they were caught in.

'They put off five men,' Reg said at last. 'They put off five men today.'

She looked at him. 'It's true then? Times are getting worse?'

'Yes,' said Reg. 'Looks like it.'

'This Wall Street thing, it really means something?'

'That's what they say. I think it's been there longer than that. It's just that everybody's taking notice now, aren't they?'

'The poor salesmen. It must be awful for them.'

'Salesmen?'

'That got put off.'

'They put the salesmen off a month ago,' said Reg softly.

She stared at him without comprehending. 'Who then?'

'Everyone who'd been there under ten years,' he said.

She started to cry again, only more gently this time, the tears covering her face that had had the colour bleached out of it.

'You,' she said, and he nodded.

Jeannie started to scream properly in the other room, and Winnie stumbled to her feet.

'Just as well old girl,' said Reg, stroking her hand with clumsy jerking movements. 'Just as well it came this time, eh? Things'll be better when I get settled in with the old man. See what we can do then, eh?'

That year, 1929, the world closed itself like a fist around them. There was no job at the stock and station. A year later it closed down and Reg's father jumped off the Fairfield Bridge and drowned, just like the Wall Street brokers, only by comparison it was peanuts, as Ambrose would say. Whereas they jumped for hundreds of thousands, maybe millions for all Clara knew, though money had never been plentiful enough for her to imagine past a hundred pounds, Reg's father went down for maybe a couple of thousand. It was all pitiful and pointless but as someone nasty over at the Junction said, it made a big splash, right across the front page of the local paper and for a day or two everyone had something to say about it.

Clara followed her mother in and out of Winnie's house while the family was getting ready for the funeral. Reg's mother let everyone make the arrangements for her. She had no idea of what to do, and it was clear that she had never had to do a thing for herself in her life. She was the sort of person who sat back and imagined that any woman who had to look after herself must have married a bad lot. Mumma said to Rita, in one of their rare exchanges, that the woman would probably die of shame as much as grief which were harder words than Mumma spoke about people as a rule. Some of the inertia washed over onto Reg and his sister Nola and they sat staring out the windows and getting up to walk around every now and then. It didn't seem to matter what Clara or Jeannie did, they were in people's way. Nobody could help noticing though, that it was Winnie who was in charge.

She had changed overnight, very grave and sad, but managing in a new way. Once or twice Reg looked at her, and it was almost as if he was scared of her, and she would look at him in an odd sort of way, resigned and grown up, in a manner that was new, too.

Of course Winnie had always acted grown up, as long as Clara could remember, and it seemed a silly thing to think now. Perhaps that was the key. Before she had been acting and now it was real.

On the day before the funeral, the undertaker called round to the house to ask Mrs Hoggard which hymns she had chosen for the service, and if she had decided how she would like her husband to be dressed in his coffin.

Winnie went up the stairs of her mother-in-law's house, in search of her. At the door of the bedroom, the pink organdie room, she heard voices. She stopped, respectfully waiting so as not to interrupt whatever family conference was taking place. The door was open. In front of the mirror, Reg paraded like a dummy under his mother and sister's watchful eyes. He was wearing one of his father's suits. Its length was right, but it was three sizes too large on his frame.

'Will it do?' said Mrs Hoggard, to Nola. 'I just can't visualise him in it any more.'

'Perhaps we should get something new,' said Nola.

'It does seem a little bit of a waste, doesn't it?' ventured Reg. I mean no one will see it for long.'

Both women rounded on him. 'We can't do it badly,' hissed Nola through her teeth. 'It's bad enough already.'

'I must say it's good cloth though,' said Mrs Hoggard, stroking Reg's thigh. 'Perhaps it will do.'

'What about his watch and chain? Do you think we should put it on him?' Nola said.

'Shouldn't it stay in the family?' said Mrs Hoggard, with the first edge of doubt in her voice.

'I would like it, you know,' said Reg.

'Oh no, he'd have wanted it kept in the family. And I mean, I already have a son, Reg,' Nola said.

'Perhaps . . . do you think . . . his nightshirt, after all? Reg?'

At the possible vision of her husband dressed in his father's nightshirt, Winnie fled.

She told the undertaker that Mr Hoggard would be wearing his best suit, which he had conveniently not worn to drown himself in, and his gold watch, and that the family wished to have 'Onward Christian Soldiers' sung at the funeral.

Afterwards, she went upstairs, where everyone was sitting, just as they had done before the dress rehearsal, and advised them of the undertaker's requirements. Nobody demurred.

Mrs Hoggard said, only, 'You will see that the sandwiches are thin, won't you Winifred? Really thin.'

It was at that time, too, that Clara became aware, in a real day-to-day sense, that she was Winnie's baby sister, another responsibility in a life which was quickly assuming too many burdens. She still wanted to be near her, but she had a new instinct that she should be careful. It occurred to her, on those days before the funeral, that Winnie resented her in some quite positive way. She would try to have adult conversations with Mumma, asking her advice, even though she was making all the arrangements herself, but Mumma wasn't much help. She kept cuddling Clara on her lap and twining her hair round and round her fingers, saying how she had to get home to get Clara's and their father's tea. Clara could see Winnie looking at her then, and she kept trying to wriggle away from Mumma so that Winnie wouldn't be angry and Mumma kept getting her back, until in the end they left, but at least Mumma took Jeannie off her hands, so that she stayed for two nights. Clara was told to look after her.

If Winnie thought she had worries it was nothing to what she would have had if she could have seen the two children, Jeannie trailing behind Clara round Frankton Junction. Clara took her up on top of the railway bridge, the one with four arches across it,

18

where the steam belched up through the boards and between your feet, from the engines' stacks. While they were up there she thought about pushing Jeannie off the bridge, like grandfather Hoggard. When she had considered the matter, she decided it wouldn't do her much good and that it wouldn't help her with Winnie at all, so instead she scared Jeannie with a fearsome tale of what would happen to her if she slipped and fell. When she was crying long and hard she took her down, like some saintly saviour, holding her hand. Jeannie insisted on sleeping in her bed that night, and became both an asset and a liability. Clara found that she could manipulate Winnie through Jeannie, but on the other hand, she was always getting stuck with her.

There was insurance money to collect after Reg's father died. Winnie supposed that he saw that as the point of dying, even though she would have called it pointless. A man like that couldn't have lived with the shame of not leaving his family provided for, and maybe he wanted to get out while there was still time, still some money left to do it properly.

As it turned out, it wasn't enough to do it properly, or if it was, nobody had the experience of a depression to know how to manage what there was. Reg took his five hundred pounds and paid off his and Winnie's little house. If he had kept some of it back maybe things would have been easier for them. It was just that nobody seemed to know. Nobody really did the right things. They had to have some place to live so maybe it was best that they kept it.

But the trouble was, when they had paid for it, they had no money left at all. Reg had had an easy life, and because his life was mapped out for him, or so he thought, he had never really trained for anything, in spite of his talk about standing on his own feet. He was going to push a pen around for a while and then be a manager. As it turned out, there was nothing to manage and the death had a backlash on him that his father probably hadn't thought of when he made what he believed was his providential plunge. People said that the Hoggards couldn't stand up to things, that they cracked under strain. It didn't matter that people everywhere were cracking up in different ways but at least they were alive, that was the difference. If there had been any of the kinds of job that Reg was cut out for, nobody would trust a Hoggard with them. If. It didn't cut much ice that there weren't any.

He started knocking on doors offering to rake up leaves, clean

19

windows, mend front fences, for a shilling a time. He got harder-looking and lost the weight around his middle.

Winnie and Clara's father was killed in an accident on the railways soon afterwards and Mumma got a small pension. She used to give Winnie a few shillings for 'minding Clara', or that's what she said, and Brian and Frank were working on farms out of town. They brought in fruit and vegetables and the odd piece of meat. Clara started noticing one or another piece of furniture gone when she went to Winnie's.

'At least we have the house,' Reg would say, more and more often, in a despairing kind of way.

'Yes,' Winnie would say, and if they were outside she would turn and look at it, one of a procession of houses squatting across the plains in the flat heavy air of Hamilton, which sometimes turned to searing heat, and then again, in the winter, to a numbing blanket of river fog. Clara could see by the look in Winnie's eyes that it failed now to have meaning for her, that the precious house was just wood and iron nailed together, like all the other houses. True, it had a verandah, which was more than some of the houses had, though for what purpose it was hard to tell, for nobody ever sat on the verandah (which faced away from the sun anyway) and it appeared to be useful for nothing except collecting dead leaves at the end of each summer, blown in from the poplar tree which stood near the gate. As she got older, Clara's job of sweeping the leaves from the verandah replaced chasing the magpies. She had become what Winnie had come to describe in complaining tones to Mumma, 'a fidgety child'.

She could see Winnie growing old as the knot of poverty pulled in. While she was older too, she was not old enough to be of any real help to Winnie. She tried hard, but that usually ended up by her being told that she was in the way. Sometimes she rebelled and didn't try at all, and then she got sent back to Mumma. At least, though, being older meant that she was allowed to get the bus back to Frankton on her own, which she preferred. There were more Maoris than European children in Frankton by then, and some of them were her friends at school. Winnie disapproved, because frail tremulous old Mrs Hoggard did, and Winnie adopted the attitudes, if not the style, of the Hoggards as she first knew them. In those days, when Mrs Hoggard was more youthful, and pretty, and adorned with floating chiffon scarves like Isadora Duncan, they would go riding in the Hoggards' car, a magnificent Daimler, and drive out past the pa at Ngaruawahia. 'Pai korry,' Mrs Hoggard would trill to them, imitating the Maoris, or inventing a whole new language for them, 'Pai korry,' and everybody in the Daimler would roar with laughter, Mr Hoggard doubling against the steering wheel, and catching his breath.

Mrs Hoggard's lifestyle might have changed, but her opinions still held sway. Winnie seemed to believe she had no choice except to think like her, even though these days she disliked, even despised her. The Hoggards had been her achievement. There had to be something left. Clara was disappointed. For a little while it had appeared that Winnie might be smarter than the Hoggards, but she had slipped into apathy and acceptance. And when she and Clara and the children got in a bus to go back to Mumma's, Clara knew instinctively that she would sit beside a European before a Maori, and even if they didn't notice, she saw it as a reproach. She would be torn in two, wanting to sit beside Winnie and sit beside her friends, and terrified in her heart of hearts that she was criticising Winnie.

One day Clara saw Winnie standing at her bench as usual, but her face was white as chalk, as white as the bench which she scrubbed with ever-increasing vehemence each day. The hallstand had gone in the morning, nice polished wood, gone for ten shillings. Winnie had found fault with Clara all afternoon. Sometimes Clara wondered why she bothered to have her there at all. Was it only for the money which Mumma gave her, or simply to keep her away from Mumma in the hope that Mumma would love her less and Winnie more? The second was a vain hope. As long as she let Mumma twine her fingers through her hair she would love Clara more. Just so long as she did not have the work of looking after her.

There was always a sense of duty to be considered, but it did not bear thinking about. She wanted Winnie to love her best, or at least better than Jeannie. It occurred to her that she was contrary in every way. Mumma's arrangement suited her very well in fact, for Clara did not want to be looked after by Mumma any more than Mumma wanted to look after her.

Though she was never quite sure why she wanted to be looked after by Winnie so much.

She supposed that it was because Winnie looked more like her mother than Mumma did. Or had looked. But then she started to get so worn that Clara thought that it would not be long before

21

they looked alike. She stared at her one day, looking for the first signs of the great ropey varicose veins that disfigured Mumma's legs and was relieved to see how absolutely smooth and tapered Winnie's still were. Her eyes travelled up her skirt and Clara saw that Winnie was bleeding. There was a big spreading crimson patch across her skirt.

Clara began to shake, afraid that her sister was going to die. For once Winnie noticed that there was something wrong and asked what the matter was. She didn't want to tell her. She wanted to protect her from the pain and terror of her illness, but at last she had to tell her.

Winnie's hand travelled slowly to her bottom and her face was wondering and disbelieving and joyful. Reg came in, and she was kissing him, and laughing for once. They spent some of the ten shillings on meat, and Jeannie had the largest portion which she didn't want when it came to the point, so Winnie fed it in little cold forksful to Reg. Clara had no idea why they were so happy or whether Winnie would get better.

Clara's friends at school paid off. She was nine years old, but she knew where babies came from and how they got there. Winnie became fascinating for different reasons from any of the previous ones, and she fascinated Clara in a way that Mumma never could, even though it appeared that Mumma had had more to do with the whole business than Winnie. The evidence was, that at one time or another, Mumma had borne seven children, of which she was one, and Winnie was another, whereas Winnie hadn't got past first base yet — as, later, the Americans were fond of saying.

But now she realised that Winnie could have more children and that the fluctuating moods which afflicted her and Reg had much to do with the process of getting babies, or avoiding getting them. She knew that Winnie was desperately afraid of having babies and that this was sad because Clara knew that once she had wanted to have more, besides Jeannie. Clara wished she would have more too. Jeannie stumped round after her on her thick legs, increasingly demanding, aware that she had some sort of hold over Clara, though over the years the mothers of the two girls seemed to have forgotten what it was; their relationship was simply taken for granted. Clara knew that she had to look after Jeannie and that she made capital out of it. At first Clara would help her niece with her reading but after a while Jeannie caught her up. She was a determined child.

Clara supposed that she and Jeannie were some sort of rivals, and that as her aunt, she had an odd place in Jeannie's life, being herself a rival to Jeannie's mother and yet at the same time as much under her control as Jeannie was.

She thought that she liked school and it didn't occur to her to wonder whether she was good at her schoolwork or not. And she didn't really know whether Jeannie was so much better and cleverer than she was either. What she did know was, that with this very determined streak in her, Jeannie caught up and learned everything she knew at the same time as she did, and, being two years younger than Clara, this made her appear like a genius. Clara decided quite early that she couldn't be very clever in the light of Jeannie's brilliance, but there was also a small warning voice inside her which made her determine to withdraw any useful information that would assist Jeannie in her bid for recognition. The easiest way to withdraw it was never to find out it existed in the first place.

She discovered quickly, and even more later on, when she got to high school, that it was easier that way, and that it won her friends. There were more people who were not clever than there were clever ones. Clara had more friends than Jeannie ever did. And, although it was never discussed within the family, Clara was pretty, with bright blue eyes and curly nut-coloured hair, while Jeannie's hair was straight and dull and nobody in their wildest dreams would say she was pretty.

Just sometimes a teacher would hold Clara's interest. Then she would start to get agitated and delighted as something clicked into place, especially in history and maths which seemed to have some curious parallel structure whereby you could unlock the secrets of the world, one by going back and the other by going forward. Occasionally she would ask a question. If the teacher had been smart enough to interest her in the first place then they were also generally smart enough to detect a spark beneath her lethargy. As soon as she saw that spark of recognition in their eyes she would close up. The result was usually a report that said 'Not working to the best of her ability' or, more concisely, and frequently, 'Clara is lazy.' She took a special pride in these reports. They increased her following enormously. Perhaps they raised an aura of mystery about her. The thought that she could have done better if she wanted to, was more interesting than it seemed, than simply not being able to do better. It indicated a positive act of will, or choice, on her part. But then she would think that she flattered herself.

23

She had no real proof that she could ever have done much better, even if Robin used to tell her that she could. But then Robin gave the impression of knowing a great deal when often she thought he was as ignorant as she was, or any of the others.

That happened later though. But the seeds were sown then, and she knew she was sick of Jeannie tagging along behind, and demanding and demanding and always being in a position to get her own way. She wished that Winnie would get her some brothers and sisters who would relieve her of the responsibility of always worrying about her.

It came to a head one day late in the winter of 1933. The oak dresser had gone in the morning. Winnie had hung onto it for as long as she could. It was a piece of furniture she was very proud of, with nice grain, and heavy leaded glass panels. Not that she was as interested in housework as she had been, though that wasn't really surprising for there was hardly anything left in the house except essentials and even the effort of keeping them seemed to be too much for her some days. She would drag herself from one task to another and end the day asking where it had gone and complaining about how tired she felt. But she did still polish the dresser at least once a week, and her crockery sat twinkling behind the glass ready for use though there wasn't much to put on the plates any more. For that reason Clara had stopped going there so often, and when she did, she usually took food from Mumma's.

But it was the holidays, and Frank had been in from the farm to see Mumma. He had cadged extra eggs and vegetables from the farmer. Mumma was pleased of the excuse to load Clara with food and send her over to Winnie's, to spend a couple of days with her. She turned up on the doorstep armed with half a dozen eggs and a couple of cabbages. At first Winnie frowned when she saw her, but when she saw what she had brought, her expression changed to a watery smile. She fed two eggs to Jeannie and two to Reg, and Clara said that she had had some at home so then Winnie had one too and there was one left over. It sat in the kitchen cupboard for more than a day while Winnie turned it over in her mind as to who was going to have it.

She didn't ask Clara for an opinion, but if she had, Clara would have said Reg, out of him and Jeannie, because Jeannie was still quite plump, all things considered. Winnie had started queuing for food up town three days a week and they made sure the children got as much as they could give them.

It was Reg who was in a really bad way because by that time he was working for the Swamp Development League. The land round Hamilton was swampy peatland and some businessmen had got the idea of burning off the peat so that the land could be brought into production more quickly and there was an abundance of cheap labour for what was really a foul job. They did make some work for the men who had nothing, but still, as some people said privately, the businessmen stood to make a pretty packet out of it in the long run. Mumma said to Frank that you could go round in circles forever on something like that, because while it was awful to see what was happening to Reg, on the other side of it was all the money that his father had made out of people by extending high-priced credit and foreclosing on farmers in the days when he was on top of things. In fact if he hadn't been so silly as to go jumping off the Fairfield Bridge he would probably have been one of the first ones to make a few bob out of it, more fool him.

But now Reg was out in these stinking swamps, and everyone knew they were stinking, you couldn't get away from it, there in the town. The fires would smoulder for months on end, and the air was laden for miles around with foul-smelling smoke, and if it got mixed up with river fog it would get down into the lungs of the townspeople, until they felt as if the air was being pushed out of them. Some mornings Clara would step outside and the sensation of choking would come up to meet her, and she would wonder how she could bear it for the day, and then at the point when it seemed as if it would just be easier to choke to death there would be a break for a few hours and some relief. She didn't know whether other people felt the way she did, but she would panic in that dense evil air.

Reg worked in the heart of the swamp with the wet underfoot and the smoke swirling in clouds above him, and some nights he was able to come home and others he camped out in the fields with the men.

There was nothing much for him and Winnie to say to each other. He was gaunt and starting to stoop and it was hard to realise that he still hadn't turned thirty. Winnie was bleak and pinched and when she did talk she tended to be sharp.

The day the dresser went started differently.

Clara thought Winnie would cry or do something violent or angry when it was carried out of the house. But she didn't. She pocketed the pound the men gave her for it without saying a word.

25

They looked embarrassed, and Clara guessed that they knew how little it was for such a good piece of furniture. One of them started to say something. Perhaps he wanted to say he was sorry but Winnie gave him such a cool look that he turned his face away from hers and said nothing.

After they had gone Winnie went to the kitchen and stood at the bench staring out onto the little lawn. It was full of magpies but she didn't remark on them. They circled around on the grass with little dancing steps, their heads held impudently on one side, and opened their beaks with stretching satisfied gestures. It occurred to Clara that they were surviving the winter better than any of them. Nothing had diminished the shine on their feathers and they were more daring than they had ever been. Winnie's knuckles were clenched tight on the edge of the bench.

'You'll get another dresser Winnie,' Clara ventured, wanting to console her.

'What?' She stared through Clara, as if she didn't know what she was talking about.

'The dresser. I'm sorry it's gone,' she tried, braver than the removal man.

'Oh. That.' She gestured with her hands, but in a way that didn't mean anything. 'It doesn't matter.'

'It does. Winnie, it does matter.' Clara started crying, without knowing why, and wished that Winnie would too, because then she would know what to do for her; she could put her arms round her and tell her that things would be all right, even if it were not true.

But Winnie only stared at her as if she was being silly, and she stopped crying almost as suddenly as she had started.

'Shall I take Jeannie for a walk?'

'If you like. No. I don't know,' she said, making an effort.

Clara waited.

'Perhaps not. We're going out later, you don't want to get your coats damp now.'

'Where are we going?'

'To queue for some lunch.' She looked grim, and at the same time shaky. Clara wondered if it was like this every time she went, but it seemed as if she had something else on her mind besides lunch.

'They don't open till eleven and I might have to go somewhere else for a while. If we make sure we're there at eleven we might get served early, but if I have to go away I want you to mind my place in the queue and look after Jeannie.'

26

'Why don't I look after Jeannie here? I could you know. I wouldn't do anything silly,' Clara said.

'Because then if I went off, I'd lose out in the queue and have to start from the back again.'

There was fine drizzle starting outside.

'It seems a pity to take Jeannie out in the weather.' Clara would have liked to go and queue with Winnie if it had just been the two of them.

As if she could read her thoughts, Winnie rounded on her. 'I thought you were coming over to help me. Are you going to help or do you want to go back to Mama's?' When she said 'Mama' she meant business.

'Help,' said Clara sullenly. She thought she hated Winnie. She wanted to give her so much and she never seemed to notice.

'You're spoiled. Mama's made you a spoiled brat.'

'Don't talk to me like that.' Clara was at once terrified of what she had said, and brave in the one breath.

Winnie looked at her. 'I beg your pardon young lady?'

'You've got no right to talk to me like that.'

'Oh haven't I?'

'You're not my mother, you're my sister. Sisters aren't in charge like mothers. Sisters are supposed to share with each other.'

Winnie's face contorted. 'Sister. Oh yes, you're my sister all right. Mumma ought to be ashamed of having had you. It's disgusting. Sister. I could have died when you were born. It nearly ruined my life. I couldn't get out of it fast enough when you were born.' She advanced on Clara, her face almost unrecognisable with loathing and anger. 'Don't you tell me what I'm supposed to share with you.'

She had her hands up as if to seize or hit her. Clara cowered back against the kitchen table, her eyes darting round looking for a way to the door. Her head banged against the corner of the doorway as she ducked. She reeled sideways, and Winnie caught her as she fell. Clara wriggled, half-dazed, trying to escape, expecting the attack. Instead Winnie was crying, as Clara had wanted her to do when the dresser went. She sat down on one of the chairs and rocked backwards and forwards with her head in one hand and the other arm encircling her sister.

'I'm sorry, Clara, so sorry,' she said.

'It's all right.' The back of her head was still hurting, and she had no idea what it was all about but she was aware of some new change, some redefinition again of their relationship, which had

27

taken place over the last few violent moments in the kitchen.

Winnie looked as if she was going to try to explain something but then she shook her head slowly and touched the back of Clara's head. 'Is it all right?'

She knew that Winnie meant is everything all right, not just her head, and it seemed easiest to say yes. In a way it didn't matter, what had happened. She had said what she thought for once. She realised then that Winnie had spent a lot of their lives, certainly a lot of her life anyway, saying one thing and meaning another.

'We'll get our coats and go now,' she said with a burst of energy. 'If we leave now we might get in at the head of the queue.'

They didn't though. There were at least fifty people there when they arrived and it was still only half past ten. Women called out to Winnie. She settled in behind one called Cora and in front of another called Ellen. They shared an air of conspiracy with Winnie. The business of getting food was a serious one, it had brought them together. Cora was thin and brittle and fair with well-bitten fingernails. She wore an air of hectic vitality that looked as if it would dissolve into a vague and puzzled vulnerability if she was pushed. Ellen was stout and untidy, and like everyone else in the queue she looked tired, but she was intent on keeping the others' spirits up. She produced marbles out of her pocket and offered them to Jeannie who accepted them and went to play with one of her children.

'D'you want to play?' Ellen asked Clara.

She shook her head. 'Later.' Winnie looked vexed, but Clara stood her ground, ignoring them, trying to look as if she wasn't interested in what they were saying, and she succeeded in so much as that they began to talk as if she wasn't there after a while, or at least as if she couldn't understand what they were saying.

Cora said, 'This the kid sister is it?'

Winnie sighed and said that it was. Before that morning, and their fight in the kitchen, Clara might not have noticed the way she said it, but now she knew that inside she resented her, she could pick her tone. It didn't really seem to matter all that much. In a way it made her more real, less predictable than when she was trying to show her nice side all the time, and therefore more interesting.

'You got your appointment all right?' asked Cora.

'Yes.' Winnie's voice was small and tight. Clara glanced at her out of the corner of her eye. She looked more out of place here than most of the others. For those who had never had appearances to keep up in the first place, it was an easier step to take, coming to join the queue. Clara wondered in the back of her mind if it was Reg's fault that Winnie was here. Then she thought of Mumma, and the enormous lie that her life was and decided that you couldn't particularly blame one person or another for things that happened. It was beginning to be boring and she was on the point of moving away but the next time that Ellen spoke, there was something in her voice that stopped her, a premonition of movement in their shuffling stop-and-go existence in the queue.

'What time?' asked Ellen.

'Twelve thirty. I might just make it if they open on time here.'

'Don't bank on that,' said Cora. 'The bastards enjoy making us wait.'

'I expect they need to get a good feed before they start work,' said Ellen grimly. 'I can see Mary Holmes up near the front. I reckon she'd change with you if I told her.'

'No, don't,' said Winnie. 'I've heard her husband's bad with asthma. Besides,' she added, 'I don't want to go telling everyone.'

Up front, the doors were opened and the queue began to move but it was a slow procession with stops and starts while people at the head of the line argued for more, or children were rounded up from wandering away, so that they could get their soup. At twelve they were still shuffling forward with nearly twenty people ahead. Winnie was anxious and fidgety. Clara had relented and gone to play marbles with Jeannie, and then skipped up and down with her to keep their feet warm, and swung Ellen's little boy round and round by his hands until her arms felt as if they were coming out of their sockets. Then the slide was closed down on the queue when they were only five away from a bowl of soup and a loaf of bread.

'You'll hold our place?' said Winnie to Clara. Her face was closed and afraid.

'Don't worry about the kids,' said Ellen. 'They'll be all right with us.'

'Would you like me to come with you?' said Cora impulsively.

'Don't be silly,' said Winnie, 'You'd miss out too.'

'There's two kids here, one could hold each place.'

Winnie wavered, then pulled herself together.

'I'll be all right. Honestly. If I need someone to hold my hand then I shouldn't be going in the first place.'

'Are you quite sure?' said Ellen, speaking more soberly than she had all morning.

'Oh I don't know,' Winnie said. 'I just don't know how to go on without doing it. I mean . . . look at us.' She shrugged. 'As sure as you can ever be.'

They muttered good luck to her but none of them looked at her or each other, as they did.

When she had gone Clara pretended to be concerned about Jeannie, and she was too, in a way, because she knew then that there was something really odd about Winnie that tied in with the way she had cracked up at her, and her gaunt look, and selling the dresser, the whole lot.

Ellen said, 'I couldn't go through with it myself.'

'It suits some,' said Cora. Her face was hard and angry. For a moment they were on the verge of quarrelling. 'You heard what she said. Look at us. I couldn't take another kid, I can bloody tell you.'

'All right, I know,' Ellen said. 'I wouldn't have given her the address if it wasn't for knowing that she couldn't take a kid. I know.'

Their voices murmured on above Clara, soothing and reassuring each other, but she had stopped taking notice of them. She knew what it was about. Winnie was having a baby. A baby she didn't want. And somehow, though she didn't understand how, these women were trying to make her stop having the baby. That was something her friends at school hadn't told her about. Winnie with a baby inside her. It didn't make sense when she had wanted so much for there to be another one.

But then there was this morning. Things had changed. And there was this queue. She hoped Winnie would come back without the baby.

Winnie wasn't sure what she had expected the house to look like. She had come to it the long way round, pausing to look over fences, wondering how the people inside were managing, listening for the voices of children and trying to see them, to see whether they looked as if they were getting enough to eat or not. She had taken the route across the bridge and when she was halfway across she looked down at the dark river and wondered if Mr Hoggard had time to find the water cold before it closed over his head. She wasn't tempted to jump herself, though it did occur to her that it would be so very much easier than what she was proposing to do, and probably cheaper for Reg. Although on second thoughts, if they fished her out, and they always did seem to find bodies in the Waikato sooner or later, hooked up in the twisted willows, there

30

would be the cost of burying her. Besides, she hadn't admired what Mr Hoggard had done. It seemed short-sighted and foolish and they would almost certainly have been better off if he had hung on and been patient about things. Sensible, was how she had been described when she was a schoolgirl. No nonsense about Winnie Bentley. Well, there wouldn't be any nonsense about her now.

Yet her knees would hardly hold her up when she stood at the gate of the address she had been given. It wasn't a mansion, one possibility she had considered. The person she was going to see could have made a fortune out of her trade. On the other hand she more than half-expected it to be a tumbledown filthy shack. But it was an ordinary-looking weatherboard house, the paintwork a bit the worse for wear to be true, but quite unexceptional. Although maybe the trees and shrubs had been allowed to grow rather close around the doorway.

She knocked once, twice, three times, slowly, as she had been told to, and waited. Nothing seemed to move. In a panic she started to beat at the door. It flew open while she was in the middle of pounding, and revealed a woman's face, round and slightly whiskery round the chin.

'Come in,' she said sharply.

The door shut behind them. The dark-stained wood panelling enclosed them in shadow.

'Why did you do that?'

'I thought . . . '

'You didn't. You knew what to do. Panicky?'

'Perhaps. Wouldn't you, if you were me?' Winnie was surprised at her own voice. It was cooler, she was more articulate than she had expected of herself.

The woman looked her over carefully, and made a small 'hnnnh' noise between her teeth. 'Mrs Hoggard?'

'Yes.'

'You're late.'

'I got held up in the relief queue.'

'All right then. I just don't like my visitors hanging round on the doorstep. It makes me nervous.'

'I understand.'

'Come on then, through here.' She was a cumbersome woman, yet oddly light on her feet. She led Winnie through the house into a large kitchen, with a scrubbed pine table running down the length of it. Winnie stopped at the door. She had heard about

31

kitchen table jobs. Everybody had heard of them, but she didn't really believe in them.

'Is this where you're going to . . . examine me?' She thought she would faint, and promised herself that she wouldn't. She needed her feet to run.

'What d'you expect? All modern conveniences? This isn't a doctor's surgery.'

'I'm sorry. I didn't mean to be rude, Mrs . . . '

The woman looked at her. 'Don't ask. I don't have a name. Look, if you want to go, go. All right. If you want to stay, it's clean. I'm not stupid. I don't want trouble any more than you do.' Then, softly, as if reading her mind, 'It has to be in the kitchen. There's running water don't you see, and the bathroom's not big enough to take a table. So it's just like you've heard. Right? Right. So if you want to leave . . . it's over to you really, isn't it?'

'No,' said Winnie. 'I don't want to go.'

'Then take off your coat and get up on the table, pants off too, I'll see what we can feel.'

Winnie took off her coat very slowly, trying to prolong the moment until she climbed on the kitchen chair and up onto the table. The woman washed her hands at the kitchen sink, and Winnie noticed that she had a pile of freshly laundered towels in the hot-water cupboard. She took one out and dried her hands methodically.

'Yes,' she said, as she completed the careful process, 'I'm clean. But poor, like everybody.'

'The depression's hit most of us,' said Winnie, stretching herself out on the table. The wood was very smooth and cool but it warmed to her body's touch.

'I can't afford luxuries. Some people think I'd be able to but it's not like that.' On the stove a pot of water boiled. The woman took out a pair of rubber gloves from a drawer, and with a pair of tongs, dipped them one after the other into the water. 'I tell you, I've done it for nothing, there's some people that down on their luck at present.'

This was the moment of truth that Winnie had been waiting for. 'How much — does it cost?' she managed to whisper.

There was a pause. 'You say you're on relief?'

'Yes.'

'How long since your husband worked? You've got a husband I take it?'

'Well of course I have. I mean I'm —'

'Pregnant,' interposed the woman. 'So what?'

'He's in the swamps. That's all he's had for a year.'

'How many others? Kids?'

'One.'

'Just one.' Again the slow-drawn out 'hnnnh'. 'Ten pounds.'

'Ten pounds?' The room seemed cold, and there was a cobweb on the ceiling. 'You said . . if people were down on their luck . . .'

'Luck? Think if you had six. That's what I mean about luck.'

'I haven't . . . I don't think I could get it. I sold something this morning. I thought I'd get more. An oak dresser. It was a beautiful piece. I'd been hanging onto it, because it was so nice. I mean, there was nothing else, but I kept on hanging onto this dresser. Silly. I mean if I'd sold it before, I'd have done better. But I sold it. For this, you see.' She could hear her voice as if from a great distance, and it seemed to be going on and on and she didn't know how to stop it. 'Well, I got a pound for it,' she finished lamely.

The other woman sighed. 'I take risks in this business. It's a lot of worry.'

'I know. I mean I can understand that, it's just . . . '

'Seven pounds ten. I can't offer you any better.'

'All right,' said Winnie, and closed her eyes, as the woman's hands descended onto and into her body. They were firm and confident, and not entirely unpleasant as they moved in their search for her baby.

'Two months did you say?'

'Yes.' She exclaimed as she was hit by a small sharp pain and had an odd desire to ask the woman to be careful. 'When would you be able to do it?'

The woman was breathing more heavily; she pushed Winnie further onto her side, then straightened up suddenly and walked over to the bench. She pulled the gloves off and started to wash again.

'Not at all. Sorry,' she said.

'But you said,' Winnie began, only she didn't finish, because she knew what the woman would say.

'You said you were two months.'

'I could have been a little bit out on my dates,' Winnie whispered.

'A little bit! You're nearer to four.'

'Not that far. I'm sure I'm not.' And I'm not, she told herself fiercely. Well, not that she could recall. A bit afraid maybe, but that shouldn't make her misjudge.

'I told you, I take risks,' the woman was saying. 'But I told you something else too, didn't I? Do you remember what it was? No, well I'll tell you. I said I wasn't stupid. So that means I weigh up the risks. Seven pound ten. It's not much return when I've got a dead woman on my hands. You know where your seven pounds'd take me? Straight to the lock-up. You know you think you're hard up, but I can tell from your ways, you've done all right, somewhere along the way. You think you're lowering yourself coming here. Oh yes, I can tell. But I can tell you too, you don't know anything.'

'I don't know what to do.' Winnie had started to cry and she didn't want to be weeping and ridiculous on this woman's kitchen table but she couldn't stop herself. She struggled to get herself upright and to find her clothes.

'If you can find seven pound ten for me, you can find seven pound ten to look after your baby. I'd get on with having it if I was you.'

'I'll find someone,' said Winnie.

'Not in this town you won't, there's nobody who'd touch you. Here's your coat.'

Winnie felt vainly in the pocket for a handkerchief and was reduced to wiping her nose on the back of her sleeve. The woman was watching her, and she said more gently, 'Look, times'll get better, they've got to. But you mightn't. Who'd look after your other kid if anything happened to you?'

'You mean that?'

'Yes.' The woman looked tired and less hostile, as if she had been through all of this many times and had no answers. 'You know, you've got a husband, it's more than a lot have got these days. You try and sort something out with him, eh?'

Winnie nodded. She didn't say it but she thought how much easier said than done that was, as she reflected on the yawning gulf between her and the stranger Reg had become in her life, these last months. 'How much do I owe you for now?' She felt the pound note crinkling in her coat pocket and thought that it was sad that this was what her oak dresser had bought her in the end, just a chance to be told that nothing could be done to help her.

'Forget it.'

'But . . . . '

'But nothing. Forget it and forget you ever saw me. All right?'

And the door closed behind her, as she faced the dank afternoon again and turned the pound over in her pocket.

Back at the queue the others had been served. Cora and Ellen had seen to Jeannie and Clara getting their meal, and they had looked after the children until Winnie came back. They were quiet when they saw her face, and waited for her to say something first.

'I'm too far gone,' said Winnie.

'Ahhh.' Their voices like wind in the grass.

They set off walking together, along towards Garden Place hill. It was a chill sour day, August, harsh still with winter but a feeling of change in the air too. Things were greening up and there was blossom glittering along the bare branches of a tree. Clara's heart was skipping. Winnie was going to have a baby. The world was going to change, all right. The prospect of change, any change, excited her. The turning of the year assumed a greater significance.

'When will you tell him?' Cora asked.

'Reg? Oh . . . I don't know. I'll see how he is tonight. I don't know, he's having such a time of it, and I don't make it any easier for him, not lately; I've been a fair cow. I reckon I ought to try to cheer him up a bit.'

It was strange to hear Winnie talking like this and Clara thought that maybe this was how Winnie had been, talking with friends, when she had been much younger. Perhaps the way she was now, was how Clara might be herself one day. Only something told her she would never be quite like Winnie.

'Are you feeling better about it then?' Ellen was asking her.

'It looks as if I'll have to be, won't I? I mean there's nothing I can do about it, is there?'

Cora looked at Ellen. 'Go on, tell her,' she urged.

Ellen looked uncomfortable and turned away.

'I told you, it's all right for some,' said Cora, and there was that sharp edge in her voice again. 'Especially cows like you that make milk like Jersey heifers. You don't notice the feeding. What if her milk doesn't come in?'

Winnie was looking from one to the other in bewilderment.

'All right then,' said Ellen, 'Mind you I don't believe in it. But there's one up in Ngaruawahia, Winnie. He might see you right. How far on are you?'

'Three and a half months. Or thereabouts. I think.'

'He might. I'm not saying he would, but he might.'

Winnie walked along quietly with them. 'Thanks,' she said after a while.

'Shall I write it down then?'

'No, I don't think so.'

'No? You're mad,' said Cora.

'I trusted her,' said Winnie. 'Sounds crazy, but this woman, I did trust her.'

'She's a good woman,' said Ellen. 'In her way.'

'I felt that. I hated going there, and she got angry. But I reckon she'd have done it if it was safe. Even though I couldn't pay the full amount. But she wouldn't. So maybe it is too risky. And I've got Jeannie to think of. It wouldn't be fair.'

She was watching Jeannie, and Clara thought, yes, it is Jeannie she thinks of, little pudgy Jeannie in her turned-over skirt, squatting on the pavement poking at a cat. She remembered that it was only this morning, although it was rapidly beginning to seem like something that she had known for a long time, maybe always, that she and Winnie had established that they were sisters and that Winnie couldn't take charge of her as if she was her mother. Clara could see how true that really was. Winnie didn't have a responsibility for her in the way she did for Jeannie and the new baby when it came.

She moved away.

She moved in other ways that day too, though not so much in the physical sense. That way, nothing really changed for years, her time continuing to be divided between Mumma and Winnie. But she did move away from the same intense feeling of thinking that she belonged to Winnie, and she looked at her in a different way, and she could see things that she had not seen before.

Even on the night of that long day, Clara watched Winnie, for now she knew even more about her than Reg did.

If there was something different about Winnie, there was about Reg too. It was so tangible that it could almost be smelled in the air the moment he walked in, but Winnie, immersed in her own thoughts, didn't pick it. Reg was strange and nervous, but mixed with that there was a curious air of relief and suppressed excitement. It was as if he was, on the one hand, in a personal agony over something, on the other, as if he, too, had moved away from something, in the same way that Clara had moved away from Winnie.

Winnie had cooked the last egg for him, and there was bread and the vegetables and a slice of bacon that Frank had brought from the farm. It was a funny mixture but substantial enough. Winnie was bright and edgy. Clara could see she was in the way so she retreated to Jeannie's bedroom and began to read *The Wind in the Willows* to her. She didn't know how many times she had read it to her before, and soon her niece got impatient and took over from her, because she could read it as well as Clara. There didn't seem to be a place for her anywhere. She took her hot water bottle to fill at the kitchen tap and found herself a corner by the stove. She began to draw pictures in her school pad; first, pictures of families with lots of children and the girls all had curly hair like hers and even the very small ones wore high heels. As if at a great distance Reg and Winnie's voices murmured in the next room.

'Please have half of it,' Reg said.

'I've eaten,' she said. 'I had soup today in the queue. They didn't give you that out at the reclamation.'

'I can't keep having more than you. You've got to eat too.'

'What's half an egg?' she said. 'Go on, it'll get cold.'

When he'd finished she took his plate and scraped it, then she pushed it to one side of the table. Usually she picked things up and took them straight through to the kitchen and banged them in the sink.

'How was it today then?' Her voice continued its forced brightness.

'The same.' He was non-committal.

'It might be drier tomorrow. I'm sure the weather's going to clear.'

'I'm not going tomorrow,' he said carefully.

There was a short silence between them. 'They've stood you down again?'

He grunted.

'Well. Probably it's just as well. You could do with a break.'

'That's the way I look at it.'

'There'll be some pay owing.'

'A bit. You know where to pick it up.'

'Me?'

'I'll be around looking out for something won't I? I can't waste the time.'

Clara, listening, thought there was something odd in this statement. Even she knew that if he'd been stood down it would have been the first thing he did, go and pick up his money, before he did anything else. Clara picked a note of panic in his voice. He needn't have worried. Winnie was only half hearing him.

'What did you do today?' he asked her.

'Oh . . . nothing. Nothing really. I was in the queue for a long time. Terrible you know. You'll be standing there, after you've waited and waited, and they'll close down for lunch, just like that, in your face. For their lunch would you believe.'

'Did you see anyone?'

'Cora. Ellen. The usual.' It was turning out harder than she had expected. She couldn't think of the right lines to give him. 'What about you? You see anyone?'

'I called in on my mother on the way home.'

'Oh, her. I thought you were late.' Winnie remembered that she was being nice to Reg and bit back the sarcasm which crept into her voice whenever they discussed old Mrs Hoggard. 'How is she then?'

'All right.'

'Doesn't she get sick of rattling round in that big old house by herself?' It was a contentious point but with an effort Winnie made it sound solicitous.

'She's taken in three boarders.'

'She hasn't!'

'She has you know.'

'She must be better then.'

'I'd say she was. One of them's going to fix up her vegetable garden.'

'I'm glad she's . . . got herself together then.' She had been going to say 'pulled' herself together. They were skating on thin ice. 'We could do with a bit of fixing up in our own. If you turned it over I could get some seedlings from Mama. If you're going to be off work that'd be as good as anything you could do.'

'I'll only be stood down for a day or so,' said Reg evasively. 'But I will when I can,' he added, anxious again and not wanting to draw her attention to his refusal. He went on, 'It's a bit early yet. The earth'll still be cold.'

'Yes, I suppose you're right.'

They were hedging. Reg yawned and belched.

'At least I'll be able to get your boots dry. Shall I put them in the oven now?' She moved to get up. Her voice was heavy.

'I had to hand them in today. They're short of them.'

'That's silly, they'll just be wet when they give them to someone else.'

'Well they did.'

'You are going back?' she said sharply.

'You're really keen on me going out there?' he said.

There was an argument in the air, one of those manufactured

38

arguments that people have when they are trying to hide something important, but whatever happens it is the argument that can be blamed. They still hardly ever argued, not in words at any rate, but Winnie could feel it coming on them, settling in the room like river fog. The odd thing was, she couldn't decide which of them was actually picking the argument. She knew she had plenty to hide from him, and yet she had this strange feeling that it was he who wanted her to be angry, and shout at him.

'No. No, I'm not Reg. You know I don't like you going out there.' She said it quietly, trying to still them both. 'You're tired. Why don't you come to bed? I'll put the dishes in the sink and come with you. We could have an early night.'

'Well . . . soon.'

'We could . . . I do love you Reg.' She was clumsy with love and there was real longing in her voice. There didn't seem much point in pursuing whatever it was she had had to tell him. Not tonight. She thought that perhaps if they could be kind to each other he would know without her having to tell him.

'Don't,' he said. 'I can't bear it.'

'Why not?'

'You know why not. I can't bear lying beside you and not being able to. It's been months since . . . . I was so scared after. I can't put a kid up you. I want you so much,' he said harshly.

So, she thought, it seems I will tell him after all, and as she opened her mouth to say what she must, there was a knock on the door, like bad movie, right on cue. She could have laughed if it hadn't been so bad for them.

Reg pushed his chair back hard. 'I'll get it.' He was padding down the hallway already. Winnie got to her feet and collected the plates.

In the kitchen, Clara heard her coming, and slipped like a speck of dust through a crack out of the room, to the bed she shared with Jeannie. She was asleep, her arms flung up above her head, her soft mouth open slightly. She breathed through her mouth when she slept. Clara put on her nightdress and got in beside her.

Winnie had started washing the plates when Reg came back up the hall.

'I'll dry,' he said.

'Who was it?' she asked.

'Oh . . . just Albie Tubbs. He might call by at the weekend.'

'Albie? Why didn't he come in then?'

'He was off to some meeting or other. The Labour Party.'

'Oh that. Don't tell me he goes along to them?'

'Lots do. Anyway, he just thought he'd see if I'd be here at the weekend.' His voice was hesitant and Winnie had the sudden quick feeling that he was lying, but Reg didn't lie. At least she had never known him to. Or maybe he did, and it just didn't occur to her. She didn't understand lies. It must be her own body, making her think things like that about him. Besides, she did tell lies now, she remembered. Something new, something she'd never done. It was all inside her.

'He's still in work then?'

'Most school teachers are.'

'He was a funny boy, wasn't he?'

'Yes. You always said his ears stuck out.'

'They weren't that bad really. Remember the picnic when he fell in the river?'

'That's because he was so short-sighted.'

'But he made it funny. That's what I liked about him. He always made you laugh at him but it was a nice kind of a joke.' She laughed, remembering. 'They were good times, weren't they?'

'You were so shy, I never knew for sure whether you were enjoying yourself.'

'It was your family. I was scared of them.'

'I know. But you were lovely. They knew you were lovely. They knew I'd be lucky to get you.'

'I never thought that. About them. I thought it was the other way round. They thought I was lucky to get you.'

'What's it matter love? Either way it's been all right, eh?'

'Been?'

'Is, then. Why don't you go and get into bed and I'll be there in a minute eh? I'll come and hold you, just hold you, we both need a rest.'

'You'll come soon?' said Winnie.

'As soon as I've locked up and tucked up the girl. Go along, I'll be there in a minute.'

He went through into Jeannie's bedroom. Clara shut her eyes as if she was asleep, with the blankets pulled up around her face. She could just see his shape by the light from the kitchen. He stood by the bed and stared down at Jeannie, and after a moment he leaned down and kissed her gently on the forehead, making a small muffled sound in his throat. As he was passing, he hesitated and touched Clara's face with his finger. Then he went out into the kitchen, and she heard him tearing paper from her pad. Clara

40

blushed in the dark, thinking he would see her drawings. He took a pencil out of her box, and there was rustling for a few moments, then he moved on to the bedroom, and the bed that he and Winnie shared. The house was still, and yet it was not still, as if it moved with their breaths.

In the dark, she took him in his arms, and moved her body towards his, but he held himself still and very careful, and said in a quiet lost voice, 'You're good, you're such a good girl Winnie,' and she didn't know whether it was a reproach for being so forward to him, or a compliment, but she didn't dare ask him, and when he began to stroke her hair she was reassured. They wrapped together in the tight dark, and the movement of his hand on the back of her head went quietly on, until she slept.

When they woke in the morning he was gone.

It was Jeannie, paddling barefoot through the freezing house to the lavatory, who found his note on the kitchen table. Clara heard their cries, and went out to find out what the matter was. Jeannie, like a mother herself, was cradling Winnie in her arms.

Reg had left at daybreak for the goldfields in the South Island. He could not bear what was happening to them all, he said in his note, and he was sure that he would be able to send them more money from down there, maybe make a little, and it would be one less mouth to feed.

Clara was excluded from their grief and went back to her room. Everything had changed all right, more than she had bargained for, even Jeannie, who was not a baby any more. That afternoon Clara went back to Mumma.

She went across town on her own, and as she left she looked back up the street and Jeannie was sweeping the verandah, not that there were any leaves on that harsh late winter day. Maybe it needed sweeping. Anyway, Jeannie was doing it.

Clara and Mumma looked to Winnie over the months till Caroline was born, but it was Jeannie she turned to.

Jeannie, that is, and Albie Tubbs.

CHAPTER THREE

Albie's ears did stick out slightly, and he had thick lenses in his glasses, but if these minor imperfections were ignored, he was actually rather nice-looking.

He and Reg had been in the same class together at Hamilton High, or at least until Albie moved ahead into a higher group than Reg. Reg had always been smart enough, but Albie was better than smart, he was clever. He went away to university, and Reg and Winnie used to talk about how he came back in the holidays dressed in rather extraordinary, but quite elegant clothes, and out to entertain them all by acting the part of the bungling young intellectual. His family were the ultimate of anyone's social aspirations in Hamilton. His father was a lawyer with a reputation for never losing a case, and it was generally understood that Albie would follow in his footsteps and join the family firm.

There were marvellous parties in the summer at the Tubbs' house, which was right on the bank of the wide river which flows through the town. Their place was hidden by willows and the young people used to go there in droves over the weekends, dressed in blazers and straw hats. Winnie had photographs of them, and they were the last thing she remembered to save out of the drawer of the oak dresser the day it went. She had pulled the drawer open and looked at them and nearly closed it again, but even on that awful day, she had decided to save them. It was a whole new world for her at the Tubbs', and when it began she knew that she wanted to be part of it forever. The Tubbs, despite their unfortunate name, had a magic that Winnie had never encountered before, or was likely to anywhere else within the confines of Hamilton.

Then something happened. None of them ever knew much about it, and what they did hear was filtered through in little snippets, so that even Reg, who was Albie's friend, was excluded.

But they did hear that Albie had fallen in love with a girl in Auckland whom his family thought was unsuitable. They fought to prevent him marrying her and stopped his allowance. They were certain that this would achieve their purpose because they believed the girl was only out for his money. Then they discovered that she was having a baby and they rushed to Auckland in a panic in order to make good what had happened. But when they got there the girl had married an old boyfriend who was prepared to take her on with the child. She died when her baby was born, and Albie cut himself off from his family.

His mother died without them being reconciled, and his father's practice dropped away. He became a dusty small-town lawyer mouldering away in his big empty offices. One day, out of the blue, Albie came back and moved in with his father to a smaller house. It seemed to those who knew them that the two men had just about forgotten what the quarrel was all about.

Albie went to teach at Tech, which was in itself a small act of defiance against the establishment and his own background, but as the school was gradually becoming respectable it could hardly be seen as a revolution. Besides, as the years passed and the depression took over, it was something just to have a job. Albie and Reg had almost been social equals; now despite the fact that neither had money nor status, Albie, with his comic name and big ears, kept the edge simply by being employed.

Reg had been scandalised by Albie's downfall and it had taken them a long time to pick up with each other. When they did, they must both have recognised the changes. They started a friendship again.

The weekend after Reg went away Albie did come to see Winnie.

During the week Mumma had gone backwards and forwards to Winnie's, doleing out what comfort she could, though every now and then Winnie would catch her looking at her in a way which made her wonder if she didn't really believe that she would be better off without Reg. But then, as Winnie knew, Mumma had some jaundiced ideas about men. Maybe with good reason, though who was to know, except Mumma herself. And sometimes Winnie thought that Clara might have seen more than she let on with her too careful and too sharp big eyes. Maybe.

Winnie sensed, too, that Mumma was anxious for her to settle down as quickly as possible to her changed style of life, to get on with things, and not fret about her missing husband. She thought bitterly that it would let her mother be free to get back to her cyclamens and orchids. Not that people bought them any more, but Winnie suspected that she might really like that, to have the fragile waxy flowers to herself, much as some women wanted to have their children to themselves without a father round to interfere with the running of things or to distract attention from their place at the centre.

Of course there was the problem of the baby. Even Mumma, batty old Mumma, couldn't overlook that Winnie had been left to have a baby on her own. She did take that part quite seriously, Winnie supposed, but there was the feeling there that she really hoped that something, or someone, would turn up to take her off her hands.

Someone did, and it was sooner than anyone could have predicted. Mumma went home on the Saturday morning to water her plants, leaving Clara there 'for company' and to 'play with Jeannie'. As Winnie and Jeannie and Clara all knew, each in their separate way, their needs had changed and it didn't matter whether she stayed or not. Only none of them was ready to express these thoughts so directly, or maybe they didn't even understand the change in so many words. It was just a different feeling in the air.

The weather had lightened, and the month turned during that week. One of Winnie's trees had developed a row of white buds like the rime of the all-too-familiar frost. In place of the constant soggy endurance test, that Saturday afternoon was a bright hard day with a brisk and promising breeze.

Jeannie and Clara had washed the lunch dishes. There was extra food that week. As news of Reg's departure spread, all sorts of people turned up with help. Perhaps Reg knew a thing or two, Winnie reflected, but it seemed a pity that a few of them hadn't done something a bit sooner. She supposed that they did their best, those ladies in furs, with the shiny little cars packed with scones and things, and she supposed too, that there were just too many people like the Hoggards for them to be able to pick out who was the worst off. People like them were especially hard to recognise, she had to admit to herself, because they would be the last to own up to their need. Winnie was still like that, but Cora and Ellen were not, and she supposed they must have put the word around about how things were with her. All sorts of food arrived, and flour and sugar, so that Winnie started baking again. To Clara it was almost like the old days, with the kitchen full of cooking smells and warmth, and the bright day outside. Winnie, though, was pale and self-contained, with heavy eyes and not much to say for herself.

That afternoon, around two o'clock, there was a knock on the back door.

'Shall I get it?' Clara called.

Winnie came out of the dining-room.

'Yes. If it's food tell them thank you very much and say I'm lying down,' she whispered.

'Shall I take it?'

She looked at Clara scornfully. 'Of course.'

'What if it's not food?'

'Oh . . . use your brains.' She pushed Clara towards the door before disappearing back into the dining-room.

It was Albie, standing uncertainly on one foot and then the other, as if he was about to give up and go away.

'Good afternoon,' Clara said, using her brightest social voice in a manner that she hoped would please Winnie. 'Mr Tubbs, isn't it? If it's food, my sister says thank you very much and she's not feeling so well.'

He stared as if she was demented. 'I came to see Reg,' he said.

'Oh.' Clara looked over her shoulder for help, but none was forthcoming. What she was almost certain that Winnie had meant was that if it was anybody else she should tell them she wasn't there or couldn't see them. But then she knew that Reg and Winnie liked Albie. She seemed bound to make a mistake, whatever she did.

'He's gone away,' she muttered.

'Is he working today?'

'No. He's gone. Right away, to the goldfields.'

'Is your sister in?'

'I don't know,' said Clara miserably, wishing that she didn't have to take responsibility for him.

'I'll get Mum,' said Jeannie. 'I expect she'll want to see you.'

Clara heard Winnie speak on a high sharp note to Jeannie. She appeared after what seemed like a long time.

'Hello Albie,' she said, without moving towards him. Clara thought that Jeannie was in for trouble this time, but it seemed that she knew better what was good for her mother. Albie came in without being invited and shut the door firmly behind him.

'Now what's this all about?' he said.

45

'He's gone.'

'So she said.' He nodded in Clara's direction and she wished that people would remember her name. She supposed that he didn't really know her very well. At least it gave her a chance to study him properly while they talked. Apart from the ears, which didn't seem so bad after all, perhaps because he hadn't had a haircut for quite a while and his hair was bushy and wavy round them, and the glasses, which didn't hide his nice eyes, he had a high forehead with rather less hair there than round his ears, and a full mouth above a jutting chin with a cleft. He had got rather stooped so that at first you didn't realise how tall he was. Winnie had to look up to him which she didn't with Reg, and Clara thought that he must be about six foot, maybe more, and he had a very tanned shiny skin, even though it was winter. It gave him the appearance of excellent health and considering that he worked inside, was in odd contrast to Reg and other men she had seen who worked on the swamp scheme. Despite the outdoor life their skins were often marked by a glassy pallor.

'He didn't tell me he was going,' said Winnie.

For a while the silence condensed around them. Winnie thought, he already knows. Everything there is to know about me. And it occurred to her then, for the last time before she dismissed the matter as not being important enough to consider further, that it was not he who had come to the door on the night Reg went away. Maybe Reg had seen him and suggested he call that day, but that was another matter, and whatever it implied, didn't concern her now. What was clear was, that whatever Albie knew, they were not things he had been told. Like the old knowledge that lies in the air over excavations, it was a matter of simple knowing. She had not had this experience with anyone before.

He said at last, 'I expect he had to go. He wouldn't have gone otherwise.'

'That's what I tell myself.'

'Do you?' He seemed surprised, pleased with her somehow.

'I feel sorrier for him than I do for myself.'

He nodded. 'I'd say that was fair.'

It seemed a funny thing for him to say at the time.

'If I'd known . . . ' Winnie trailed away, tried again. 'I could have stopped him.'

'Could you?' Albie's eyes were searching.

'Oh yes.' She said this with quiet certainty. Without thinking she placed her hand on her stomach. Albie saw. Again Winnie had

46

the feeling that he knew exactly what she was talking about and she glanced up at him as if his height was an irresistible force that she had not confronted before. Their eyes met and she coloured, but she didn't look away.

'Yes,' she said, though he had said nothing.

'Would you have?' he asked.

'Stopped him?' She hesitated. 'Of course. That night I would have. That would have been the natural thing to do wouldn't it?'

'And now?'

She gestured with her hands, partly a shrug, partly an acceptance of what had happened.

'I expect not. I couldn't have seen it then could I? Though I'm not glad, if that's what you mean.'

He smiled slightly. 'Of course not. I didn't mean that.'

'We'll manage. I won't try and have him brought back.'

He stood looking at her. 'Get your coat on,' he said.

'Why?'

'We're going for a walk. It'll be cold by the lake, you'll need something warm.'

Winnie looked at the two girls.

'Jeannie'll be all right with Clara,' he said. Clara smiled, pleased he had remembered her name. The way he handled it there was no question of her and Jeannie going with them.

Winnie looked as if she was going to protest but when she looked up at Albie again it was clear that she must go with him.

They often walked by the lake through the spring and the summer that followed, though it got harder for Winnie to get around as the months passed. At first they walked rather stiffly, side by side, being careful not to touch, but as her pregnancy advanced it was more natural for her to take his arm, and lean towards him.

Clara never heard what people thought about this state of affairs. In Hamilton, when a man stopped to talk to a woman it was usually because they were related to each other or about to become so. It wasn't done to stand around talking to men in public unless there was some immediate connection with each other, and married women didn't stop to talk with other men even if they were their husband's best friends. In fact, that was probably the worst person to be seen talking to. And yet Winnie and Albie slipped into an easy pattern of being seen together, and seemed somehow careless about what they were doing. It had to be because of some difference in Albie, for on her own, Winnie would never have dreamed of behaving like that. Yet with him, it was almost as if she followed in a trance; certainly, in those months when she was waiting for the baby to be born, as though in some mysterious way he had taken charge of her life.

Mumma appeared to accept it as a quite natural turn of events. Perhaps the uncharitable could say that she was relieved, but then again, it was not so much unkind as a simple truth. Albie released her, maybe not in the practical sense, for there was still plenty to be done to help keep the Hoggard household going, but in that Winnie stopped relying on her. She did not have to concern herself whether Winnie was happy or unhappy, whether she might be confronted by her tears or not, and whether she would have to exert her own inner life to meet her daughter's needs. It was all taken care of. Winnie would rather be with Albie. It was as straightforward as that.

If neighbours talked, Winnie seemed unaware, and if the family gossiped they did not do so in front of Clara. It had happened so easily, the transition from Reg to Albie, that in a way nobody noticed. Or so it seemed to Clara, when she thought back to that time. And for a brief period there was a difference about many people, too, as if for the moment judgement was all but suspended. They were most preoccupied with what happened to themselves. Maybe what Winnie did with her life was less important than it might have been in more ordinary times.

There was one thing though, and Clara and Winnie in their own ways both noticed the fact, that the good ladies with the food stopped coming. Presumably they thought that Winnie had someone to look after her so they didn't need to any more.

When Winnie did think about it, that was how she would like to have seen it, but she knew that really those particular ladies in Hamilton were not quite like that. They were funny about the bishop too, who had recently married his housekeeper. It was said that the Cathedral was often half-empty.

Gradually the need for food stopped being so desperate anyway. Reg started sending money home once a month. He had got in on the gold scheme down south, subsidised mining as it was called, and in some ways it was just about as miserable as the swamps but he wrote that at least you were your own boss and you could make a bit of money. He was quite hopeful about things.

After a while the letters stopped coming, or certainly did not come often, but there was money deposited for Winnie every month and he never missed, so that after a while she came to take it for granted that she had a small regular income. Albie helped with the garden at weekends and he and his father had more vegetables round at their place than the two of them could use, and enough space for a hen run, so there were eggs too.

Sometimes they spoke to each other as a man and his wife might do, with the ease and familiarity of two people who understood each other's old habits, and tolerated silences as if they were actually communications. Yet Clara did not think of them like that, for Albie never stayed at the house, except later, when the baby was ill (which, admittedly, turned out to be often) but then he would sit up all night in front of the stove with the oven door open to keep him warm, and often with the cot alongside of him so he could reach out when the child cried. This way Winnie got to have a rest.

And although they touched each other, they did not embrace, and Winnie always referred to him as Mr Tubbs when she was speaking of him to Jeannie and Clara, and that was what they called him. Yet it was he who chose the name of Caroline for the baby when it came, a more colourful and ambitious name than Winnie might have chosen for her, having for so long put aside the manner in which Clara had come to be named. Mumma asked her once if Reg liked the baby's name.

'I haven't got round to mentioning it,' said Winnie shortly.

Mumma looked at her then. 'The baby or her name?' she asked. By Winnie's silence it was clear that she meant both. Even Mumma seemed shocked for a moment, but she didn't ask again.

Sometimes Winnie thought about the gap that there was in her and Albie's lives, for it was true that she had come to think of him as a husband, except in one vital respect. She wondered whether it was fair that they were not lovers, and supposed that if she had a conscience about the matter it worked in reverse to what it should, because she seemed to take so much from him and to give so little in return. She wondered why he kept coming to her and if he was waiting for her to let it begin. She thought that if she had not been having the baby when he first came to her that it would have happened, but then it had not seemed proper, she was sure as much to him as to her. Until at last there was no point where it could begin. Or so it seemed. The time for it had slipped past them. Besides, there was Caroline, the sick grumpy little girl, and after a while it seemed that Albie found it enough just to take care of them all. Some days, standing at her window, looking down at the peach tree and the magpies, and the fresh silver beet sprouting in the newly hoed earth, she would wonder what to do about it, and how he felt, but she did not know how to begin in this respect and had no way of accounting for what he thought about it. It occurred to her, on other days, that looking after them was a means of atoning for his own past.

Yet they were lovers. In a way. And in a way they both knew it.

Later, when Winnie turned self-righteous and matronly, Clara would remember that. The way they looked at each other. The turn of their heads. The secret containment of glancing touches. The way they laughed.

By the summer of 1934 Albie was persuading Winnie to go on outings with him, so Clara was much in demand again to stay with the two girls. Albie had to be clever to get Winnie to accept things, because she wouldn't take money from him and so he had to invent gifts of the things she needed — and sometimes didn't need but gave her pleasure. He had got her to take a wireless as a Christmas present, even though she was shocked by its extravagance, but he said that if she would accept a Christmas present at all (and as she had got one for him there was really no argument) then it was only extravagant if he couldn't afford it. They listened to 'Scrim' and after some initial resistance from her, they would talk about the Labour Party, and she went to some meetings with him.

That was the beginning. After that it was the races. That did surprise the family, because she wasn't the type and he didn't seem to be either. Clara, looking back on that too, thought they were probably right about this because she herself was crazy about the races and when she first knew Ambrose they would go as often as possible; she knew that neither she nor any of the friends they went with were like Winnie and Albie.

But it seemed that this slightly stooped, rather eccentric (for that was how some saw him) school teacher of Winnie's was a racehorse fan and knew how to study form. It was from him that Clara first learnt how bets were placed. Later he talked Winnie into going to the Summer Show at Claudelands with him, and Clara, who would normally have expected to go herself, had to stay home with the girls. Mumma said that Winnie didn't get many outings and it was the least she could do for her. Secretly Clara thought that Winnie was doing rather well for herself. She and Mumma didn't have a wireless.

She wasn't old enough to make herself heard, and it was still a couple of years off the Show being the major event of the year to meet boys, or nothing in the world would have made her look after Winnie's kids for her. She did as she was told.

She was expecting them back round lunchtime but they didn't come. She heated some soup and spoonfed Caroline who never seemed to like anything, and tried to get Jeannie to help her but Jeannie showed a great reluctance where the baby was concerned and Clara was just about in tears by the time Winnie and Albie turned up after four in the afternoon.

They burst into the kitchen where she was mixing up cocoa in a fresh attempt to tempt Caroline, and Winnie's face was shining in a way it hadn't done for years.

'Hello there,' she cried, with a sweeping theatrical gesture which wasn't like her at all.

'Where have you been?' Clara said angrily.

'Where have we been? Where *have* we been?' she cried to Albie.

Looking at her face it was easy to forget that she was wearing a shapeless old coat with patches in the sleeves and down-at-heel mended-over shoes.

'We went to the races,' said Albie with an air of triumph.

Clara stared at them. Caroline started to cry again, and Clara picked her up and thrust her at Winnie. 'Perhaps you could race some food into her then,' she said. 'It might shut her up.'

For once Winnie took notice. Clara had tears in her eyes, and she felt stupid for being so angry, and unkind because she was out to spoil their pleasure. For all that, there was a passing satisfaction that Winnie had stopped and seen her when she said, 'You poor thing. I'll see to her.' She took Caroline and the little girl stopped crying at once.

Winnie said, 'I'll give you five shillings for looking after her all day, it's the least I can do.'

She sort of tossed this off as if she did it all the time, or rather she tried to, but it came out in a rather stilted and awkward way. Albie looked at her sideways.

She said, 'Yes Albie that's fair. Clara's always looking after the kids for me and I can afford it you know.'

'But you can't,' said Clara.

'Yes I can, because Albie made me place a bet today and I don't think I've ever felt so guilty about *anything* in my life, but he made me, didn't you, tell her you made me,' she implored, turning to Albie.

'Took it out of her purse,' he said solemnly, joining in the story. 'Tell her why.'

'Because if I'd put it on for you, you wouldn't have taken the winnings, even if you paid me back for the bet.'

'Right. A pound. A whole pound Clara. I don't know whether I should tell Mumma, what do you think?'

'I don't think she'll care if you won,' Clara said, for of course by then it was obvious that she had. 'How much did you get?'

Winnie looked as if she had had her story spoiled a little by being anticipated, but she said, as if she was doing a conjuring trick, 'Twenty-nine pounds, Clara. Can you imagine it?'

It was Winnie who couldn't imagine it, really. She didn't know of anyone having so much money all at the one time, not the actual money in their hand. But she had it. It was folded up in notes in her purse. She held one of them up to Clara.

'As soon as I get change for this I'll give you five shillings.'

'She'll get the change on Monday,' said Albie, 'because that's when she's going shopping.'

'Oh I can't Albie,' she said, as if continuing a conversation they had already begun.

'I'm not taking you to the races in this again,' he said, touching the sleeve of her tatty old garment. 'You do want to come again, don't you?'

On the Monday she bought a Donegal tweed suit and a green hat and matching green shoes, and gave Clara her five shillings.

They didn't go to the races every time they were on but still they went quite often; after the next time Winnie was able to buy an oak dresser much like the one she had sold, and slowly the house was refurnished.

Meanwhile, Reg's money kept on coming. One day in an idle moment Winnie said to Mumma, 'I wonder where he is nowadays. Reg. You know, I wonder where he is.'

'If you really want to know, you can trace where the money goes into your account, young lady.' Mumma's tone was unusually sharp.

Winnie's face closed like a trap. Still, she had taken to giving Mumma presents lately, and Mumma didn't refuse them. Winnie didn't know what had prompted her to mention Reg, for she seldom thought about him these days. But after that conversation she found herself staring down the garden more than ever, and he kept creeping in, through the corners of her attention. It had become increasingly difficult to recall exactly what he looked like, which seemed extraordinary when she considered that there had been a time when his image was imprinted on her like part of herself. It came to her one morning that that was partly the explanation, that she had always expected him to be there, and he had gone away, and with him he had taken any certainty of him. She became less surprised by the lack of his image in her mind.

The other thing that occurred to her was that she was happier now than she had ever been, and with this came the knowledge that the reason she thought of Reg so often now was because she was afraid he would return.

And that she loved Albie.

She wondered if other women were so slow and ordered in the progression of their thoughts, and why it had taken her so long to understand what was so obvious, now that she had come to this point. 'I am older,' she said aloud, in the kitchen, one morning. There was nobody there, but she needed to hear herself talk. 'It's not like I was a silly kid.'

All that day, and in the days that followed immediately afterwards, she was animated and laughed a great deal. But the mood didn't last long. In the progression of her thoughts there were the other considerations, which she had, for a time, put aside. She wanted him now, with her in her bed. He could not fail to notice, and her new awareness of him changed the way he was when they were together, too.

They were sitting together on the sofa one evening. There was a good fire burning, marking an early autumn. Pine cones were spitting in the grate and there was a glow in the room. Albie moved towards her, but instead of letting him come closer to her she moved down the sofa, away from him. They had the wireless on, and there was static in the air.

Albie got up to adjust the set.

'Shall I turn it off?'

'No. I don't know. There might be something on.'

'There might.' He walked around the room.

'You're restless. Can't you sit still?'

'Not really. No, as a matter of fact it's very difficult.'

'Perhaps you should go home and have an early night.'

'Is that what you want? Is it?' He was close to shouting at her.

She sat very still. On the wireless a singer began to croon, 'What'll I do?', anticipating parting and the loss of love.

He sat down again and they looked at each other, their faces aching and painful.

'Why can't we?' said Albie. 'I can't bear this.'

'I'm still married,' said Winnie. Her voice was strained.

'That's an excuse,' said Albie harshly. 'You would have at the beginning.'

She didn't answer him at once, then she said, 'But we didn't did we?'

'Don't you want to? Don't you want *me*?'

'You know I do.' She was surprised by her own violence.

'Then now. While we both want it. While it's right.'

'But it's not right, don't you see. The children . . . any of the girls could get up . . . they're too old . . . '

'Too old for what?' he said.

'To know that we . . . that it was like that, when we haven't the right.'

'It's killing me Win,' he said. 'D'you understand?'

'What'll you do?' she said, like the song.

'Do?' He was trembling. 'I think I'd die if I couldn't see you every day I live,' he said. 'That's what I think I'd do.'

She put her hand on the back of his neck.

'It'll be all right soon,' she said. 'It'll be all right love.'

He lifted his head. 'What d'you mean?'

'I'll work something out, you'll see. So that it is right.'

He gripped her hand then, and was still. The music was gentle and only the flames moved.

In the kitchen where she had gone for a drink, Clara slipped away back through the shadows, and lay awake beside Jeannie.

It was less than a week after they had talked that Winnie and Albie gathered them all up for a walk to the lake. The two adults walked behind Jeannie and Clara pushing Caroline in her pushchair. It was a grey flat day, and they were wearing their heavy coats for the first time of the year, except for Clara who had reached the age where she didn't want to be different if she met any friends. The ducks at the edge of the water went round and round in aimless little circles, waiting for stray scraps to float past. The older girls fed them out of a brown paper bag filled with crusts. Clara remembered when there had been no crusts to spare. Mostly they had their hands filled with looking after Caroline.

For all she was a pretty yellow-haired little girl, she was restless and still irritable. If she was crossed it always seemed as if it was their fault and even Clara and Jeannie found themselves uneasily lined up together to defend each other when she grizzled.

They tired of feeding the ducks. Clara felt as if she had been tired of it for years. The feathers of the birds eddied around them in small dusty clouds and there was nothing to do. Some mothers sat with their children near the waterfront and it was the kind of day when they all seemed cross. Behind them eight very tall pine trees stood in a cluster. They had had all their branches removed right up to the bushy tufts at the very top. Clara wondered who on earth could have bothered to strip them like that. Probably someone as bored as them, with the advantage of axes and ropes. At least they had done something. That was what she craved, that something would happen. Anything.

She was nearly thirteen now, and she had seen two boys from the High School kicking stones along the lake front. She was glad they weren't Tech boys. They would have run a mile if they had spotted Albie even though it was said that he got on well with his pupils. She fancied one of the boys in particular, for she had seen him often. He lived down Winnie's street. But though she had seen him around for years, she hadn't really noticed him till just recently. She could see that he noticed her too.

She put Caroline in her pushchair and strapped her in.

'Sit with her a while, she'll settle down,' she said to Jeannie, making her voice as callous as she could.

'Where are you going?'

Clara wondered how many times she had heard Jeannie ask that same relentless question.

'Just for a walk.'

'Can't we all go?' But it was clear that Clara would say no even before she had asked. Clara was learning to say no.

She walked rapidly, with her head down. She ran a hand through her hair and felt it fluff out beneath her fingers, and arched her spine so that her waist pulled in tighter, though she knew that is was already very small and neat, and she gave her bottom a little wiggle the way she had seen Jean Harlow doing it on the screen, or at least it felt as if she was doing it the same. But when she looked round furtively to see if the boys were watching, they had gone. She was almost relieved. She had not really worked out what she would do if she met them. At least she had had a brief respite from Jeannie and Caroline.

As she turned to go back to them she heard Winnie and Albie's voices. They were sitting together on a seat behind the bush alongside the drive that encircled the lake. She stopped, thinking she was going to be caught for leaving Jeannie and Caroline, or half afraid that they might magically divine that she had been chasing boys.

'I've done everything I could to trace him,' Winnie said. 'They don't know where he is.'

'What about the last deposit he made?'

'They tracked it down to Christchurch, but they didn't know anything about him there. They think he was just passing through. And that was two months ago, Albie, so it looks as if he might have stopped sending money altogether. I don't think he'll ever come back.'

'Does it make you feel any better?'

'About us? Oh yes.'

'It'll be all right then?'

She looked up at him. 'I've been hard on you haven't I?'

He picked up her hand and turned it over in his. 'It's all right now though. It doesn't matter.'

She turned her face towards him and he kissed her, holding her close, and said, against her sensible short brown hair, 'Oh my sweet love. Don't ever leave me Winnie.'

Soon they got to their feet for in the distance Winnie heard Caroline's fretful cry. Jeannie and Clara pushed the pushchair up the hill again between them. Clara was pleased to see that the boys had gone.

She looked back at Winnie and Albie and they were following a little way behind. Albie was swinging along, jaunty and certain, and his shoulders were straighter than she had ever seen them. Winnie had a dreamy silly sort of smile hovering around the corners of her mouth. As they turned out of the gates and back towards the water tower, Clara felt absurdly pleased for them, not knowing quite why, but glad that for them at least, something was going to happen. She was sure that it was so.

And that was the way it was when Reg walked along the street to meet them, just a few moments later.

After Reg had kissed Winnie's cheek he shook hands with Albie and thanked him for keeping an eye on his family while he'd been away. It was as if he had been gone for a week rather than three years, the way he spoke.

He and Winnie slipped back into a routine, and he never asked where the clothes or the furniture had come from. He didn't need to ask about Caroline though the records would have been sufficient to dispel any doubts. But he didn't ask to see them. Caroline was just like the Hoggards which was something none of them had really noticed before, and so pretty that she delighted her father. She stopped being cross within a week of him being home as if something missing had been put in place in her life. Clara was glad for Reg's sake.

Albie didn't die, but he didn't come round any more either. Winnie cut the Donegal tweed down for Jeannie, and Caroline tottered round the yard a few times playing at dressing up in the brave green shoes and hat until they were relegated to the rubbish tin.

Reg got a job at the dairy factory and it wasn't long before they gave him a job in management. He and Winnie began to prosper and if she was quiet, she looked well enough. As for Clara, she had other things to do besides worry about them.

CHAPTER FOUR

Clara always painted Hamilton in the most gloomy colours when she described the town to people afterwards. The way she talked about it, anyone would be justified in believing that it was always foggy and cold, frosty and bitter, or grey and leaden. It is true that it can be all of those, but it can be beautiful too. When the sun shines it is a great ripe ball in the sky and the green land at the edge of the town glistens like a soft coat on the earth. The river, to be sure, is always sombre, but in its steady and unhurried flow there is the heart of the matter. There is a movement, a deep current. And if the water is touched with the hand, it is clean and lovely water. Not everyone bothers. People don't always take the time to study the Waikato river. But on a good day, one of the high-domed shiny days, it is worth it, as Clara came to know over the years.

It was a day like that when she finally got to talk to Robin. He lived near Winnie's, and it was he whom she had watched with such admiration, the day that Reg came back from the goldfields. A High School boy.

She was sent to High the next year, or rather she elected to go there. In a way it was because of Robin, although she couldn't have spelled it out as being the reason then. She was certainly interested in boys, there was no doubt about that, and he was the one that she could watch secretly every weekend that she was at Winnie's place. He came to represent high school to her and the tantalising possibilities of boys in general. When the question of where she would go to school came up there really wasn't any doubt about it. She was going to High too.

She was enrolled for French and Latin and mathematics; everything that had a difficult ring to it. But if her teachers had thought that she had a glimmer of cleverness, they hadn't reckoned on the baleful influence of clever Jeannie, or how Clara already knew how much easier it was to be popular than clever. By the end of the first year she had dropped out of French and Latin. Her stray and strange passion for history and mathematics, which was more evident in class than in her exam results, kept her uneasily in the second class down from the top. She could only disrupt the lower classes; she was manageable where they placed her. It suited her and later she was grateful for it when she met Robin, properly that is, for he, glittering and brilliant, would not have taken kindly to the competition of a really top girl, and would have been embarrassed by a dull one. It was ideal. It was where Clara stayed, without distinction, for her entire time at high school.

Towards the end of her first year, she got to know Robin. She would catch glimpes of him walking to school if she stayed over at Winnie's at the weekend and went to school from her place on the Monday morning, although by then that didn't happen very often. She would see him around school too, but only from a distance. She was a year behind him and besides, the girls and boys were not encouraged to mix.

In a way it didn't matter, because he was still just one of the whole hairy-legged, pimply, and amazingly exciting horde of boys that teemed around the place, whistling and appearing to jeer at the girls.

On a Saturday morning in late November, Clara went out to Winnie's letter box. Winnie and Reg were having a rare outing. One of the Hoggard cousins was getting married and they had asked her to stay over with the girls while they went to the wedding. She was resentful because she thought they were old enough to take care of themselves. Besides she felt she was only invited there these days when Winnie wanted something. She was particularly incensed that weekend because there was a dance on at the Junction and, although she hadn't yet turned fourteen, it was amazing what she could get away with. Mumma never seemed to notice what Clara did. In spite of that she had never actually had the nerve to go to one of the dances, though she was one of a group who hung around the door of the hall on the way home from the pictures some nights, and crept round parked cars before retreating with their breaths flapping in their chests like a line of washing. This night was to have been the night when they ventured across the doorstep.

Instead Mumma had put her foot down with unusual force.

Perhaps she had an inkling of what was on Clara's mind, and with it an attack of conscience. Clara wasn't sure what it was, but between Mumma and Winnie they got her over to stay with the girls. The wedding was at eleven o'clock and Winnie and Reg didn't expect to be home till late in the evening, for they were being driven out to Cambridge by relatives who were sure to stay the distance.

The postie's whistle shrilled at Winnie's box and Clara ambled out to see what was there. A couple of bills and a circular from the Labour Party which had probably been delivered by hand the night before.

What a morning. The trees and shrubs had come to life and were shiny and flowering, there was a smell of summer in the air. Across the road a forsythia blazed like yellow fire, an enormous spreading ball. Clara was surprised that the Council hadn't cut it back, it took up so much room on the street. Robin Mawson appeared from behind it on his hands and knees, coming out backwards. She couldn't believe it at first, it was such an absurd sight, which he must have known, or would have if he hadn't been so concerned about something else. Instead of being embarrassed or rushing off without looking at her he called out.

'Have you seen a pup by any chance?'

'Have you lost one?'

'I wouldn't be under a bush if I hadn't.'

There were several reasons why he mightn't have been under a bush but she didn't say that. She asked him, instead, what the pup was like and how long it had been lost. It was a very small puppy he said, too small to be wandering about on its own, and he had only had it a week. It was a Labrador and its name was Chip though he supposed it wouldn't know its name yet. It had been gone since the night before, and even though the weather was warmer now he was afraid that it might have suffered from a night in the open. Would she watch out for him, he beseeched Clara.

Would she? She had admired Robin from such distance, for so long, and here he was asking her to do something for him.

And she looked at his mass of wavy fair hair and his almond-shaped eyes, his pimples, and his anxious overworked Adam's apple, and couldn't believe her luck.

Nor could she when she found the pup cowering in Winnie's woodshed, less than an hour later. She called out to Jeannie and told her she was taking the pup over to Doctor Mawson's place. She was as offhanded as she could be, and when Jeannie wanted to

60

go with her she rebuked her in a sharp grown-up way for thinking of leaving Caroline on her own. She was, she implied, committed to attending to the busines of the moment without having to worry about nonsense like that. It was an old and useful trick with Jeannie and it nearly always worked.

She met Robin in the street on the way to his house. When he saw the pup his face lit up. She thought then that that might be an end to it but he insisted (insisted? maybe she let him think he did) that she go back to his place so that his father, who had paid a great deal for the dog and was furious with him, according to Robin, could thank her, and she could see it fed, and so forth. There seemed to be a whole string of good reasons why he wanted her to go with him, but only one very good one why she should want to go, which was, quite simply, that she didn't ever want to be anywhere for the rest of her life except walking along beside Robin Mawson; and if walking alongside of him took her into the huge white house with gables and pillars, set back from the street behind oak trees and fine silver birches, where Doctor and Mrs Mawson and their family lived, that was fine by her.

When she thought back to that time, it was almost impossible to retell how she felt then, either to herself or anyone else. She fell in love with Robin and Robin fell in love with her. She entered that tender world of loving for the first time. There is never another time like it again in all the world, no matter what happens in the future. The mind changes. The body changes, not so much as at the beginning of womanhood, but with a blossoming as if there is a purpose for everything. She walked differently. And she dreamt, in a new way. She dreamt of marriage.

So did he. They went to church in the cathedral where Robin had sung as a choirboy, and they thought of themselves as being already married. It was summer and they learned the languages of love beside the river and beneath the trees. Summer ripened everything.

The butterflies hovered above and birds sang as they made their explorations. The pennyroyal bloomed profusely along the banks of the river and they crushed it so that strange tangy smell of it clung to their clothes afterwards; there were willow trees twisting everywhere, screening them from the world, the thistledown touched them as a reminder that they must be gentle with each other.

If it could have stopped there. If a summer had been enough. Perhaps, quite simply, if they had been older. If at the end of it

61

there had been no war. If his parents and hers had not been so different.

If all of these things had been so, her life might have been different, she would think afterwards.

For his parents did not approve. It was Winnie's story all over again, only worse in a way. Some people in Hamilton tried to propagate the notion that there were no differences amongst them, that they were of one class. It was not so, and Clara, who moved from the Junction to that part of Hamilton where the Mawsons lived, knew that as well as anyone. And the gap between the Junction and the people who lived in the pas made an even greater nonsense of the idea of equality.

Even within the one group there were differences. As the depression receded and became a memory, a lot of the people in Hamilton began to prosper; many of them became very rich. What made the difference was when, and how, they got rich. With the Hoggards, in their heyday, it had been commercial, with the Mawsons it was professional.

Most of the children ended up at the same schools, often private ones in the cities, but the Mawsons had left it too late for Christ's, and decided, as some of the quite notable families in town were being experimental and liberal about their children's education, that they would try High. Later, when Clara entered Robin's life and persisted in it, they tried desperately to get him into Collegiate or into King's but it was too late, and he wouldn't have gone anyway. He simply said he would fail his exams if they did, and he meant it.

Certainly the families ended up at the same twenty-firsts and some of them did marry amongst the different groups, but it was definitely stepping up if you moved from commercial to professional. As for Clara, she was the worst sort of outsider. If it had been Jeannie and they had both been older it might just have been possible, but not Clara. She was the wrong side of the tracks, and the railway tracks at that. Robin could not have picked worse company to keep.

Nor could his parents have handled it more badly. They did all they could to separate them, and the more they did the more inseparable they became.

Clara turned fourteen in the January after they met, and on that same day she made love for the first time. Robin was fifteen, and although what they did was as new to him as it was to her it seemed as if they had been lovers for a long time. She often felt when she had been with him on the riverbank like a ripe melon that had been split with an axe. She was very happy.

It was over a year before she became pregnant, and she missed the first fifth form exams recovering from the abortion she had at Doctor Mawson's house.

Winnie thought the Mawsons must have taken leave of their senses when Clara was invited there to stay. They told her to tell Mumma that she wanted to study for the exams with Robin, and then, that she'd got the flu and couldn't sit them, and all the time she was staying in their immaculate primrose spare bedroom and Mrs Mawson brought her cups of tea, snivelling, and not looking at her. Before she left to go home Doctor Mawson came in and sat on the edge of the bed in his most professional manner. He waited expectantly as if she was supposed to say something. When she didn't he sighed and said in a tired voice, 'I suppose you've got ideas about him?'

'What ideas?' she said stupidly.

'Marriage. Things like that. Young girls get ideas like that.'

'We know we're too young. I mean, that's why . . . ' she blushed and trailed away. 'That's why we couldn't have the baby,' she finished lamely.

'You and Robin can't have babies — ever,' he said.

'But when we're married, when we're older . . . '

'Exactly. That's exactly what I mean. You girls get ideas.'

She didn't understand. Not altogether, though she had a horrible feeling that if she tried she could work it out. He looked as if he might try and explain it to her carefully but then changed his mind. He spoke sharply and with authority.

'When Robin marries he'll find a decent girl. He's got a career ahead of him. She'll be the right sort of person to help him.'

'He won't give me up.' She was fierce too.

'Oh don't be silly. A few years at medical school, he'll soon forget you.'

'And if he doesn't?'

He was clearly astounded and angry as well. 'You'll have a long time to wait. He can't marry anyone till he's twenty-one without my consent. You don't really think I'd allow it, do you?'

He was a grey, suede-coloured man with fine soft grey hair, thinning above the long grey stripes in his face, and he held his papery grey hands in a tent with the tips of his fingers while he talked. She studied those hands and thought about what they had done to her.

63

'If you love him as you say you do,' he went on, his voice colourless and quiet again, 'you'll let him go. You don't even do well at school. I've found out, you know.' His voice rose a pitch higher again, as if to say that the very least she could do to earn the love of his son was to get good marks at school.

In a way, he was right. A funny thing had happened to her since she met Robin. Before she'd been lazy, but it was true that she could have done better, as the teachers said. Then when she was with him something changed. She didn't want to do well under any circumstances. He was bright, very bright, but every now and then she would be a jump ahead of him about something, and she would see him look at her with a small, hurt, indignant look so that she shied off, scared of what she had done. She stopped being good in history and maths, stopped being good at anything except being Robin's girlfriend.

It was good enough in terms of popularity at school, but she got sick of the place. She wanted to leave and start getting her box together. It went without saying that when Robin left for medical school she intended going too, and that they were going to get married, in spite of what his father had said. It had become more important to get some sheets and pillowcases and towels and crockery than to stay on doing algebra and Tudor England. Besides she had come to hate the school itself. The corridors were like endless tunnels. The small windows were like the tight smiles of Hamilton's matrons.

She called in at Winnie's after she left the Mawson's. Winnie fussed over her pale appearance. She told her she was leaving school, that there was no point in going on because of the need to save in preparation for getting married to Robin. Winnie's face darkened then. She could have been a Mawson herself.

'You silly child,' she said, and glanced over her shoulder to check that Jeannie couldn't hear. 'You can't have the Mawsons, don't you know?'

'Why not? You had Reg.'

She thought Winnie was going to smack her face then but she checked herself. 'It was different.'

'Why?' Clara shouted at her. 'Why are you always different? You were worse than I ever was. Our father was still alive when you married Reg. The Hoggards can't have liked that very much.'

Winnie shook then but she said, regaining her usual even way, 'I was older. You must see that. And I'd made something of myself. And I'd got away. You must see that it was different.'

'You think I should leave Mumma then? Where shall I go? Come and live with you and pretend you're my mother? I could you know.'

'Go home,' she said tiredly. 'Stop being stupid.'

'I'm not too young to have a baby.'

'I shall speak to Mumma about you if you go on talking dirty,' she said.

Clara laughed then. 'What would she do?'

'Then I'll speak to Reg.'

'Reg can't stop me having a baby. He can go up to Doctor Mawson's and fish mine out of the garden if he likes. That's where he put it on Saturday afternoon.'

She went very white then. 'You didn't?'

'I did, and I'm having another one as soon as I'm sixteen and he's not getting his dirty paws on me then, I'll have it and they'll have to let Robin marry me the way he wants to and I'll go away to Dunedin with him. So there.'

'Clara. Clara, go back to school. Please. Please stop this.' Winnie was near to tears. Clara didn't really understand why she hated her being with Robin so much, especially, as she pointed out to her, after she had gone off with Reg and upset the Hoggards all those years before. She thought she might have been a bit proud of her following in her footsteps now.

When she thought about it later she could see why Winnie was frightened. She really had had more to offer than Clara did then, and even though the Hoggards had fallen on hard times, she had used her marriage — or most of it —to build up a careful life for her children, those two precious daughters, and if Clara created a scandal that the Mawsons couldn't live down, her efforts would count for nothing.

'What's the matter Winnie? You'd have had an abortion if you could. Do you wish you could have had one like me?'

Her face sagged.

'I wanted my baby, Winnie, but they wouldn't let me have it. That's really why you're mad, isn't it?'

Winnie smacked her then, and it was too late for either of them to have regrets, although they both did.

Clara left school and she stopped seeing Winnie. She didn't go near her for nearly a year. Mumma didn't seem to care whether she went to school or not and she liked the idea of being paid board. As for her teachers, they visibly sighed with relief. She worried a little about Robin still being a schoolboy and her being at work but by that time he looked so grown up that it wasn't really important. If it hadn't been for his huge hairy legs sticking out of his short pants he could have been a member of the staff.

Things had been decided for her anyway, because a week or so after the trip to the Mawsons she did get 'flu and it settled on her chest. She was ill for three weeks and Mumma nursed her, as tender and attentive as the most careful mother in the world. She rang Doctor Mawson who wouldn't come. She was puzzled because she told Clara he had questioned her a great deal about her illness and then refused point-blank to come because he wasn't their doctor, and he had told her to get one in Frankton. Clara was relieved. She hadn't known Mumma was going to ring him.

It wasn't easy to get a doctor in Frankton either because the Bentleys' previous one had left to go to the war and they were getting scarce in the area. In the end one did come, by which time Clara had pneumonia. Mumma and Robin took turns sitting up with her for several nights in a row and eventually she recovered, though she was weak. She supposed that she should have been in hospital. Her chest was always weak afterwards.

She liked that time with Mumma, though Mumma herself was angry and uncomprehending that Winnie didn't come to see Clara, or help. Clara understood, but she was angry too.

From then on, Robin lived in clear defiance of his parents, and continued to see Clara.

But the two of them also lived with tensions that had not been there before. Because she had been so ill, her job in a millinery shop left her exhausted at the end of each day when he was waiting to pick her up at the shop, still in his school uniform with his bag of books slung over his shoulder. She was learning with painful slowness to make hats but she wasn't good at it. She would be bad-tempered and irritable with him, often when he was skipping a meal to see her, and she couldn't understand herself, why she was like that. Then she could see, sometimes by about Sunday night when she had started to recover, just what she was doing to him, and so they started spending some of her wages on meals in town. They bought big plates of fish and chips and bread and butter and a cup of tea for four shillings when she was only earning two pounds. It didn't go far. Her savings suffered. Clara had to pay for him to get into the pictures as well.

The other thing that bothered them was the war. Neither of them could take it seriously, and yet slowly they were starting to realise that they might have to.

'If I'm at medical school I mightn't get called up. At least not straight away,' Robin said one evening. They were sitting in the caf.

'It can't go on that long,' she said. 'You won't be eighteen for ages.'

'That's what they said when it started, that it wouldn't go on for long.'

'Are you really worried?'

'You know how long the last war went on.'

'It can't,' she said stubbornly. Only she guessed it could.

After they had eaten at the caf he would walk her home and then catch a bus back across town, or take the long walk around the lakeside, to start his study again. Some nights she thought he shouldn't come and she would say this, then tremble with anxiety in case he agreed. He never did. Their lives were beginning to revolve around the Junction. Around the Roxy on Saturday afternoons. It was easy to blot out what was happening beyond themselves in that thick little pit of darkness. They saw 'Gone With The Wind' three times, and laughed themselves sick at the Marx Brothers and the Keystone Cops. But disconcertingly, the world beyond would creep in some afternoons. The first war commentaries were coming through in the shorts.

Usually they didn't talk about them afterwards. It was better not to. Or if they did mention them they would say firmly that it was a long way off. It couldn't happen to them. And Robin would go off again to his school books.

She wasn't really worried about his work. He had always done well. He had left her far behind and the school saw him as a shining hope. He was one of their top scholars. Everything he did seemed easy. His mind glided effortlessly round mathematical problems which by then her own mind could only dimly comprehend. Occasionally she would make a comment, put in a word, get excited by something he saw when he talked about it, and that was enough for him. His face would shine eagerly as he rushed on, outlining a problem, talking it out to its logical conclusion, not noticing whether she could see it through to the end with him or not. Her mind would wander off on a tangent, concerned with the technicalities of blocking the new season's hats and not much liking the prospect. Every now and then, if she attended to him, she might pick up a flaw in his argument, but she never said so. She had abdicated, just like King Edward. Of course she understood. It seemed natural to give up everything for love.

So she counted off the days until they would go away together.

67

She looked forward to the summer when at least they would have the riverbanks to return to in the weekends. Their lives had been restricted as far as their lovemaking was concerned. Sometimes when Mumma was out in her glasshouse they would snatch a furtive and too quick encounter in Clara's bedroom. It did little for either of them and they comforted themselves that it would not be for much longer. Soon they would have a place of their own, in another and distant town.

Neither of them were prepared for what happened next. It was more unbelievable and more devastating than the war. At the end of the year Robin failed his exams.

CHAPTER FIVE

When the results came out in January Robin's name simply wasn't there. At first they thought there had been a mistake and his parents were positive that this was so.

His father rang the Education Department in Wellington. They brushed him off and told him to wait for the results to arrive in the mail. They came the next day and it was there in black and white, forty-five percent for Chemistry and forty for English. Doctor Mawson send for a recount and rang every two days to hurry it along because it was important to his son who was going to be a doctor. Only of course he wasn't going to be, not that year. In retrospect Clara knew that she had accepted the inevitability of that fact from the moment they had opened the newspaper and his name had been missing. She could see how impossible it was to build a world on such assumptions of order. They believed in themselves too much. They had taken things for granted.

On the riverbank that summer, she saw things she had not seen before. The water rippled like heavy brown metal. She saw the thick mud where the ducks swam. She smelt them on·the hot still air. There were crowds of arum lilies in flower casting a sickly sweetness. They had been on the coffin at her father's long-ago and almost forgotten funeral. There was convulvulus, dense and clinging.

She had never loved him so much. So she believed.

It was decided that Robin would return to school. It was a humiliating and awful decision but there was nothing else for it. His father re-opened the subject of him going away to school. He refused point-blank. He would not go back to school at all and they could forget about him being a doctor if they pursued it. He was big enough for his father to take him seriously.

In some ways their lives were surprisingly improved in the year that followed. The Mawsons stopped fighting Clara so much. She was invited back to the house again, first for a still and silent meal and then from time to time she would go there on a Sunday afternoon. Robin was given an allowance which wasn't substantial but it allowed him to go out without depending on Clara. As well, his father provided him with contraceptives and for the time being she shelved the idea of having babies.

This new approach to the problem of their son had its drawbacks as well. There was some elaborate devising of social events at their home which Robin was required to attend in exchange for the new concessions, and from which Clara was excluded.

The socialising was in the form of parties which included everybody they knew who had daughters of a suitable age to be friendly with Robin. They were unsuccessful in their attempts. In the first place Robin was only interested in Clara, and in the second, most of the girls had left school by that time, and none of these sophisticated young ladies with their lipstick and first cigarettes were interested in a schoolboy, however big and handsome he might have looked out of school uniform. If they were going to go for a uniform it would be khaki, or with luck, blue.

About the only person who was even remotely interested in him was Sally Carver, a rather oddly shaped girl, and barely suitable by the Mawsons' standards. Her father was a dentist in Frankton, and new to the district. His profession made him at least worth cultivating; his choice of location showed him for what he was, new to the game despite his age.

He may have appealed to the Mawsons in another respect. He had taken up his profession when he was older, qualifying after the depression. It was not a bad example for Robin, that you could get somewhere if you wanted to enough, even if you had had a bit of misfortune along the way.

But Sally had unfortunate teeth, despite her father's ministrations, and a horse laugh, and she didn't always keep very good company. Robin and Clara could have told the Mawsons this but Sally didn't seem important enough to embarrass. Though it did annoy Clara, if she stopped long enough to think about it, that Sally gave Robin sidelong glances as they were coming out of the pictures, as if she knew him really well. And she had stayed on at school after everyone else had left, because in spite of her unpleasing appearance she was clever, and younger than the other girls who were being sent his way. She and Clara had briefly been in the same class at school. But Robin saw her only as a target for peanuts on a Saturday afternoon. To Clara who felt she had put childhood far behind her, he still seemed a schoolboy in some ways and she the older of the two.

His mother and she had taken to having stilted conversations on Sundays and she was starting to handle them in a way she could not have done before.

'It's very important that Robin passes, you know Clara. He must. You do understand that, don't you?' she said one afternoon.

'Of course I do,' she replied. She could not understand why anyone should feel the need to make such an obvious statement.

'His grandfather was a doctor too. It will make it three generations in a row.'

She had large moist eyes; surprising, because her face was angular and bony and her mouth as thin as her husband's. She turned them on Clara with a very intense gaze.

'If it's what Robin wants you can count on me.' It sounded silly and Girl Guide-ish, but Clara couldn't think of anything else to say.

'But of course it's what Robin wants.' She was quite certain of herself.

'Of course,' said Clara too, and wondered why it was so necessary to convince her all of a sudden. She had never doubted that Robin would be a doctor, even if it was going to be later rather than sooner.

She left their place, walking with Robin. His dog Chip snuffled along at their heels. They skirted round the end of the street where Winnie and Reg lived, as they had been doing for the past year, but as they passed the corner they suddenly came face to face with Winnie carrying a billy of milk. She had missed the milkman at the gate and caught up with him down the road. They all stopped, said hullo in small awkward voices, and stopped again.

'You'd better come in,' she said at last.

They tied Chip up at the gate and followed her inside. Reg was sitting at the kitchen table with his shirt sleeves rolled up, smoking, with a morose expression on his face and reading the '8 O'Clock'. He seemed surprised and at the same time pleased to see them.

'Long time no see,' he said, folding the newspaper. He looked appraisingly at Clara and she felt herself go hot. She hadn't seen him since the time of her abortion the previous year. She guessed he would have heard about it.

Jeannie had her mid-term report and Clara asked to see it. It was hard to believe that she was in High now too. She had forgotten that, although Robin had mentioned seeing her there. It broke the ice and they started to talk, almost like old times. Clara knew they had been getting by all right because Mumma had been seeing Winnie again, but not when she was around. She didn't know whether she still thought about the way Winnie had avoided her. It was hard to fathom what Mumma thought.

When they were leaving, Winnie followed them to the gate.

'It was good for him, seeing you,' she said.

'Reg?' Clara had never thought Reg cared much one way or another whether she was around.

'You can see what he's like.'

Clara had to admit that if she had noticed anything, it hadn't really registered, though now Winnie mentioned it she supposed he hadn't looked so good when they went in. She said that perhaps he was looking a bit older.

'That's exactly it,' Winnie said, pouncing on this as if it was a really important observation. 'He's too old and he won't accept it.'

'Too old for what?'

'The war, of course.'

'You mean he wants to go?'

'He says he does but he doesn't really, you know.'

'How d'you know? I mean, he might.'

She turned tired cloudy eyes towards Clara. 'He says it would make something happen.'

After that both Robin and Clara started seeing Winnie again from time to time, dropping in as often as not on a Sunday afternoon. She seemed pleased now that the Mawsons entertained Clara and, like them, she seemed to have accepted that she and Robin were together.

Robin worked very hard as the exams approached again and they missed whole days of seeing each other. It made their times together even more important. Clara was still making hats, but Miss Cresswell who she worked for used to sigh and shake her head over some of her efforts. She was better at selling them than making them, and this kept her in a job. She had let her hair grow below her shoulders and she washed it twice a week, staying up late to let it dry, so that it was always glossy and her curls sprung around her face. When she modelled hats for customers they could fancy they would look like her, and they almost invariably bought what she showed them. She moved quite a lot of Miss Cresswell's old stock that way.

Just before the exams Wirth's circus came to town and set up their tents at the showgrounds. Clara bought two tickets and showed them to Robin. He said he couldn't possibly go, didn't she know that he had to study? She said it was the best thing he could do, have a night out like that. He had studied till it was coming out of his ears and now he should switch off it for a few hours, give himself a rest. In the end he agreed.

They loved every moment of it, each, as it turned out, in their different ways. For Clara, in that tent, could see herself up there. Clara Bentley, cavorting on tightropes, swinging through the air by her teeth from spinning hoops, dancing, pirouetting. If it was she who was under that spotlight, she decided she would choose to wear tights covered in emerald-green sequins. How beautiful, how powerful, a solitary figure, shining, glittering as she turned under that light.

After, they went to the caf and had their usual meal of fish and chips. They had been going there for so long now that they got a double quantity of bread and two cups of tea for no extra charge. Robin poured tomato sauce over his meal and she could see him thinking. He was so deep in thought that the chips starting floating in the red liquid. She pulled the bottle out of his hand and sat it on the table.

'Penny for them?'

He shrugged. 'I don't know. Not really.'

'Yes you do. Tell me.'

He smiled cagily at her. She loved his smile. Women might be cat-like, but so are some men, and it is an attractive thing. In time, there would be Ambrose, and she though of him as cat-like too, or of the cat family. A panther perhaps. It was the one thing, perhaps, that these two men would have in common. With Robin it was something about the eyes, long and narrow and curving up ever so slightly at the corners. If she looked at him alongside his parents, she could see that he had inherited the best of both of them and nothing, that she could see, of their less attractive characteristics. Come to that, neither of them were particularly attractive, but if you took certain features and put them together in a package the result was rather good. Despite his size there was a great delicacy about his features, from his mother's fine bone structure she supposed, and he had his father's excellent hands. She studied those hands now, as they played with the salt and pepper. The fingers had rather large joints but they tapered elegantly, and he had strong thumbs. The hands of a surgeon, she thought as she looked at them.

'I was thinking,' he said after a while, 'that if you wanted to walk on that tightrope you would first of all need to know how to get off it.'

She didn't understand. She asked him which clown he liked the best. He said, 'You.' They left it at that.

He passed his exams with brilliant results. It had all been for the best, everyone kept saying. He had been too young the first time. He could never have got marks as good as that. Now he had topped the whole of the country in chemistry. It was a miracle. The failure was behind him.

His family threw a party and everyone was invited, even Winnie and Reg and Clara. Mrs Mawson asked Clara nervously if she thought Mumma would like to come and she said no. She didn't tell Mumma about the invitation. Afterwards she was sorry.

It was a good party and everyone behaved well. Sally Carver had passed her exams too. She was off to train as a dental nurse in February. Only talk of war subdued the party, but never for long.

The Sunday after the party Robin and Clara were down at the riverbank. They had taken a bag of sandwiches and cakes left over from the night before to feed to the ducks. Clara had a fleeting idea that her whole life had been spent feeding ducks, that she could qualify as the great gamekeeper of them all, even if she wasn't much good at making hats. Nobody came by their place. They were longtime squatters on that bank. It was almost as if they owned it. Clara often sat on in the sun with her blouse off after they had made love, Robin stroking her without looking over his shoulder to see if they were being watched. The willows formed a curtain and they never worried that they might be seen.

Robin heaved bread well out into the river and a large bossy drake dived quickly and deeply, beating off rivals with his wings as he did.

As it surfaced Robin cried 'Eureka!' They often did that, both of them. It was more than Archimedes' Principle, though water was bound to provoke it. To them it signified a private mystery.

74

Once, on a summer day, they had borrowed bikes and ridden into the country. It was an undisturbed landscape yet Clara had felt a fretting unease in it. The morning, which had started with a sky like a great uncut sapphire, had turned sombre. They both fell quiet as they pedalled, stopped calling to each other. Clara thought of death in quiet places; that people might quietly kill each other without changing the appearance of things. As they passed through the countryside, they might be dying before their eyes, absorbed into the earth, or simply fading behind the shaded windows.

The rain began to fall and they would have been soaked except that they came to the small settlement of Eureka, and they shouted the name together, laughed and, relieved, took shelter.

'I wonder why it's called that,' said Robin.

They never found out. They often asked people if they knew, just to see the dumb looks on their faces. Somebody ought to know, but nobody did. It was what Hamilton was like.

But, 'What about?' she asked on this occasion, blowing cigarette smoke into the lazy air and watching it spiral away.

'I have it this time,' he said.

'Don't keep me in suspense.'

'I'm not going to med school,' he announced cheerfully, and stood up dusting his pants.

'Don't be silly,' said Clara, throwing more bread out to the ducks. The big drake got it again.

'I'm not. I mean it.'

She looked up at him then and saw that he did.

'What d'you mean?' she said. She knew she sounded stupid because already he had said all that needed saying.

He sat down beside her again, resting his hands loosely against his knees.

'I don't think I was ever going to go,' he said gently. 'It's not me.'

'What'll you do then?' She felt she should be shouting at him, making a scene, or asking him to explain himself better. Instead it felt like a very old movie where you know what is going to happen, and why, and you don't know whether to laugh or cry or if, simply by doing neither, you can stop it from happening. Only you know you can't.

'I don't know. I honestly don't. Well yes, I suppose I do in a way, in the short term anyway. I mean, they'll call me up in April, and then they'll send me off. I should think we ought to get married then, shouldn't you?'

She stared at him dumbly.

He went on. 'After it's all over . . . I don't know. Maybe I wouldn't mind being a vet. I wouldn't mind that. It makes more sense to me. But if I couldn't . . . I don't mind too much. Accountancy maybe. I'm good at figures. You can't look that far ahead. Not when there's a war on.'

It had happened at last. He had grown up too. She had been the adult, or so she had thought. She thought too, that she knew him. Now it was all back to front. Looking at him then, she thought with a sudden fierce bitterness, that he had known this all along, or at least, for a long time. Then she thought that perhaps she had been meant to know and failed him.

She hardly saw him that week, or not for more than half an hour or so at a time. On the Sunday she went round, at his bidding, to his place. They had scones and tea with his mother and afterwards he left them together while he walked Chip. Clara had had one of her increasingly frequent colds during the week and he told her to stay in.

When he was gone his mother turned to her and hissed, 'You did this, didn't you?'

Her moist eyes glistened and she drew her thin lips back over her teeth.

'No. I didn't want him to do it,' said Clara.

She looked at her then and Clara could feel her contempt and fury washing over her. 'You can have him now. You must be pleased about that.'

'I don't know what you mean.' Clara didn't move but in her head she was frantically devising ways of escape from the chintz room with its Wedgwood ornaments.

Mrs Mawson scooped up the tea things from between them. 'He might as well get married. He says he wants to. He does whatever he wants. He always has. It makes no difference now.'

Clara saw Winnie the next day. She was seventeen and it seemed that she was about to have her heart's desire. Night and day since she was thirteen she had thought that some day she would marry Robin Mawson and now she was to be allowed to, because there was a war on. It didn't make sense.

'I'm only seventeen,' she said to Winnie.

'Yes, well that can't be helped,' Winnie said, the way she might say it if Clara had spilled something on the bench or dropped a cup. Nothing important.

Only of course it was.

'He's only just left school,' Clara said.

Winnie gave her a funny look then. 'Yes, that's true,' was all she said.

But it was for that reason, as much as anything, that the marriage was delayed until his embarkation. For the sake of appearances. Not that it was said like that, but that was what it was. That was Hamilton too. Even if there was a war on.

He was sent to Papakura for training and his going was a wound in itself. The night before he went away he stayed at the house in Frankton Junction and Mumma drank gin and never heard a thing. They lay with their arms wrapped around each other, talking all night, though it was hard to remember, even within days, what they had talked about. Trivial things, not plans for the future. She had planned a future for so long, yet now that one full of positive happenings and events was being handed to her, Clara was afraid. She wanted things to go on the way they were, for time to run its own course with them.

The months that followed were dream-like. Robin came and went, and the date for his embarkation was set for the end of October. They would be married quietly in the Cathedral on his final leave, in the third week of that month, with only their two families present. Clara would wear a pink silk dress and Miss Cresswell made her a hat swathed in silk tulle with a crown of feathers. Mumma was specially training orchids to be ready when the time came.

He had leave on a weekend in September. It was to be the last time she saw him before the wedding. After they had had lunch with his parents they walked up town, heading towards the riverbank. It was a curious still day, inclined to greyness with a temperamental sun appearing fitfully behind the clouds. Spring had begun and the neat gardens were rich with flowering bulbs, tidily banked with earth. As they passed Winnie's place Clara saw that her peach tree was in flower too, abundant and beautiful. She could still remember it stringy and struggling for life, with the hard little fruit that never properly ripened, when she was small. Now all that had changed. Like everything else in Hamilton, it flourished.

Victoria Street yawned empty before them as they walked towards the riverbank. There wasn't a car to be seen and very little movement. They paused for a moment to look in Paul's bookshop but it was just something to do. Robin said he would like a bit of reading material and she said she would try to get him some books or magazines when the shops were open and send them up. They admired the new post office, a big solid building, the most impressive in town. A couple walked by, pushing a pram. Clara kept thinking to herself, this is the last time, the very last time we will do this.

She told herself that there was no real reason for her to think this. Robin would come back, they would have their lives together before them. He might die of course. She had thought of him being killed, but it was just as likely that he wouldn't be. The real thing was that it would never be like this again, whatever happened. They would never be a boy and girl just walking out again. She couldn't put that thought aside.

'They say the Jap thing's serious,' Robin said.

'Yes. That's what they're saying. So I hear.'

'You'll pay attention to the drill, won't you?'

'Yes, of course.'

'I wish you'd think about living at my parents' place,' he said.

She stopped in the street and stared at him. 'Why?'

It was an unspoken rule between them that they both simply tolerated his parents. Mumma both did and didn't count. She was a strange lady, stranger than Robin, or anyone else except Clara, knew. She had never made any difference to or difficulty in their lives since they had been together, but at the same time her presence, and the house at Frankton Junction, had been a focus for them, a place to go when all else failed. She would be pleased to see them and at the same time unseeing. She demanded very little. Amongst her stuffed and crocheted doilies there was a different kind of order to the Mawsons' opulence. She provided order out of long habit, not through any particular desire to impress. Once it had been a defence against a harsh and judging world. Nobody cared now, nor had cared for a very long time, whether Mumma was bats or not, though her reputation as being so had doubtless scared the Mawsons as much as anything. But she certainly made life easier than they did. Clara didn't want to go and live with them or anyone else but Mumma, if she couldn't live with Robin.

'I think you'd be safer in an attack,' Robin said. 'They'd be more likely to go for the railway yards first. Cut off communications, you know.' He sounded military already.

'I'll be all right,' she said. 'I know how to take care of myself.'

'Not against bombs you don't. Besides, my parents are building an air-raid shelter.'

'Good on them. I'll call if I need it.'

'You're being silly now,' he said sharply.

'Will we see the eclipse, d'you think?'

'What eclipse?'

'There's an eclipse of the sun in the Caucasian mountains. It's due today.'

'Caucasia? That's the other side of the world.'

'So. We'll see part of it.' She was pleased to have diverted him, and to know something that he didn't. 'Think how black it will become. Think of the world going black in the middle of the day. That would be kind of like the end of the world.'

'I suppose it would.'

'Anyway, you'll be on the other side of the world soon.'

His face lit up. 'I know. It's exciting isn't it?'

'It might be awful.'

'D'you think I don't realise that? That's why I'm worried about you . . . it'll be awful just not being certain whether you're all right or not. But it'll be something different, won't it?'

She found herself thinking with some bitterness just how different it would be. It occurred to her that the reason she had been so certain that nothing would ever be the same again was because, the next time they walked up Victoria Street some Sunday afternoon, not only would they be a married couple, but he would have gone away and changed, while she stayed the same. He would have been to different places, and seen the hues of other skies, and the shapes and outlines of other countries, their hills and valleys, towns and cities, the splendid and the dreadful; and she would have seen nothing more than this. They had planned to change their lives together but now it was he who would be changing it on his own. She would still be making and selling hats, and walking up empty Victoria Street with the new post office to look forward to as the highlight of each day.

They lay down on the bank together, the first time that spring. It was still squelchy and damp beneath the undergrowth and Robin laid his khaki jacket inside out on the ground before he covered her. The sky began to turn a strange yellow before they were done. From beneath his shoulder she could see a cloud move from the sun's face and a black edge cutting across the light. It hurt her eyes to look at it and yet it was impossible not to try. She buried her head against Robin's shoulder. O lover, lover, cover me for one last time.

They drew apart. The strange colour of the world engulfed them, this odd yellow light, as if the invasion had actually begun. It grew colder, and they drew together again, shivering. The birds gave disbelieving little chirps and squawks, then lapsed into frightened silence. Still. Cold. Half-dark. It only lasted a few minutes and then the sun emerged again as rapidly as it had faded. Robin and Clara turned to each other, their hands gripping as if they were afraid the other might suddenly slip out of sight, out of reach.

So much for love. Why should it suddenly stop? She tried to answer that question in her head over and over again in the week that followed. For when Robin boarded the bus back to Papakura that evening, she didn't love him any more. It was not for any reason that she knew, and at first she thought she must be mistaken. But the next morning she woke up and it was still true.

Later, she came to believe that she learned things from the awful time that followed. She learned that ceasing to love does not alter the fact of having loved. But love can stop.

She supposed, too, that it must be true that being in love for the first time, really in love, is special and it hardly ever lasts. Perhaps everyone knew that. Everyone, that is, who has been there, and who it has happened to. Nobody can know it is true while it is still happening.

She told a friend about it afterwards, and the friend did not take it very seriously at first, not until she told her about the wedding that nearly happened, and the difficulty it caused for so many people. Then Janice, her friend, said that it was the war, and that it would never have happened, that none of it would ever have gone so far, if there had not been that to contend with. Clara thought she was probably right.

That and the differences between them. Maybe they had thrived on those too much, as a kind of excitement. Her especially. She had always had a quiet passion for the dramatic. Sometimes she thought she was angry with Robin because he did not change her life in the way that she had hoped, first by failing his exams when they both believed the time was right for them to go away and leave Hamilton behind them, then by deciding not to go to medical school at all, and finally, whether of his own choosing or not (and who would really choose a war?) by making the change without her.

But she thought eventually, that she had been too hard on herself. She thought that it was simply the end of love. Maybe they had delayed its end, but who could be that wise when there was still so much to learn?

She went to see Winnie the next Saturday morning. Reg was sitting at the kitchen table, smoking and silent behind a newspaper, as he almost always was these days. Winnie chattered around him, making pikelets, a shade too hearty. Clara tried to tell her but couldn't. She wanted Winnie to tell her what she should do, because at that stage it seemed unthinkable that she should cancel the wedding.

It was impossible to talk to her with Reg sitting there. Once or twice she caught him looking at her and for some reason she couldn't look back at him.

But she could look at them together, and she was appalled by what she saw. Love did die. Just being married wasn't enough and she hadn't even got that far.

She left Winnie's and walked on round to the Mawsons'. She believed she owed them something, though afterwards she reflected that in this she could have been mistaken.

Mrs Mawson was turning out cupboards of Robin's and his younger brother Peter's clothes, to make up for Red Cross parcels. Chip barked a welcome to her. He had a lean disgruntled look about him these days. She wondered if it would help him if she lived at the Mawsons' but she guessed Peter would take him over in time. Once Robin had gone overseas, and he didn't see him on occasional weekends like he did then, she was sure he would start believing he was Peter's dog.

And there was no way she was going to live at the Mawsons'. That was the only thing she was sure about when she walked into the house. At least she thought it was until she started talking to Mrs Mawson.

Then she heard herself telling her that she didn't want to marry Robin. At least not yet for a while. It was too soon for them, she heard her own stranger's voice saying. That was how she tried to explain it. If they wrote to each other while he was away, then they would be more sure when he came back. She was babbling and making excuses, anything to fill the silence that seemed to be going on and on.

Mrs Mawson called her a whore then. Only she said it 'whoo-er' the way the children did at school, or over at the Junction. She said

81

Clara was 'a dirty little whoo-er', the same as in a swearword, with her lips pulled back over her teeth, the way Clara had seen her before. She knew then that her once-beloved Robin's mother was no better and no different really from her or Mumma or any of a lot of other people she knew. Somehow that made it easier.

One more thing happened. She went back through town, intending to catch a bus over to Frankton. She had just missed one and she thought of going to the pictures but the Strand was full and they were showing 'Gone With the Wind' yet again at the Theatre Royal and she thought that she couldn't stand all that renunciation and parting and stuff that afternoon so she headed down to the riverbank. She wondered if maybe she should fling herself off a bridge or something like that, like in the remote and hushed-up story of old man Hoggard, but she knew that wasn't what she really wanted. She needed some time to think out something. It was only an idea that was beginning in the back of her head, but give it time and it might take shape.

She thought she should be feeling something for Robin and their past but there was nothing. It was clean and new inside her as if it had never happened. She realised uneasily that she still had to tell him. With the zeal of the convert she thought perhaps she was doing him a good turn. She decided to write to him that night, after she'd washed her hair.

Reg found her there. He could have followed her, but she didn't think that this was so. Rather, that he knew he would find her there. Suddenly the willows in their new season's green didn't seem as safe and protective as they had always done. When he sat down beside her she knew at once, without him saying so, that he had seen her there before.

'Hullo,' he said.

'Hullo.'

'Cigarette?' She took one and he lit it for her. She noticed that his blunt fingers shook slightly.

'Thanks.'

'Come here often?'

'You know I do.' Within minutes suspicion had become fact. He sat watching the smoke curl in the air. 'Clara. You all right?'

'How did you know?'

'Takes one to know one.'

'What?'

'Problems. You've got them too.'

She grunted through her nose. 'Not now. I did.'

He looked sideways at her. 'You going to marry him?'

She shook her head. 'You going to the war?' she asked.

'I dunno. I honestly don't know kid.'

He was bulging under his fly. She reached over and started to unbutton him. He grabbed her hand and held it.

'You don't want to do that Clara,' he said thickly.

'You want me to though, don't you?' she said.

His thin sandy hair was sticking out unbrushed from his head, and his blue eyes were wet and despairing. He made 'mmm' noises in the back of his throat as he fumbled to help her, and his cock, dark and plum-coloured at the end, stood up in the spring afternoon.

'They can see us, people can see us,' he whimpered as he pushed inside her. It flashed through her mind what excellent sport Robin and she had provided for goodness knows how long, there in that same place, and then that it was time the watchers were given some variety amongst the players. Reg came very quickly and tried unsuccessfully to pull out of her. He wanted to cover himself straight away but he was still erect and she knew she could bring him again. It was a revelation that neither of them had expected. This time he murmured, 'Nice, nice,' repeating it on and on, like an incantation against her ear. She knew then that it was possible after all, to make love to other people in other places; in the long slow afternoon she shouted and tore at the grass beside her, as he stroked steadily inside her.

When it was over she lay smiling up at him as he scrambled to his feet, pulling his trousers up over his knees.

'Get up Clara,' he said urgently.

'Soon.' She felt very relaxed.

'You have to get up.'

You might. I don't.'

'Cover it. Please cover it,' he said, pulling at her skirt which was riding round her thighs. To please him, for he had pleased her so much, she straightened her clothes and lay back again in the sun.

'You worry too much. It was good wasn't it?'

'Yes,' he said, looking down at her grimly. Then more softly, and half to himself, he added, 'It was lovely.'

'Next time I'll bring a blanket,' she said, reaching out and picking grass from his trouser cuff.

He nodded. 'Yes. Do that, Clara.'

There was no next time. Reg joined up on the Monday morning. She saw him only once more on his final leave, and then it was like talking to a stranger. She often saw Winnie, who was an odd mixture of being partly relieved that he had made up his mind at last, partly sad for herself and the girls, but overall, proud that he was doing his 'duty'.

His joining up took the heat out of her decision not to marry Robin as far as her own family was concerned. Jeannie and Caroline, the latter particularly, missed their father and it pleased them to have Clara around. Mumma said she was glad she had got the material for the wedding dress before Clara changed her mind, or she would have had to go without, and it was a shame for her not to have such a pretty dress. She wanted Clara to have something nice.

Mumma looked very old the day Clara left Hamilton a few months later. It was a day of the river fog rolling over the plains, the onset of another winter and the bleak cold settling in. For all the sun does shine there, it was perhaps because of that day that she remembered it from then on as a bleak place of bitter cold. She took the pink silk dress with her. She was sure that she would have plenty of use for it in her new life in Auckland. The idea that had begun, months before, on the riverbank, had become an exciting venture, full of promise.

When they asked her what she would do, she said war work. When she got a job in the Nestle's factory instead, she wrote and told them that she was in a factory doing war work in Parnell. She was sure then, that she would get into Mason's next door before long. It was war work as far as she was concerned, but people got funny ideas about luxury goods these days, even if they were going to the troops. She kept meaning to tell them what she was doing when it became obvious that she was going to stay on in the chocolate factory. There was nothing wrong with it, and all the talk about the black market wasn't worth listening to as far as she was concerned. Only she was no letter writer and it got harder to put down on paper and then, bit by bit, things started to come apart, and nothing she wrote would do, because later it was so full of half-truths, it wasn't worth telling. Besides, after Reg was killed, only a month out in the Western Desert, she didn't want to write to them much more anyway.

She didn't see Robin again either. But at least Robin was alive.

84

Part Three

THE PUZZLE

CHAPTER SIX

It is the letter that has begun it all, all this long night of happenings.

There is the sound inside the Puzzle and the sound outside. The children's voices penetrate most sharply. It is school holiday time and there seems to be no end to children milling around. When Ma Hollis, who lives across the passage from Clara, looks out her window she can see them three storeys below her on the pavement. They scream all day beneath the windows of the chocolate factory, with their demanding cry for 'choc-lit', until at last the workers throw gobs of the stuff down onto the street, and then their shrieks mount even higher as they scuffle over each other, fighting and brawling to get to the steaming mounds, and some of the little ones get trampled when they lick the pavement. Their yells seem to go on for hours and often their mothers join in too, sticking up for one or other of them and starting their own fights among themselves.

Not that anyone blames them, at least not round these streets, though someone coming from the outside might be less tolerant. But if you live in Paddy's Puzzle it is different, and it matters too, what happens to one another.

Ma Hollis opens her door and goes a little way down the passage, cocking her head from side to side, stopping to listen.

'They're something dreadful today,' Biddy Chisholm says. She stands at the end of the passage trying to decide whether to go down to the street or not. Under her mop of streaky blonde hair, one eye glows with a blue and purple venom.

'Did you put an onion on that eye like I told you?' Ma Hollis asks.

'That's for bee stings,' says Biddy.

'Same difference. Draws it either way.'

87

'I couldn't put an onion near my eye. Hurt like a bastard as it was. I oughter go down and see if Kathie's with that mob again.'

'I'd stay away if I was you,' advises Ma Hollis. 'They landed you that lot yesterday.' She indicates Biddy's eye.

'I know. But I can't go letting her get herself knocked around, now can I?'

'I reckon as that kid of yours can take care of herself, if she wants to get herself in it again.'

'Oh damn her,' says Biddy with sudden conviction. 'You're right. I've got enough to put up with as it is. I could have killed her last night, I can tell you. I was too sore to see anybody, but I'll have to tonight. I mean, I will won't I, I'll go broke at this rate. I'll have to take my customers in the dark. Thank Gawd for the blackout heh?'

'What they don't know won't hurt them. Don't do it with your eye.'

'Some of 'em want an eyeful first, that's the trouble.' She draws on her cigarette, coughing on a lungful of smoke, and pulls her frayed green robe around her. Now that she has decided to leave her daughter to the mob below the effort to move seems more than she can bear to contemplate. She shivers and looks up and down the passage in a disconnected fashion as if she is not entirely sure why she is there. Outside another shriek rents the air, but either Biddy doesn't hear it or can distinguish that it is not Kathie for she doesn't flinch this time, even though Ma Hollis shifts uneasily.

'It's not the kids' fault, the noise they make,' she says. 'When you can't buy chocolate for love nor money in the city, and there's a whole factory full of it right next door, and the way it smells, you can't blame 'em can yuz? 'S'enuff to darn near drive me crazy let alone them kids.'

'Clara used to get it out to them when she worked there. There was nobody like Clara for getting the stuff out to them.'

'Janice does her best.'

'But not like she did when she lived here. Makes a difference.'

'Clara's a good kid,' says Ma Hollis.

'Yes,' says Biddy sombrely. The air is thick and slow between them.

'I better get along the wharves,' says May. 'You want fish heads?'

'I should shouldn't I? But I don't know that Kathie'll eat them again tonight.'

88

'Reckon she should take what's offered.'

'I reckon we'll have sausages. I could do with a sausage. Ta, anyway.'

Ma Hollis and Billy walk down past the gasworks to the wharves. She wears a cherry pink velvet dress that is stained with this and that, though neither she nor anyone else would be able to tell you what any of it was, the stains have been there so long. She takes little short steps on her fat ankles and her breathing is heavy. Beside her walks her grandson Billy, or rather, sometimes he walks and sometimes he breaks into a run, jogging on ahead of her, peering into people's letterboxes, kneeling down and shouting hullo into them, and running before he is caught. Not that he is afraid of the consequences. Ma is near. She will take care of everything.

He smiles over his shoulder at his grandmother and she smiles back, the warm vacant loving smile of an old woman enjoying the subtle hint of spring, still slightly acid, but there, hanging in pockets of air. She supposes she should be thinking of the war. That's what everyone thinks about these days, but the war has been there forever, or so it seems, and it is too nice a day. Certainly it had started before Billy came to live with her, so it might as well be forever. She wonders briefly where his mother is now, not in the way that mothers usually think of their daughters, but rather with a vague fear that she might materialise. She pushes her fear away. Her daughter wouldn't want Billy back anyway. She had never wanted him much in the first place.

Billy's head lolls slightly to one side as he stands in the street looking back at her. At least she thinks it does, just momentarily, but she dismisses that thought too, for fear that it is disloyal.

Down by the gasworks the fishing boats are tied, heeling in a breeze that is keener now that they are close to the sea. Ma and Billy hold out their sack between them and a fisherman fills it with heads in exchange for a sixpenny bit. The round dead eyes glitter up at Ma. She looks with love at Billy.

Clara is asleep when she takes her letter in to her. Billy had pulled it out of the letterbox when they got home and whooped at her, shouting that a letter had come from his father at the war. He'd raced down three flights of steps and out into the street to inform the kids before she could catch up and tell him not to be silly because he doesn't have a father at the war — which makes him shout with rage — and that the letter is not for him; and that he shouldn't even have opened the letterbox because it isn't his. But they always look in Clara's letterbox. Like theirs, there is so rarely anything in it that a single letter is reason enough for excitement.

Clara has been dreaming. She often dreams these days, as she did in her childhood. There had been a time, somewhere in between, when she used to go to bed and fall into a deep and dreamless sleep and keep her dreaming for waking hours. Even in Hamilton, where the land stretched away in interminable flatness, where the dark river fogs melted the edge of morning in winter and the peatfires blotted out the sun in summer. She dreamed then of a time when she wouldn't live there any more; of a time when she would wear tights covered with emerald-green sequins and sing in night clubs; and of eating fine foods, knowing only that fine food would mean that it wasn't cabbages and mutton. She had dreamed of love, and of a time when there would not be talk of war ahead and the poverty of a depression so close behind that it leaned on the shoulders of everyone she knew and reminded them that having lived through it, it would never leave them all their lives.

She had thought then that if she lived her dreams and believed in them, she could make them come true. It seemed to be unwise ever to turn her back on them or to commit them to the uncertainty of sleep.

But now, in the middle of the day, the children's noise has quietened while they go off to wheedle bread from their mothers for lunch, and she has dozed off.

The dreams come again. She is still on a wide plain, but this time she does not know what country she is in. She is trying to decide whether or not it is America when Ma Hollis comes in. At least she thinks that is when she comes in though she might have been standing at the end of the bed for longer, it is hard to tell. In her dream there is a perimeter of faces around her, only the ones she sees are black; then she hears singing as if in church and as she opens her eyes it is not a church at all but the children in the street below. They have come back and snatches of their song drifts up: '. . . mairzy doats and dozy doats; and liddle lamzey divey, kiddly divy too, wouldn' you?'

The plain recedes to a ghetto smelling of whisky and urine, and in the split-second before she knows exactly where she is, Ambrose's face and hers float together across continents, and she knows that all places are one and the same.

Like a choir, the kids come in with the refrain, '. . . if the words sound funny and queer, and maybe a little childish to your ear/ it's mares eat oats and does eat oats/and little lambs eat ivy/and kids'll eat ivy too /wouldn't you?'

Ma Hollis stands with her hands on her hips; a grubby apron stretches across her bulging stomach.

'You needed that sleep,' she remarks.

'You can't get any peace around here,' Clara grumbles. 'Those bloody kids.'

'Yeah, well what d'you expect?' She sighs. 'I give little Billy a shillin' to get me some kummy kum for dinner and some cig'rettes.'

Clara guesses she has done it for her, because Billy is one of the ringleaders; but she knows it won't keep him quiet for long because the shop is just across the road from the factory. She hopes he'll be smart and steal some sweets the way he usually does. That will keep him quiet a bit longer. His grandmother has taught him to be quick with his hands.

Ma holds out the letter to her. 'For you.' She squints at the envelope then and Clara guesses that she will have shown it to someone, Biddy Chisholm perhaps, for there is no way Ma could have read her name and address on her own.

The sight of the letter scares her. At first she thinks it must be from Mumma who is the only person who writes to her, but it is not her writing.

'You want me to go, heh?' Ma blows out her cheeks and lets the air escape slowly through her teeth.

'No.'

The older woman looks relieved. She settles herself on the wooden chair beside the bed and watches the girl turn the letter over in her hands.

'It's from my sister,' says Clara. She studies the handwriting, square and somehow upright, which is how she thinks of Winnie herself, and there is her name, Miss Clara Bentley, Flat 19, and the number in Cleveland Road which looks so unusual written down like that, because it suggests an address such as other people have, when really it is this strange dark web of concrete tunnels in the place they call Paddy's Puzzle. She puts the letter down on the patchwork spread that covers the bed.

Ma creaks in the chair, or the chair creaks with the weight of her, it is hard to tell which, because Ma's bones might as easily shift in their sockets as lengths of wood fitted into each other.

Clara wishes she had some more comfortable chairs. Everything in the room is upright and hard, wooden and straight. She thinks of the times when Ambrose sits up straight and uneasy beside her, for often now if he can, he will stay and watch over her through the night. On such nights she will wake from time to time and somehow divine his black face in the blacked-out night that the war has imposed upon them, his head rolling a little to one side, a gentle snore issuing from the wide flaring nostrils, and she is afraid then that he will fall and hurt himself on the floor.

When he first started coming to see her it hadn't mattered about the chairs, for then he shared her bed. But that is past now and she is rarely comfortable enough to have him stay in bed with her for long. Even though the weather is still cold she will be hot, sometimes dry, with skin like sandpaper; at other times she will be saturated with sweat.

So that that is all she has to offer him, the hard chairs, and she says to him that she's sorry, and wonders why, when he is so good at getting so many other things, why he doesn't try to get himself a big easy chair to sit in, but it doesn't really seem to bother him. There is never anything that he seems to mind, at least not inside this room. It seems odd to her, for there is so much to mind; the iron bed, the stark furniture, the dirt creeping through the cracks despite both their efforts to keep it at bay; the crooked carpentry, the harsh unshaded glare of the gaslight, the peeling wallpaper, the appalling plumbing.

'How's your lav?' Clara asks Ma Hollis.

'Overflowed again. Gone right down May Abbott's bath this morning. Serves her fuckin' right.'

There is a long-standing feud between May and Ma Hollis. Ma smiles and sucks her badly fitting teeth up and down round an ulcer on her tongue.

'Sitting in the bath and up to her neck in shit,' she says with satisfaction. 'I suppose I'll have the bleeding plumber in again though,' she adds on a gloomier note. 'Not that he ever finds nothing.'

It is true. The plumbing in Paddy's Puzzle is one of the marvels of the Western world. Experts have come from England to look at the plumbing, just for the novelty of it. The building is a vast sprawling seven-storey place made of concrete, its walls packed with waste metal and old railway lines. Between them snake metal pipes, connecting into each other. It took so long to build, seven years to be exact, that the plumber who joined it all together often

92

forgot where he'd put one or other of the pipes and so they came out in odd places with no apparent rhyme or reason. Ma Hollis has been known to say that the inhabitants (May Abbott, who considered herself a cut above Ma, said 'residents' but that made anybody who overheard her in the Puzzle laugh) shared so much shit of one sort or another that a bit more made no difference, as long as it didn't come from strangers. It was, she said, like the people themselves. They don't take shit from anyone outside the walls, but if you are on the inside it is all right. That is in her mellower moments.

'Perhaps the plumber'll put the Condy's down again,' Clara says.

It is Condy's Crystals that the plumber uses to try to trace where one pipe goes into another in the building. They turn the water all on and then watch to see where it comes out coloured.

Ma nods, 'Crystals got in Biddy's wash last time. She wasn't that pleased.'

'She could get worse.'

Sometimes they use ink, there is one particular plumber that does, and in his wake there is strife over bad drinking water and ruined clothes.

'You going to open that letter?'

Clara knows that it is what she has been waiting for. She is still afraid.

It is hard to say why. She thinks it might be to do with authority which she has always mistrusted. She is not certain whether or not she is entitled to a benefit. Several of the people who live in the Puzzle say she is, but the thought of going through the formalities of getting one intimidates her. She is sure that the authorities will ask her questions, and try to direct her life. She is sure too, that they will find some way to make her leave Paddy's Puzzle, and that if she tells them that that is her home, and that she wants to stay there, they will not be impressed. She thinks they will find a way to send her back to Hamilton, or, worse, to place her in a hospital or an institution of some kind. Biddy's sister and the mother of her friend Janice have been in sanitoriums, and both Biddy and Janice have told her there is nothing to it, that they are good places to go. You can even have a bit of a laugh in the sans, they say. Janice has related how her mother had gone up the back of the boiler room with some of the lads one New Year's Eve, and had a bit of sly grog and a cigarette or two and some slap and tickle. Her old lady had been quite chuffed about it, seeing as how she had never stepped out of line in her life before, and they all got caught and nearly expelled just like at a boarding school, can you imagine that?

Clara had no wish to be convinced. It doesn't make sense, what they say. Janice's mother died in the end, and Biddy's sister is still inside.

Once, maybe, Clara thinks, but she has left it too late now.

Sometimes she thinks that if there was some point, some future, she could still be persuaded; but it seems more likely that they would talk her into it and the worst might still happen and she has no wish, she has told them, to die alone, away from them all, and away from Ambrose. Biddy argues with her that this would not be so, that she is being stubborn, and points out that whatever has happened to Janice's mother, her sister is going to be all right. She is down in Christchurch, and Biddy says she'll be back working the Wigram base in no time.

There are times when they nearly talk her round, but then something will happen to stop her going along with them. She will intercept a glance between them, she will catch herself listening to the sound of her own body and believe that she hears the flesh shift under the skin. She will look at Janice then, and Janice will say nothing. Janice misses her mother.

But there could be another element to Biddy's concern and it is one that might be shared by other mothers in the Puzzle. If Biddy cares deeply about anything or anyone, it's about Kathie. Clara thinks she would understand if Biddy wanted her to go because she is a health hazard. But she also thinks that, if you look around this place, there are plenty of health hazards without being too concerned about her. Kathie will get tuberculosis if she is meant to and that is all there is to it.

Still, it's another reason to fear the appearance of a letter of any kind. Nobody shops anyone else in the Puzzle, except, just possibly, for that one reason, that they are afraid for a child. The children may run wild, do what they like, see sights which are not for the eyes of the nice well-dressed children up at the other end of Cleveland Road towards the Rose Gardens; but if there is a mortal danger the mothers are like wild animals. They might even shop a friend.

She knows it is nothing like that. It is from Winnie.

'My sister Winnie,' Clara says again to Ma Hollis.

The soft grey fur on her upper lip settles into line as she sucks her mouth back.

'My older sister,' says Clara. 'Actually she's twice as old as me. Just double my age.'

'You don't say,' breathes Ma Hollis. 'Your mother, she must have been a stayer.'

Clara smiles and reflects on that. The description doesn't quite fit Mumma. Clara thinks of her more as accident-prone. She is someone to whom things just happen. In lots of ways Ma Hollis reminds her of Mumma. They have the same straggling grey hair cut straight round the bottom somewhere in line with the lowest chin, and they have the same indeterminate figures, witness to many children and bad eating habits.

But there are differences.

Whereas in Ma Hollis there is a kind of durabilty, in Clara's mother there is, rather, an inept decision not to abandon the situation. It is to do with the business of existence. Clara wonders uneasily now if she might have contributed to her mother's sense of purpose in the same way that Billy seems to make Ma's life worthwhile. She shivers. The parallel is uncomfortable.

And there are other differences too. Ma Hollis is a big lady encased in vulgar strawberry-pink velvet with food spilled down her front, but Clara's mother who, equally, has no dress sense, manages to make her unsuitable clothes look like a penance. No, Clara cannot think of Mumma as a stayer.

Rather than open Winnie's letter, she wants to explain these things to her visitor, to talk about Mumma and Winnie and all of them in the place from which she has come. But she knows that she cannot postpone the moment any longer, that to open the letter is inevitable.

It occurs to her that this is significant in itself, the inevitability of Winnie, and supposes that it is because she too represents authority, just like hospitals and doctors and all the other people who might see fit to interfere with her life. In a flash of panic she wonders who has told Winnie that she is sick, but then she thinks that that is impossible. There is nothing Winnie could know about her now. Nothing. She has covered her traces too well. She has not, until that moment, told anyone in Paddy's Puzzle of Winnie's existence, though she has mentioned her in passing to Ambrose. She has told him none of the dark secrets that, in the end, divide her from Winnie.

'I was a mistake,' says Clara, as she tears the letter open. 'Mum never really meant to have me, I guess.'

'I'll bet she didn't. I'd have tied you in a sugar sack with the kittens,' says Ma.

'She might as well have. They get you sooner or later, don't they? One way or another.' And then she is crying and choking and there is bright blood on the pillow again. Ma Hollis cradles her against her shoulder. Her plump strong arms surround her; her stale breath rattles tobacco against her ear.

When the spasm is over she lays Clara back against the pillow and opens the window. The hot chocolate smell sweeps through the room again, as close as if she is standing over the vats. The children's voices chant their hard incessant cry for chocolate. A little sweetness in their lives.

'I'm sorry lovey,' Ma says. 'I'll leave you to it.'

'No don't go, please don't go,' she says, like a child. 'It's me. I'm being silly. It's just Winnie, she makes me nervous. She sort of brought me up you see. I mean Mumma had given up on me. I guess she kind of got tired by the time I came along.'

Ma nods. 'Figgers.'

'Yes I know. But Winnie was bossy and she had her own little baby when I was three.'

'Ah, you don't say. She married?'

Clara almost smiles, for the first time that day. In Hamilton it would have been taken for granted. Nobody would have asked if she was married, they would have just said something like, 'She must have got married young.' It simply wouldn't have occurred to them that she might not be married at all.

'He was killed in the war, her husband. Nearly a year ago. He should never have gone. He was too old. He was like that though, Reg was. Took off to the goldfields in the depression, never told Winnie he was going. Nearly killed her.'

Or was it she who had nearly killed Winnie? It doesn't pay to think about it.

'When he made up his mind he just went,' she says. 'He was like that. She couldn't have talked him out of the war. Jeannie, that's the older of the girls, she's sixteen. Actually Winnie'd been married two years when she came along.'

She thinks how like a Hamilton matron she sounds herself, having worked to inform Ma Hollis that Winnie is respectable and had got married and had her children in the proper sequence.

Maybe, she reflects, she really is a bit proud of it. It's like saying that your family has connections. My sister knows Clark Gable. My mother was spoken to by the Prince of Wales. Something like that. All would be equally remarkable. She has other thoughts about Winnie, but she pushes them aside.

In a way it calms her, talking about her. It makes her sister real and ordinary again and she starts to read the letter without any more fuss, avid for news of Mumma who, for all her fat sorrows and wrestling with life, is still a force to be reckoned with, particularly her fluttering futile adoration of Clara herself. Clara often thinks that Mumma's love would be better directed towards Winnie who has always wanted it so much more badly than she did, or to Rita, who is to have yet another baby. She scans the page for news of Jeannie and Caroline too, because it is they who are always uppermost in Winnie's mind, those two girls who are really talented and might do exciting and impossible things like getting educated. Clara thinks what a great relief it was to Winnie when her children offered so much more promise than their aunt.

But there is none of the news she seeks. The words blur on the page before her, then stand out in mocking relief.

'She's coming here,' says Clara at last.

'Your sister?'

'Yes.'

'She can't though.' Ma Hollis' voice is flat and disbelieving, but emphatic at the same time.

They have no need to explain to each other why it is wrong — Clara has aired Winnie's respectability.

'Of course she can't,' says Clara. 'It's mad. She'll try to take me away.'

Ma looks hard at her then, but her voice is gentle. 'No way?'

'Never. Why, are you sick of me being here?' She is ashamed of her sharp irritable voice which she uses more often than not these days, but she doesn't seem to have any control over how it comes out. Ma's big old breasts rise and settle again. 'I just asked, little Clara. I best go and see if young Billy got my things. He's just as like gone spend the money on his self.' She lumbers to her feet.

'I'm sorry Ma.'

'No. No, you don't want to be sorry. You got no need to be sorry for nothing. I'm just . . . ' she stops. 'So sorry too.'

Clara thinks that watching people being consumed with grief on one's own account is hardly uplifting, but she knows what Ma Hollis means, and if she feels like crying some more for herself it's in a different detached kind of way, a sadness for a condition over which she has no control. She thinks she vaguely understands about reversing the role of the comforter, the afflicted one taking

97

care of the healthy. You learn about people very rapidly in Paddy's Puzzle and she has set herself to learning so much in so short a time; she supposes it is the key to why she stays there. That, and Ambrose. Though it is hard not to see Ambrose as the reason on his own. But if she distances herself ever so slightly from the matter, then she can see that he has become part of the learning too, so she has to consider him alongside of everything else.

'About your sister,' Ma Hollis is saying. 'What does she want?'

'She's got some business with the War Office. About Reg's pension. She wants to come and stay.'

'What will you do?'

'I suppose she'll have to come. If I say I've got no room . . . well, she'll come anyway. Winnie's like that. Can I borrow your camp stretcher do you think?'

Ma nods, but looks confused.

Clara sees that it must seem odd, her turning back on what they have both agreed only a moment before. But then Ma really doesn't know Winnie. 'I can't stop her,' she says. 'The thing is, she doesn't have to know. About everything, anyway.'

She looks around the room and knows that there are some things that cannot be concealed.

'She'll know you're sick,' says Ma Hollis.

Clara is silent.

'Is she dumb, this sister of yours?'

'I'm not that bad. I'll tell her I've got a cold.'

'You said . . . well, I git the idea she's not like some of us. She might be diff'rent.' It is both a statement and a question.

'She doesn't need to know.'

'You can't take away Paddy's Puzzle. You can't turn it into a fairy castle.'

There is an inescapable logic about this. Clara sighs. 'I'll tell her it's part of the war effort.'

Ma rolls her eyes then. 'I'll send the camp stretcher over. You want for Billy to put it up?'

'If Ambrose doesn't come. Thanks, Ma.'

'Ambrose! You'll tell her Ambrose is part of the war effort too?'

They laugh as she closes the door but Clara has an uneasy sick feeling which grows and burgeons into full-blown terror when she has gone. What if he doesn't come tonight, and she can't tell him that Winnie will be here tomorrow? And what about Janice? She will have to get in touch with Janice somehow and tell her not to bring the goods. On the other hand she needs money and food for Winnie's arrival. She needs Ambrose to find Janice. She thinks of sending Billy but he'll never get near Janice at the chocolate factory. Whereas they just might let a Marine through. They are so strict with the rationing and the factory is like a fortress; there is a great temptation for the corrupt going both in and out of that place. She knows. She's been there.

She worked in the factory through '42 and till the summer. She thought that it could have been the cold air when she walked out of that hot place that speeded up the consumption. The air was so thick in there and it had been a damp winter. Even though the Puzzle was directly across the road the cold hit you when you came out, and when you got inside it was not much better, what with the dripping plumbing and the seepage. You were never really bone-dry and warm. Nor were the two buildings well-placed for the winter.

There is a long road, Cleveland Road, which runs right down from the Rose Gardens, connecting with Garfield Street which runs on up to Parnell; almost in the heart of Auckland City, the suburb is a world in itself. Cleveland Road dips down into a steep gully while Garfield Street rises at the far end, thus trapping the smell of chocolate. Clara is not sure which end she prefers. The Rose Garden end has nobs living in it. Their tall elegant houses stand back from the road and it's interesting to consider what it would be like to live in houses like that. It takes her back to possibilities now a world away. What might have been, had she chosen it so. And the summers in the Rose Gardens were unbelievable. She loves the colour and sees herself as a sumptuous romantic person in the presence of the flowers; she thinks they are as pretty a sight as any you could ever want to see. On the other side of them is the sea, and although you have to pick your way through the trenches and the air-raid shelters there is a path beneath the pohutukawas to Judge's Bay where the water is very bright and clear and it is easy to forget that in the same stretch of sea, just around the corner, there are warships at anchor. She has included the seaside in those many coloured dreams all her life, for Hamilton is an inland town and until she came here to live she had hardly seen the sea at all. It is the river she knows.

At the end of Garfield Street there is a ramshackle slum which is Parnell: delapidated shopfronts and higgledy-piggledy bungalows which house the oddly assorted people who live there. The Maori man with the club foot who sits in the sun all day waiting for the Americans to come and have their shoes shined. The woman with St Vitus' dance whose face contorts into anguished grimaces and who still hopes to sell her twitching wreck of a body; she waits all day too. There are tired lonely women everywhere, fed up with trying to get enough food for the children and sick of standing in queues (how little things have changed, thinks Clara, only now we're supposed to be pleased to be doing these things, for the war; now it is glorious to stand in line). There are workers who keep industry going, rolling out of the pubs, richer than they could ever have imagined now that there are Yanks everywhere demanding their services. At least *their* dreams have come true for nobody could have thought, ten years ago, that there could possibly be more work than there would be people to do it; there are women around too, who are, if not smart at least confident, now that they are in demand for their labour as well.

Then there is a woman dressed in robes telling fortunes and though Clara thinks, like most people, that she's so loony she's unbelievable, on good days there are kids in their teens sitting at her feet in the sun, listening to her. There is everybody and everything, and in a way that is the end of Parnell she has liked the best because so much happens there. If it's not happening you can make it happen for yourself. That is what she has always liked about life, to have things happening.

It is chilling to think that she stays exactly in the middle now, in Paddy's Puzzle, because she can no longer walk to either extreme of Parnell. So really there are no choices; but at least, in a sense, things go on happening. If she were to move to either side of that centre-line, it would be the end of her. In one direction there would be no protection from the hurly-burly, on the other there would be too much protection and a quiet death amongst muted footfalls. She cannot bear to contemplate it.

And so she stays, waiting for Ambrose and her friend Janice who works in the chocolate factory.

Suddenly she's missing the factory. That's really strange. Nobody could believe what the inside of the factory is like unless they had seen it, and once they had, they wouldn't want to know. Yet it's true, she does miss it.

Every inch of the inside is painted dark chocolate-brown. That way no one can see where the chocolate has splashed. Everybody wears brown overalls so that you can't see chocolate spilled on them either, and on their heads the workers wear little biscuit-coloured hats. The only parts that aren't this dark sludgy brown are the floors and they are brick — rather nice if they were anywhere else — and very slippery; you have to be careful how you walk. And then there are the huge vats that go day and night, and the vast copper mixing bowls shining in the gloom, mixing and dispensing the sweet liquid through miles of tubes and pipes until, at the end, the final product, the slow trickling stream which becomes a chocolate waterfall, rains down onto the sweet fillings, covering them as they slide past on trays.

The vats had been Clara's job, down in the bowels of the factory where the heat was high, a sullen ongoing humidity. Janice's job was better. She got to sit down at the machine where the chocolates were covered with foil, popping chocolate after chocolate into the little hole lined with coloured paper, smoothing it, ejecting it, thousands of them day after day; but clean, and she was able to sit. Janice said it was monotonous, but if she could have got onto that, Clara thought, it mightn't have been so bad. She might have been working still.

Would she? She doesn't know. What difference does it make now? She's not, and that's that.

But it was fun in there, for all its darkness and strangeness, all of them having to make their own light and laughter. You got to know everybody, there was so much talk; you knew what everyone did in the evenings, who the girls had gone out with, whose sons had written home from the front, and if anybody had a death, a telegram from the War Office, the whole factory was in mourning. You knew whose kids had done what and what girls had taken up with a Yank — even some of the women whose men were away fighting had too — and everybody, even the really straight ones, had learned to stop criticising. These were just the facts.

Janice and Clara were the only ones who had lived in the Puzzle. In a way they were scarlet; marked, because of all the brawling and fighting, the carry-ons, the military police making raids, the strange garments that flapped in rows drying across the roof of the building, the never-ending stream of taxis disgorging clients onto the footpath. But in the factory, their friends were more entertained than critical, and mildly curious as well. In those days while Clara was still working, they were just girls who wanted a good time, like everybody else; if they had been the real pros that some of the girls in the Puzzle were, they wouldn't bother to work in the factory anyway. Clara didn't know any Yanks then; not to speak of, just to dance with, sometimes when she was out with Janice or the other girls. That was what she liked. To dance till she collapsed with exhaustion, till her lightning feet gave out on her. It was all as exciting as she had dreamed it might be.

In the evenings the workers would spill out into the soft

evenings as the night shift was coming on. If the day-shift workers were suspicious of anyone it would be the night shift for they were another world with a separate set of secrets and conversations which had nothing to do with them. In a sense, they were simply moving into their vacant rooms. They actually knew the crowd coming along from Mason's next door where they made hand grenades better than they knew the night shift.

That was hardly surprising, for there was a constant war waged mutually by the two factories against the rats which streamed backwards and forwards between them, rats as large as cats with long soft fur, sheltering in the fennel which covered the wasteland; they were bound to see more of each other.

Clara had walked out with one of the Mason's boys for a while until he got called up. He had stayed back a bit because his father was dead and there were a lot of little kids at home. He'd been ashamed until he got the job at Mason's but then he felt better because it seemed as if he was helping the war effort making hand grenades, almost like being in munitions; then they called him up when the last of the children went off to school and his mother was able to take his job. He was happy then.

Clara used to wave and call out hullo to his mother, until one day she said her son was dead, and that was that. Soon afterwards, Clara saw a Yank waiting for her; and then she saw the littlest child waiting outside the factory for his mother on a few occasions but she never turned up. The child would trundle home in the dirty baggy pants that had been handed down to him and a streaky hungry old man's face. Clara slipped him chocolates a couple of times which was all she could think of to do.

Will Janice or Ambrose come this evening? She has worked out a plan and if just one of them comes she believes she can make it work.

In the end it is Ambrose, although she hasn't really expected him. It is half past five.

'Ambrose,' she says, and smiles and moves in the bed, as if she is having a dream.

He steals a little closer, and she is overpowered then by the scent of another armful of roses and early spring flowers which he bears, and they block out all the other powerful forces in the room. She can't help herself and begins to laugh as he pounces on her, burrowing his hands under the bedclothes, his long bony fingers finding parts of her body that will react irresistibly to his touch, but so very gentle that if she were a butterfly in the bed she would still be intact.

'You were awake all the time,' he accuses her.

'Not all the time, truly. I've just this moment woken up.'

'How's it been today?'

'Not so bad.'

He looks at her searchingly. She can never hide the truth from him.

The children below are screaming still.

'The cough's been good,' she says. 'Only one bad lot.'

'Because you rested?'

'I was tired. Yes, you could say that. I haven't moved much today.'

He is silent. He knows that what she has said is neither good nor bad and there is no response he can make that will comfort her. She knows that he is pleased that she has had some relief from the cough, but it is not really a good sign when she is so lethargic. It has to be one or the other. They both know she is no better.

And he knows her too well, knows also that she is hiding something from him. He waits, watching her. She tries to turn away, but he takes her chin in his hand and turns her back to look at him.

'What is it eh? Come on, doan' make me drag it out. Like pulling teeth tryin' to get things outa you sometimes.'

'It's my sister,' she says at last. 'My sister Winnie. She's coming to stay here. I got the letter today. Ma Hollis brought it in.'

CHAPTER SEVEN

Clara is filled with the sudden need to be active, frenetically so. She swings her feet on the floor. There is so much to do. She feels that if she doesn't get moving now she never will. Ambrose watches her anxiously.

'Hey, who is this sister then?'

'Winnie. I told you silly, you don't listen to me.'

'I forget. I'm so dumb.' He drawls the last words. His mouth has changed.

'No you're not. Don't hand me that. You're smarter than I am.'

'That ain't no way for a white lady to talk.'

She looks at him, narrowing her eyes the way she'd seen Joan Crawford do it when she was playing things cool, but she isn't trying to be funny. It is the only way she can stop herself from crying. She hates it when he talks to her like that, there is something of a sneer in it. Right now, she needs, more than anything, for him to understand.

'Auckland's full of "ladies" like me. Maybe some of them are smarter than me. Or whatever.'

'Or whatever,' he mocks. 'We are afraid to say it, hey? We still some lady.'

'You said it first.'

'Lady. Lady. Afraid to say bad words. Whatever. Shit. What sort of word is that?'

'All right, I whore.'

'Better. What do whores do?'

They have never quarrelled like this before. It is a sudden ugly confrontation with both of them going down and neither able to pull back. One more word and she senses that all will be lost between them. She looks at him, bracing herself to say the word that is hard for her, that she is not used to saying though she has

104

said it in passion when she understood what it meant; but it has nothing to do with what they have just been saying to each other. She puts her hands over her face and thinks that it is true, that at last she is going to lose him, after everything. After surviving so many tests and against so many odds. He has watched her fall ill and yet he has still seemed to love her. She has said goodbye once to him when he has gone back to the Pacific and never expected to see him again, and he has returned. Not only returned from death, but to her. A war, black and white. A soldier and a prostitute. Illness. There couldn't be much more. And yet he has continued to come, and now they are on the edge of saying something to each other that they will not be able to mend. She does not know why it is the words they say that matter. In her head, it is not important. It is language such as her friends in the factory and here in the Puzzle use every day, casually, with no special intention to offend, and she has never been shocked. What they, or she for that matter, do is more important, and probably more shocking. But it implies between her and Ambrose a world of meaning and intent. It is not what Winnie would say, or think, or maybe has ever heard. (Even at Frankton Junction? Well perhaps.) That's it, she supposes, and marvels that within seconds he has placed her in the context of Winnie's world. Placed her inside Winnie's head, so that they are against each other.

She edges her fingers apart and looks at him. She can see that he looks as ill as she feels, and knows he is afraid. Relief overwhelms her.

She drops her hands, speaks quietly. 'You do know who Winnie is, don't you?'

He looks towards her, and as she has not wounded him as he expected, he nods. 'She is a white lady,' he says and there is still some venom in his voice but it is not directed at her.

'I thought it didn't matter. That's what you said.'

'It always matters,' he says harshly.

'She's not a lady. She's ordinary.'

He curls his lip. 'She'll like this? Us?'

'No.'

'You see then.'

'It's only because she's Winnie.'

'It ain't,' he says fiercely, and there is no denying his intensity or the power of his feeling. 'It is only because it is me.'

He holds her eye. He doesn't need to say any more. What he says is true. There are a million Winnies and a million Ambroses

105

and it is always because of the Ambroses and not the Winnies.

'She's my sister,' Clara says, and starts to shiver violently.

He comes at once then and puts his arms around her, drawing her feet up onto the bed again and pulling the covers around her.

'I have to get up,' she says, resisting feebly.

'Shush, shush, yes soon pretty baby, soon little girl, little Clara.'

'Come in beside me.'

'You need food. You haven't eaten all day, eh? Eh, tell Ambrose.'

She feels like a baby, but that is how they both like it to be, now that she has come to depend upon him in such a physical sense. Her childishness shuts out what they are really about, it disguises her illness, at least for the moment.

'It doesn't matter. Just be beside me. Please.'

He slips off his shoes as he has done some hundreds of times now but not his clothes. When her face is against the rough material of his uniform she says, 'Will you love me again?'

Those long hands of his with the black knuckles and the pale palms. He holds her by the chin and tilts her face up towards him.

'Always will, no matter how long.'

But she cannot leave it alone. 'Will you fuck me again?' She has said it now, like an offering. The fingers tighten around her chin and he looks deeper into her still.

'I would surely like that, Clara.'

She can think of nothing to say except his name. 'Ambrose,' she whispers.

'What now?'

'Nothing. Just Ambrose.'

Ambrose Johnson. She doesn't know a great deal about him. He says there is nothing much to tell, that he has told her all there is to know. In a way this is probably true. She knows his mother's and father's names, Rose and Jacob, and the numbers of brothers and sisters he has, in just the same way as he knows such basic facts about her. She knows that he grew up in Harlem (don't ever say brought up, he has told her, because that, Clara, would be a lie).

'What is it like, Ambrose?' she has asked him.

He has been silent then.

'Try and tell me.' She imagines it as exciting and full of life. He says it is not. His eyes with the sepia flecks in their whites narrow when he replies.

Only once has he volunteered any opinion on the place he has come from, and that is when the sewage has jammed the drains in

106

the Puzzle. His nostrils flared at the smell of shit, and he said 'Harlem,' exhaled, changed the subject.

Another time, when she urged him to tell her what it was like, he said that it was a bad place for women. He had a sister and the only ways she could make any money were bad. She pleased white men, he said.

Sometimes Clara has wondered if there is a peculiar satisfaction for him having a white woman whom he has met as a prostitute depend upon him; as if the wheel has come full circle. Once, in an evil moment, Biddy has hissed at her, 'He screws white, baby, he'd kill white too.'

But if it is so, she does not ask. She has too much love for him and there is always the chance that to scratch beneath the surface of what they know will damage them. They have come close enough tonight.

And although she is six years younger than him, she knows how to hold back as well as he does. She wonders what he would tell people about her back in America. She suspects he will never even try. Their history is written in this room.

There is one thing he has said though, and it makes her wonder about him and the kind of man he is. He feels freer in this country than he does in his own. This war will have been a bad thing for black people, in a way that is different from other people. They will know, the young men, what it is like to live as free men. There has been an ease in the ignorance which they will no longer have.

She says that New Zealand has no special reputation for being free, that it is a country where it seems to her, and other people think so too, that it is hard to be yourself. But when she says that he looks at her as if she is talking in another tongue. Then she argues that the war can only be a good thing because if they have lived like free men they will make a greater effort to be free when they go home.

He has thought of that. He says that they should be more organised in their anger, that the whole way of thinking must change and that this might be the time that it will happen. Only he becomes uncertain and afraid when they talk like this, and one time he says that he is done for, ruined for anything like that. He had gone away to the Excelsior hotel up in Parnell and come back after closing time, towards seven o'clock, swaying on his feet. When she asked him why, he said, softly, that it was because he would have to hate people like her, and she had done for him in this respect.

Is that what he wanted, she asked him, a new world fashioned out of hate? She was surprised at herself, what thinking did for you, how far she had come. Well, at least past emerald-green tights.

No, he had said, that was not what he wanted but that was what it would have to be. Until they (the whiteys, he said, when she asked him to explain who 'they' were) were afraid of them, they would not begin to comprehend. Or want to try. Once, before New Zealand and the war in the Pacific, he'd thought that making them afraid through hate might be the answer. He doesn't know any answers any more.

In fact, he says, he has nothing to take back to America except a clean pair of heels and his number and his name, and in his opinion even the last one doesn't really belong to him.

That is Ambrose. Or as much as she knows. The rest is what she has here in this room, and he is black and very beautiful, angular with bones pressing against the planes of his face like plates, and he is tall, at least six foot three, with a spare hard body.

When she says 'Ambrose', she has said just that, Ambrose, everything she knows.

'Noisy little devils.' Now that her senses are alerted again the sound of the children fazes her. They sing the same song over and over again, and chant the same old rhymes. There is a group of girls with high piping voices who are still chanting 'Mairzy doats and dozy doats' in the crisp and deepening evening. Their voices go through her head.

'It's the school holidays,' she says. 'They go on and on. It's time they went back to school.'

'I'll bet you used to like them. The holidays. I'll bet you were the first one out the schoolroom door.'

'Yes I did too. It seems like only yesterday since I'd be waiting for them as if my life depended on it.'

'I reckon it was only yesterday too.'

'Four years. Left when I was fifteen. No keeping me.' She begins to cough and he moves to close the window.

'You don't want no noise and draughts, eh?'

'Don't you get out of this bed, Ambrose. You won't get back in it, will you?'

He lies staring at the ceiling. 'How old is your sister's little girl then?' For now they have talked about Winnie coming and he has accepted it as a fact, as she has accepted that his fear is real and that his anger is directed not at her, or even at Winnie herself, but

108

rather towards the way that she might possibly alter things between them.

Even as she lies watching him she can feel other things turning over in his head. He is like that, very quick and sharp in his ideas, and once he is onto something he works it through, way beyond her. She is not sure whether his asking about her niece is what he is really thinking, or to cover something else, but she knows better than to question him until he is ready.

'She's three years younger than me.'

'Hey, sixteen. That's pretty grown-up. Where I come from, that is o-old. Huh? Maybe I should get to meet her.'

'You wouldn't like her.'

'How d'you know that, heh?'

'She's a swot. And she's got thick ankles.'

'I like smart women. Oh, and I could be very partial to a good solid ankle . . . Heh, heh don't bite me.' He is doubled up with laughing and it makes her feel powerful that she can do this to him. She longs to sink her teeth into every part of him and she suddenly desires more than anything to hurt him until he screams. But doesn't.

'She got something you want?' he says, when he has stopped laughing.

'Brains,' she says carelessly.

'No. You can do better 'n that.'

'I dunno. Winnie maybe.' Her confession surprises her. She hadn't meant to say that. He regards her soberly.

'I don't know,' she says, tracing her finger round the stitching on the old patchwork quilt that she had brought from home. 'Honest, I don't. I mean I don't know why it's like that. It's just that . . . well, Winnie really is her mother, she just kind of filled in for mine. And she was young, you know?'

'Your sister. Mmm. I guess so. In Harlem, all mothers are old. Old before you're born to them.'

'But so was Mumma.'

'And what you got that Winnie ain't?'

'Eh? Oh that's easy. I've got Mumma.'

It all seems so plain to her that there is nothing to explain. Even though she was too tired to bring her up herself, it is still Clara, her youngest born, that Mumma loves the best, which is not fair because it is Winnie, her first born, who loved her more than any of the rest of them and craves her love the most. Funny old world.

'She got any more children? This Winnie?'

'Caroline. She'll be pretty. And smart. I'm glad she's only ten, I really am.'

But he is only half listening to her. His hands knead her shoulder, and he still stares up at the ceiling, as if what they have been saying is a part of his thoughts but somehow only on the fringe of what is central to them. It is better to wait. Although he is quick he is also impatient. Still, as he lies there thinking she has to try something to penetrate his thoughts. She feels shut out.

'Ambrose, when d'you think the ship's going to sail?'

'I told you little one, they don't tell us Marines nothing like that.'

'D'you think it'll be soon?' Suddenly she is dreadfully afraid that she has come close to the truth.

'Could be six months. Could be tomorrow.' There is a small knot in his silk skin.

'Would you leave me if it was tomorrow?'

'I've got to go an' fight for my country don't I?'

'What's the use of fighting?' she asks, and for the life of her she cannot see that there is any point to it. If it is to bring about coincidences like her meeting Ambrose, or making people better off, like the Americans coming here have done, or anything she can actually relate to the people she knows, then maybe it's all right. But when she counts the things against it, such as the loss of Reg, and the people who have got their lives all torn to bits, as opposed to the ones who are in easy street now, she can't make sense of it. As a rule she has no great thoughts about the meaning of life, except, increasingly, perhaps, about her own. But for once she would like it explained to her why they have to put up with things as they are. There is no order or sense to it.

'You mustn't say that,' says Ambrose. 'We Americans, we fighting for your little country too.' But it comes out flatly and she is not convinced. She doesn't think he is either.

'I'll die if you leave me,' she says angrily, and she doesn't give a damn then about her country or anyone else in it except herself. She goes on dwelling on her own needs and concerns but she cannot help herself. There is so much she wants to understand and if she does not know herself, as a point from which to begin, then where else can she start? She is not sure whether it is her illness that makes her so self-centred in her thoughts or whether this is really the kind of person she is. Either way she believes that she is possibly good at hiding it because people in the Puzzle act as if they like her and not altogether as if they are sorry for her, although that is a part of it, and then she starts thinking that she is cunning as well. It's hard to like yourself when you are wilting before your own eyes, and she is full of self-reproach.

In this spasm of anger her cough begins, and she thinks that she is actually going to die then, but Ambrose holds her until it is over.

'I'm going to die anyway, aren't I Ambrose?' she says, as he mops up the sputum and wipes her wet face.

He lies her back on the pillows. 'I'll get your medicine,' he says.

'I don't want it,' she says.

'You got to,' and there is a hurt desperate look in his eyes. He is such a mixture, one moment confident to the point of arrogance, the next so vulnerable. In that moment she feels that she has more power to hurt than if she had bitten him a hundred times.

'You must take it,' he repeats.

'Just make me a cup of tea.' She doesn't think the medicine will do her any good, though she does not tell him this. It is just a collection of patented powders and syrups that Ambrose has bought from the chemist. He sets great store by them.

It has also been recommended by her neighbours that French brandy, or cold strong black tea mixed with cream, is helpful. She'll take the brandy anytime, if he will give it to her, and she never reminds him that they also suggest cod liver oil, though sometimes he thinks of it himself.

'No med'cine, no tea.' He is back to himself. She has had her moment and she will take her medicine. Ambrose and her illness have decreed it. They rule her life.

Her illness. She shrinks from it. She has tuberculosis. Janice has given her a book. She wheedled it from her, seeing it at her place before any of them knew how ill she was although she had already suspected it, and thought that Ambrose had too.

The book had belonged to Janice's mother. It was called the *Homeopathic Vade Mecum*. She had asked Janice whether her mother had used it during her illness, and Janice, unsuspecting, said yes, it was what she used for everything, but Clara had already been through it and seen the thumbed pages under Consumption. Janice was furious when she found out what she'd been up to, but when Clara put it to her, she had to admit that she would have done the same.

So she had it in black and white. 'A wasting constitutional disease in which the lungs are destroyed by the caseous degeneration of morbid deposits, tubercles, pneumonic exudations and consequent ulceration. The terms Tubercular Disease, Tuberculosis, and Phthisis are synonymous.'

Charming. It really sounded charming. '*Symptoms*. The early

111

indications are often obscure. The chief symptoms are impaired digestion, loss of appetite, red or furred tongue, thirst, nausea, vomiting; more or less cough, chiefly in the morning; hoarseness or weakness of voice; irregular pains in the chest; dyspnoea on slight exertion (she doesn't know what that is but she expects she has it); debility, langour and palpitation; persistently accelerated pulse; heightened temperature; night sweats; and progressive emaciation . . . Emaciation, one of the earliest symptoms, extends to nearly every tissue of the body, the adipose, the muscular, and the bony; (so much for thinking herself slender) and even the intestines and the skin become thinner . . . '

And I want him to make love to me, oh my God, thinks Clara. Ambrose, remember I had thick curly hair once, and that my blue eyes which have always seemed marvellous and strange to you, just because they are blue, were once very bright, and do not think, just, that it was the onset of fever, even then at the beginning, because I was always told they were bright, Robin said they were bright . . . only I don't think about him because he's not important now . . . and remember that my body was quite rounded and full . . .

'. . . even the intestines and skin become thinner . . . ' Oh my God, that *is* horrible.

'I'm all right now,' she says aloud. 'I really am.' She has made so many false starts at getting up but now she has to believe that she will go through with it, for both their sakes.

'Your sister will look after you when she gets here,' Ambrose says. She looks at him to see if he means it. 'No,' she says sharply when she sees that he does.

'What d'you mean, no?'

'I mean that I don't want her to know.'

He shakes his head. 'That you're sick? Girlie, now you is dumb, she can't miss it.'

'Yes. If I'm careful.'

'You mustn't hide it from her,' he says carefully, and she senses that she is getting close to what has been in his mind all along. 'You mustn't try. She might help you to get strong again.'

It is out now, she can see quite clearly what he has been thinking. She can hardly speak for the panic which is overwhelming her, it feels as if it is clogging her pores and closing her throat and mouth.

'No, no you don't see . . . if it's strength you're talking about, she's strong all right . . . she'd do all the right things . . . take me

112

back to her place . . . fuss over me . . . I don't want any of that.'

'I don't understand you,' he says. 'You say you care for her. You care for her enough to let her come here, see how you live.'

She closes her eyes, trying not to see the things he is seeing. Sometimes she pretends to herself that he sees her room in Paddy's Puzzle as if it is an ordinary place, as if (and she feels condemned in her own eyes for thinking this but she cannot escape it) he accepts it because he is used to it. But now he is saying, in effect, that he has no illusions about its awfulness, that it is a dreadful place and a terrible lot that she has come to. Suddenly she wants to tell him about Mumma's stuffed cushions and her crochet work on all the tables, about the china cabinet with all the good glasses in it and the little plot of garden where she used to skip rope and knock the heads off the dahlias. It hadn't seemed much at the time, but now she can see that it was not so bad.

And she closes her eyes against something else too.

'Well, you care for her or don't you?' he says.

'Yes I do, Ambrose. You don't understand.'

'No, you damn right I don't understand at all girlie. Why don't you tell this sister of yours that you's sick? This sister, this one who is so sensible, gonna see right away that you sick, why you want to try an' hide these things from her?'

'I'd have told her by now if I wanted her to know.'

'You're stubborn, that's all Clara. And proud. Don't get you nowhere, no ma'am.'

'That's not what you told me. You told me being proud is the only thing kept you alive sometimes. You said that Ambrose.'

'All right. All right then. Make me understand then. Tell me how come you's don't want her to know, even if she could help you get better.'

'She'd make me leave you.'

'What's more important to you, Clara?'

'Staying with you, Ambrose.'

There is a silence between them. He sighs, sits stroking her hand.

At last he says, 'We better straighten things up nice for her, eh?'

They straighten up as best they can. Even though it is so awful Ambrose has made it brighter than it was when she first lived there. For a start there are the mats he got up in the Pacific; they are bright and cover the worst of the ugly congoleum, and they have hung some on the far wall from the window too. The cloth on the table is unpleasant, a thick heavy oilcloth, but as it is hard for Clara to get much washing done and Ma Hollis is already doing so much of it for her with a bit of help from Biddy and one or two of the others, she has had to cut down where she can. At least the cloth is basically white though the impossible flowers which can never have grown in any known garden are luridly coloured. The centrepiece is the gramophone which Ambrose bought for her. It is grander than anything she ever thought she would own, but there it stands, His Master's Voice, with nice wood panels and a pile of records sitting alongside of it. The greatest pleasure.

Then there are the flowers, the real flowers that Ambrose brings, and they have cut-glass bowls for them, for he has insisted that if he brings flowers they won't just be pushed into jam jars that are too small to contain them. The bowls are his doing.

So is the arrangement of flowers which he does this evening. And he goes up to the roof and gets down the towels and tea towels and sheets that Ma Hollis had hung there to dry in the morning. The early morning damp which had threatened to hang in the gully all day had lifted before lunch and a small breeze had whipped the clothes all afternon, so that everybody is up there, he tells her, getting in bundles of sweet-smelling clothes, crisp round the edges where the fresh air has caught them. When he brings them in Clara buries her face in them and inhales their freshness. So often clothes will hang for days in the alleyways of Paddy's Puzzle, grey and turning to mildew, fusty and as unpleasant as before they were washed, by the time they are dry.

Now everything is folded, and she has helped him, hanging onto the ends of the sheets, tugging them straight so that they sit neatly. They have enough to change her bed and to make up Winnie's too. Clara has decided that she will sleep on the camp stretcher and although Ambrose is unhappy when she tells him this she says that Winnie would find it queer if she didn't give up her bed for her.

He inspects the camp stretcher with some misgivings when Billy brings it in but he can see that her mind is made up, so he says nothing more about it.

She is really glad that he is there when Billy comes because she doesn't like being on her own with the kid. He is fifteen, but he spends his time with the children. He is strange, this Billy, and his grandmother knows that he is, but she loves him so much that Clara feels that she must never let her know that she minds about him so much.

It is not that she cares that Billy is strange, it is just that he scares her when they are alone. He seems all right until you look closely, and even then it is hard to describe just how one detects that he is different, but you do know, all the same. It is not that he steals with such dexterity, as he would have done when Ma sent him to the shops earlier in the day, because every kid in Paddy's Puzzle has learnt to steal from the time it could toddle; it's not because you have to read the most simple things out to Billy; not even, altogether, because he is always with the little kids, though that does have a bearing on it, and Clara knows that Biddy worries from time to time as far as Kathie is concerned, though she would never say a word because of what Ma is to them all.

No, it is something else again, a sort of fanatical gleam in his eye and the sense of him being very strong, and that neither of these things show in an obvious way, so you don't quite know what he's going to do next.

Billy brings the camp stretcher in, dangling it under one big arm as if it is a box of matches.

'Put it up eh Clara?' he says. He stalks in, full of importance, knowing that she cannot refuse him entry this time on the pretext of not feeling well, as she usually does.

'Oh thank you. Thank you Billy,' she says, making her voice hearty. 'Isn't it lucky Ambrose is here? He can do it.'

Billy scowls. 'I knows how to put it together,' he says, defying them to send him away.

'All right,' says Clara. 'You put it up then Billy.'

But it turns out that Billy has forgotten how to put it up and gets the struts jammed the wrong way round and Ambrose has to do it after all. It is smoothed over with a packet of candy, and a handful of loose change out of Ambrose's pocket, and Billy goes away smiling.

They both survey the room with pride.

'It looks all right now, doesn't it?' says Ambrose.

She is feeling much better. Everything looks clean and bright. Well, almost. That might be going a bit far, but at least it looks homely and livable. Yes, you could live in it. Her spirits rise.

'We can have tea now,' she says. It is the first time she has felt like eating all day.

'Not me girlie, I got to get back to base.'

'Oh no, please.'

'Hey, c'mon you know how it is.'

She does know, and has promised that she will not make it hard for him to leave. For all he does for her, it is the least she can do by way of return, and he knows that she has company around her and will not be alone. It makes many things about Paddy's Puzzle more acceptable.

'It's all right,' she says, and she tries hard to make it sound as if she means it.

'I'm going to fix you up a little somethin' to eat before I go.'

'You don't need to, I'll get something for myself. I promise I'll cook one of the eggs you brought and have some hot milk.'

'True?'

'Yes, true.' And she does mean it too, because she knows it will make him happier if he believes she really is going to look after herself. She goes to the sink and starts getting out a pan and a pot and lights the gas stove.

It is quite dark outside now and the damp is coming down again, a foggy August night. Ambrose has lit the gas mantle, and its harsh white light illuminates the room, leaving no shadows. He watches her as she starts to prepare her food.

'It's good to see you's doing that,' he says.

'You make me feel so much better. You've done me the world of good. And the roses . . . oh Ambrose, they're so nice. However do you find things like that at this time of year?'

He pulls the blackout curtain across the window. 'I got ways.'

'Did you steal them?'

'Why should I steal them, it's easier to buy them,' he says, and she knows from the lazy edge in his voice that he wishes he could stay, which in a roundabout way makes it easier to let him go. It is not so bad when you can sense that someone is longing to stay with you, it's holding them back against their will which hurts.

'You Americans. So much money,' she says. 'Nobody buys flowers.'

'Flowers just keep on growing, little one,' he says. 'If you know where to look they're there. Even when everythin' else run out you just can't stop the flowers from growing and the trees from burstin' into their green dresses, come the springtime. And it's nearly here, real near.'

'Are the trees out in the park now?' she asks him.

'Jes' coming on, the very first.'

She can see them in her mind's eye, the bright growth starting on the bare branches in contrast to the dark pohutukawas that stand above the bay. If she breathes deeply she believes she can smell the scent of the newly heaped earth in the rose beds, and she is so close to it that she can hear the sad cry of the shunting in the railway yards below and the sweet sound of the tide slapping on the shoreline as they walk beneath those bursting trees.

'Will we walk out to see them soon?' she asks.

'When the days are warmer,' he says. But she knows he doesn't want to talk about it any more. He goes into the bathroom and comes out wiping his hands on his handkerchief. She guesses that he doesn't want to dirty one of the fresh towels seeing as she is having company. 'You hardly got any soap,' he says.

'You know it's rationed. Don't look so worried. Maybe she'll bring her own.' She laughs. 'Winnie probably won't expect me to have any.'

Still he fusses and fossicks around, and his eyes light on the crockery she is taking out of the cupboard. He picks up a cup, fingers a chip.

'Now just don't you be silly,' she says crossly. 'You know we tried to get me some more cups the other week, and there was nothing you liked when you went to look and you said these would do.'

'They've gotten worse. You goin' to get some germs sticking round in these chips, huh?'

'Don't carry on.'

'You should mind. With her coming.'

'Who are you worrying about, her or me? Oh go on, leave them alone Ambrose.'

She tries to snatch the cup from his hand and between them they break it. She stands glaring at him. Suddenly he sits down at the table and puts his head in his hands.

'What is it?' she says. He continues to sit, and if he is not exactly weeping, it is something close to it.

'I'm sorry,' she says. 'Ambrose, it was my fault.'

She feels that it is too, for her moods veer all over the place, high one moment, sharp and bad-tempered the next. Half the time she doesn't understand what is happening to her, but for the moment that seems a bad excuse.

'She'll take you away,' he says.

Clara doesn't know whether to laugh or to join in his sorrow. So recently they have been quarrelling because he wanted Winnie to look after her.

He straightens up and glances at his watch. She knows that, as usual, there are no resolutions, and no way that he can stay with her tonight though that is what they both want, both of them,

117

more than anything. She is overcome, as she has been before in moments of belief, that Ambrose actually loves her. She is sure that he surprises himself. He might as easliy despise her and possibly would like himself better if he did.

'Ambrose, what colour would our children be?' she asks on an impulse.

'Children? Why d'you ask me that?'

'I just wondered.'

Which is true. She has often wondered, but she has never had the nerve to ask before. She doesn't know why she has unexpectedly had the courage now, except, she supposes, that some sort of impending change seems to be in the air and there is urgency in what they say. And often, as the long days of her isolation have passed, she has dwelled on what would be the outcome for other people — those who in some sense must be considered ordinary in a way that they can never be — of their tangled nights together, and the loving. He had always been careful, protecting her with one of the tightly rolled little rubbers that come out of the Peacock tin, so it never seemed immediate, but the possibilities were no less real. And when, in the past, she had put her mouth to his, when they had fitted together with the snug tightness of a couple invented just for those particular encounters, there must be more to it in the end, she thought.

But if one of them is intended to reach an end without the other then it is not unreasonable to consider what might have happened. It seems clear that it would have been children, because that's what happened to most people sooner or later. Surprising how people's hopes (her own in particular) change. She was older now than in the days when simply to escape was enough. And the escape had been achieved, she supposed. You had to look ahead from one undertaking to the next, and she didn't want to dance on a tightrope any more.

So that she could see herself and him in a tidy little house, somewhere on the edge of Auckland, with nappies flapping in the back yard and a baby-sitter on Saturday nights so that they could still go to the cinema or somewhere downtown to eat; some day in the future, when there would be no more rationing, and they could look in the shop windows on the way home; some day when they turned the lights back on, and people could see each other again. They would plan what to do with his next week's pay, whether it would be spent on something for the children or something new for the neat little house with carpet on the floor.

118

And in her imagination she saw them getting home and paying the sitter off and going to a room next to the children's after they had checked on them together and kissed them and tucked their blankets in; and then lying in on Sunday morning, lazy, till they were awoken by them.

It is not surprising then, that she wonders what colour those children might be.

'You ain't going to tell me we started on them?' he asks.

'No. Of course not.' She is indignant, but only with surprise, for she hadn't thought of that. In spite of her dreams that is where her children stay. What he is suggesting she thinks of as impossible, not just because of his care, but because she believes that somehow her body has decided against some things for itself even though there had been a time when it had had different ideas. But that was in another life, and before Ambrose; she doesn't think it will offer her a second chance. It is too late.

Besides, it has been a long time since he has been able to touch her, and despite her talk she knows that the desire she feels is really all in her head and it is this that has finally convinced her that what is between them is exceptional. For in this strange wilderness, they have come to the point where they make no more love and it seems that they love each other more.

'Promise?' He is anxious and she can see that he has forgotten just how long it is. She sees no point in reminding him.

'Cross my heart and wish . . . ' she trails away. 'I just wanted to know, honest. You know I'm not going to have children, not ever Ambrose . . . so, I just wondered.'

He is prepared to join in the game then. For that is what it is.

'Shee'it then, they be about half and half I guess, but sometimes they turn out more one half that the other.'

She tries to imagine them, but can't. It is something she can dwell on afresh when he has gone. For the moment it is enough.

'You call on Janice on your way? Tell her about Winnie?'

'Sure will.'

'We can keep in touch through her. She'll know when Winnie's gone.'

They say goodbye but it doesn't upset her now. She feels he will still be with her in the room afterwards.

He says, 'So long then.'

'Hey,' she says, calling him back with one last thought.

'What?'

'I wish they were more your half than mine.'

119

'Now why would you wish that?'

'Scare off Winnie.'

He laughs at her then. 'You're the one that's scared.'

'I sure am that.'

The door closes silently behind him. She is left with the heavy smell of force-fed roses, the pan of milk boiling over on the stove, the cold blue light of the gas, and the unsteady yet persistent sound that makes up the life of Paddy's Puzzle.

It is then that the difficult day of laboured breathing and intermittent coughing overtakes her. She knows that she has been fighting it off all along, but now that the day appears to be over and done with she can't fight it any more. The spasms rack, and tear, and shake her apart.

She staggers to the bathroom and what she had brought up when Ambrose was with her proves now to be only the beginning. The disease in her body is spread across the bathroom; there is blood on the walls, in the cracked handbasin. The light fragments before her eyes and for the second time that night she believes she will die. The room is full of the presence of Ambrose, but she can't reach him. She tries to cry out to Ma Hollis through the wall and wonders that she has not heard her. Somewhere, maybe in the passage outside, maybe a thousand miles away, someone is singing a blowsy plaintive melody. A whistle splits the night, the first toms in their green suits are calling. The Puzzle is open for business. She will die alone.

At last it is over and she is still there, sitting on the edge of the lavatory. Better now. She will be all right. She has got rid of the rubbish in her system. I will be all right, she tells herself aloud. There will be a tomorrow, and a tomorrow and another. I am at the turning point. I am going to get better.

Homeopathic Vade Mecum: 'Finally all the symptoms are gradually intensified: the dyspnoea becomes *very distressing,* so that the patient is unable to make any active exertion, or even to read a short paragraph without pausing, the sputa is more purulent; the pus is often expectorated pure, in roundish masses, that remain distinct in the vessel; the disease often spreads to the other organs, as the lymphatic system and the intestinal canal, in which a deposit of tubercle takes place similar to that in the lungs, and which afterwards bursts into the intestines, leaving an ulcer; and thus the alimentary canal is affected, and Diarrhoea produced. The respiratory mucous membrane may also be ulcerated, producing

huskiness, and even loss of voice, but more frequently the former, from the thickening and increase in vascularity which it undergoes. It is, therefore, but seldom that the local affection of the lungs alone causes death . . .
The mind usually remains bright, often vigorous, and so hopeful that, even amidst this general wreck of the material frame, the patient dreads not the future, and thinks he "would be well but for his Cough".'

It is only a book. It is nothing. She should never have borrowed it from Janice. Her mother probably gave in to things too easily. She probably believed what the book said. If you believed everything that's printed you'd be in a sorry mess. It's a quaint old-fashioned thing anyway. It's probably dangerous.
She takes one last look at it, though she's read it twenty times before. It will be the last time. She believes that she has done with it.

'Healthy Residence: The position of the house, the prevailing winds, the aspect of the room (of the bedroom especially), the windows, the position of the bed, and the provision for ventilation without draught, should be considered. The climate should be moderately warm, dry, and uniform, to suit the consumptive. A *voyage* under favourable conditions sometimes wonderfully renews the constitution, if the patient does not suffer from sea-sickness.'

She laughs out loud.
Somewhere, as if in answer to her, there is a burst of high quick laughter, out there in the Puzzle. It *is* a desirable residence. A rat's face peers at her from the corner of the skirting, and as quickly withdraws. There is a surge of water in her hand basin as the tenants above her release their sink, and some of it splashes over the edge. Not exactly dry, but dry enough. At least, as it sucks out down the plughole, it takes some of the rubbish she has deposited there. A sign that things are better. Yes, tomorrow she will be all right. Come Winnie, come spring. The milk has dried to a thin brown skin on the stove. It slides off easily with a knife.

121

CHAPTER EIGHT

May Abbott's teeth snap shut on a chocolate. It splits and the soft peppermint explodes in her mouth, trickles to the back of her throat. Oh yes. Oh lovely. She loves peppermint chocolates so much she dreams about them. She thinks she pays young Clara too much for them, but she cannot resist. That, and whisky. She sips first, then takes a long slurping gulp of Johnny Walker, glances surreptitiously about her as if someone might be watching. There is no one there. Peppermint and Scotch, twin fires.

May looks at her bottle and sees that it is getting low. A part of her hopes that there will be callers tonight, for by tomorrow she could be a little short, but another part of her wishes that it could be a quiet evening.

But the night is not over. In a way it never is in Paddy's Puzzle. There is the laughter, the singing and the shouting and sometimes the weeping, going right on through until the dawn.

And the night goes on in another interminable way all over Auckland, with the solid layer of the blackout sheltering all things and all people, under a thick and solid mantle.

This is such a night. When Clara has composed herself and eaten her meal, she puts her ear to the wall and listens to the rustling sounds. She wishes for a moment that she could be part of it all again. Sometimes she feels that being in this room is like seeing the world through glass and wonders if that is how she appears to others now. It is as if she is waiting for something though she has no idea what it is. Just to be able to walk out perhaps, as if she owned a share of the night and could be in charge of herself again as she moved through the dark.

It is almost an artificial night, with all the lights out. But that is not quite true for in the darkness the isthmus lies as it must have done a hunded years ago, before a city had been built, and if she were to put out the light and draw the curtain then the shape of Auckland, its hills and valleys, must stand out as on a moonlit night much as it did long ago. She has walked on the beach under a heavy red moon and looked out to Rangitoto with the city in blackout behind her. It had been like the beginning of time. But she supposes that that was artificial too, for you can't turn the clock back and begin things over again, not unless disaster strikes and razes to the ground all that has ever been, in a matter of seconds.

There are people here now, and they have designed a life with colour and light and sound that belongs to the present. Moving in this muffled vacuum is not reality. But then there is nothing absolute about anything really, because of course they could be razed to the ground right now. Any second it could begin. She supposes that it wouldn't take the Japs long to demolish Auckland.

She shivers. She has thought about this often, these winter nights. She has more reason than most to dwell on it. The air-raid warnings come often and when they do everyone is required to evacuate buildings and take to the shelters. The wardens come round checking that everyone is out, the people huddling in the cold, taking sleeping children in their arms, wheeling the old in their wheelchairs, covering up the sick with blankets, while the shrill sirens rend the air.

Only it is two months now since Clara has been to the shelters. It is difficult to check Paddy's Puzzle properly and the wardens hate doing it. In fact it is rarely completely evacuated. Although nobody has organised any system there are unspoken agreements for people to take turns at getting out and putting up a reasonable show of a crowd. As no one has any way of checking just how many occupants there are in the Puzzle at any one time, the wardens prefer to make do with this rather than venture in. The main problem is with the Military Police, the ones they call the M.P's, from the American base.

Every now and again they will swoop on the place and make sure that there are no personnel still in bed with their lady friends. It is one of their few legitimate excuses for entering the premises. There are, of course, organised systems of getting them out if a raid from the M.P's begins. Ambrose has taken advantage of it in the past. If any marines are hapless enough to get caught, the last sight of them is likely to be as they are thrown into the jeeps and beaten by the M.P's batons. Then they are not seen again for a long time, maybe never. If they are going to look for their pleasures it will probably be elsewhere; they will be off the Puzzle for good.

May goes to the mirror and studies her reflection with care. It has paid off, all the years of caring for that fragile complexion. The way they stay in the sun, these girls. No wonder they look like scrawny old hens with their feathers plucked off by the time they are thirty. No one would guess to look at May that she is seventy. It is not just her vanity that declares this fact. She is always challenging people to guess her age. They are never right. Fifty? Sixty? No? Too old? Fifty-five perhaps? She smiles, never tells them. Her ruffled mauve collar stands up pertly around the elegant curve of her chin. That of course is a matter of good fortune. She has to admit that. God gave her a good chin. But it is the difference between a profile and ordinariness. So her mother, the admiral's wife, always told her. And her father, the admiral himself, was equally pleased that it was so.

She pours herself another finger of Scotch, looks anxiously at her bounty. It is lower than she thought. Or perhaps had cared to admit to herself. She thinks that she would like some callers after all.

It has always seemed silly to Clara that the authorities are so set against the Puzzle. There are few places as free and easy and accommodating as this, and those who suffer the treatment meted out to them will probably go off and fall in love or get into steady things that are really hard to break, and if they are married, as lots of them are, then it is going to be worse in the long run. Or that's that way she looks at it. She wonders, in idle moments, if Ambrose could be married. She would never ask him, and she cannot see that it would be fruitful for him to tell her if he was. Somehow though, she doesn't think he is. The main thing is that his presence with her makes sense and she has no desire to see him taken in and made prisoner by the police. Being black has its own advantages these dark nights and his movements, which are like those of a cat, mean that he can slide like a shadow into oblivion before the police even have time to get out of their jeeps.

As for her, she can see no point in moving out to shelters. It is cold out there and if she goes to the trenches under that rusting corrugated iron she will spend the rest of the night sick. She has decided against going again and, as she says to others around her, it's her business really, now that she has made that decision, and they must not come to see whether she will go with them or not. They must simply assume that she is taking responsibility for herself. Then, if anyone asks them, they can look them in the eye and say they don't know a thing. 'You're all good liars,' she says. 'It shouldn't be difficult for you.'

Ma Hollis doesn't like it much, and once or twice she has called in, despite Clara's warning, but she has threatened to throw a bucket of water over Billy if she doesn't go away, and she knows what his adenoids will be like if he goes into the shelter in wet clothes. She looks so fierce that Ma believes her, though Clara's not sure whether she would actually do it. Billy makes her too uneasy; he might just remember the next morning.

Under the bed she has her bucket of sand, which is supposed to be for putting out fires if the bombs begin to fall; though whether one bucket of sand would do much good is hard to tell. At least the strange concrete construction might contain fire a little. And maybe it would take more than a Japanese bomb to do much damage.

But when most of them have gone, she sits in bed and waits for the all clear and wonders what it would be like if it caved in on top of her, and what would be the last things she would think about, and whether she would be very afraid. Sometimes she fills the bath with water, which is another thing they are supposed to do, although with the Puzzle's plumbing problems, it is not always very practicable, and besides she hates putting her arm down into the cold water to pull the plug when it's over.

Mostly she is not afraid. She finds this curious because although she doesn't want to die there is absolutely no resistance in her at this point. She would almost welcome a bomb.

Tonight, because nothing is happening, she peers out through a tiny chink beneath the curtain. A car is edging down Cleveland Road with its headlights masked off, and she can hear the steady clop of the milkman's horse. The horse neighs, and as the car inches past she sees a fine spray of the horse's hot breath caught for an instant in the pale glimmer cast by the lights. The car is a taxi and it has stopped outside. More soldiers?

But it looks like a girl, and a familiar one at that, though it is almost impossible to tell in the night.

The shadows of two men walking together slope up the street, and she hears a nasal voice call out, 'Ullo Sailor,' and she knows that she is right. There is only one voice like that, and even though she is imitating someone else, Janice's voice is, nevertheless, inimitable.

In a moment she is in the room, breathless, husky, amused, Janice the blonde clown from the factory. The door has been flung open and they are both laughing before she is properly through it, though neither of them really know why. For Clara's part, probably just relief that she is there.

Behind Janice, Biddy Chisholm is talking to the soldiers who have followed her in. They sound disagreeable but it is impossible to make out what it is over, and then Janice shuts the door on them.

'What's it all about?' Clara asks.

'Dunno. One of them was kicking up about taking Biddy.'

'Oh. It'll be her black eye, I guess. Wasn't it one of her regulars?'

'Gawd knows. Hey, why doesn't Popeye's cock go rusty?'

'Tell me.'

'He keeps it in Olive Oyl.'

'Ah shucks.'

There is a knock at May's door, a loud commanding rap. She jumps, spills chocolates and the novel she has been reading to the floor. She is not used to such loud and peremptory approaches. Even before she opens the door she has decided to send the caller away. But there are two of them and the first one has his foot across the threshold before she can refuse. He is a captain and he carries a bottle of whisky. It catches the flickering light of the gas lamp. Twinkles at her.

'Wanta game of cards Billy?' says Ma Hollis.

Billy sits with a very large doll in his lap. She doesn't know where it came from, it just appeared one day. The doll makes her uneasy. Somehow it doesn't seem quite natural. But then Billy has had a hard time, and his mother has been the one that's unnatural if you really thought about it. No wonder poor little Billy needs something to cuddle to himself. He doesn't show it to the other kids so she supposes it must be all right. Still, it seems best to take his mind off things now and then.

'Play snap?' says Billy.

'What about euchre?' she says hopefully. It has always been one of her favourites.

'Snap,' says Billy.

126

There is something droll about Janice. Just looking at her can make Clara laugh, though she can't explain why. If anything, she is beautiful. Clara would give a lot to look like Janice. She is very blonde, probably too blonde for some people's tastes, and of course it's not real. This of course is because Janice intends others to expect the outrageous in her, and it would be disappointing if she wasn't peroxided. But even if the colour is hectic her hair is still cut stylishly and much shorter than the current fashion. It hugs her face tightly and just covers her ears which are decked out with huge gold hoops.

She is twenty-six, and sometimes Clara wonders why she bothers to hang around with her.

'Mind if I smoke?'

Clara is about to say yes because it doesn't really suit her, but then she thinks that she is being cantankerous and has got too much into the way of suiting herself, here alone in this room. Out there in the world that she has been peeping at and yearning for only minutes before, nobody would even bother to ask if she minded. Besides it's not so long since she gave up smoking herself, and that was only because she had to. Sometimes she's dying for a drag, let alone anything else.

Janice heaves herself onto the end of the bed after pulling a chair closer, so that she can stretch out with her feet up. She is wearing a grey flannel skirt — a nice piece of cloth — and a bright red silky blouse. She looks lovely, Clara thinks, with her blonde hair and pale skin, and slightly tarty too, just the way she means to look.

'What's been happening then?' Clara asks.

'Happening? Whatever happens in this town?'

'Everything when you're around.'

'The usual. You know.'

'Tell me.'

She takes a long pull at her cigarette and blows a fine spiral of smoke towards the ceiling. 'I met a bloke,' she says quietly.

'You did? I thought you were looking get up and go.'

'Yeah. He gave me these.' She indicates her clothes.

'All right. What else?'

'Just these. I wanted to give them back but he wouldn't have it. He had the rations, he said. Well of course he did, he's an American.'

'You like him, don't you?'

'How d'you know?'

'Oh Janice . . . what d'you mean, how do I know?'

127

Clara has to wait for an answer, but after a while Janice sighs and rolls over onto her stomach, flipping a finely silk-clad leg in the air.

'He's a padre.'

Clara stares at her, waiting for the next line of the joke. Her friend isn't laughing.

'Tell me the one about Pat and Mike,' Clara says at last. She is anxious in case this is serious.

Janice flicks her cigarette ash into the saucer of Clara's cup. It sinks in a little puddle where the milk has spilled. Janice's fingers are rather blunt and dry and her nails are bitten right back. There are signs of wear and tear round Janice if you know where to look. Clara had seen her get undressed once and she showed her the stretch-marks on her stomach. Clara couldn't ever remember seeing Winnie's stomach, she kept herself covered up just like Mumma and Father used to; she wonders if her body is scarred from having children, and what her own would have been like if she had borne the child she had once conceived.

Janice has had two children. The first one she had adopted out when she was sixteen. The second one died. She said that when she was younger she blamed her mother, because her mother couldn't stand the shame of the first; when she had the second, to replace the one she gave away, her mother relented and looked after it and was still doing so when she died. A little boy and a little girl, a pigeon pair, both gone. Then her mother died and she stopped hating her, only it was too late for her mother to know she didn't blame her any more. Janice even thought her mother might have died of a broken heart over things and not TB at all (which gives Clara some encouragement; she is sure she will not die of a broken heart, except maybe if Ambrose left her for another girl). She says that having the children taught her very little about love. Between men and women anyway.

Clara believes her when she says this, for Janice has little direction in her life and sometimes the clowning and the nonsense which is fun most of the time can get overwhelming when one is feeling ill and tired.

But the real thing about Janice is a sort of honesty which overrides everything else. At the factory when people were at the limit of their sorrows and could go no further, they would often tell Janice. Clara used to wonder why, because some of the things she said were cruel and not what people might have wanted to be told at all. But she came to see that that was the secret. These last

128

two or three years people they knew had been running all over the place looking for help; most often they tried religion, priests and the like, and as far as Clara could see it hadn't worked. Not for many of them, anyway. She had seen that it didn't help, prayer and trust in God. It didn't make for the resurrection and the life of lovers and husbands who were dead, and it didn't transport you onto some higher plane where you could understand it all. Not that she could see.

She used to be scared of God and do good things to please Him, but it never seemed to change anything. She used to tempt Him too, things like stepping on the cracks in the pavement (some children said 'step on a crack, marry a rat!' but she didn't, she said 'if I step on a crack, God will strike me dead') and walking under trees with dead branches when she'd disobeyed someone, usually Winnie or a teacher (Mumma's instructions didn't really count).

God never got the upper hand and He never came to her rescue when she was in trouble either. If she thought that He would she might have turned to Him over the past months. Instead, like the other people at the factory, she chose Janice.

She didn't offer pious things, she talked about what was real. And she didn't pretend to be anything better than she was, a girl who wrapped chocolates in tinfoil and a part-time hustler for the Americans. And she didn't go on about it being the duty of New Zealand citizens to show hospitality to the 'boys'. She was in it for a good time and easier living.

'There's hardly anyone in tonight,' says May.

'In?' drawls the captain. 'Now lookee here li'l lady, my friend here told me that you could fix things up real good in return for a little favour or two. Are you telling me that my friend is not a gentleman of his word?'

May peers at his friend. She knows she needs her spectacles all the time these days, but so far she has got by without them except to read her novels. And that is a private matter, between her and the sweet romance of the young virgins who people the stories between those covers. The second man's face is familiar. Jim, she recalls. He has been a generous 'friend' as she would describe him. He looks nervous and embarrassed and she has no wish to offend him. Clearly it is at his suggestion that the captain has come armed with gifts. She tries not to look too longingly at the bottle.

'Well, Ai always do my best to help, as Jim knows,' she says, mentally congratulating herself for remembering the name. 'But

129

you see, Ai really don't have many friends in tonaight. Most of them seem to have gone out.'

'Out?' The captain's voice is incredulous. 'Say, what sort of a place is it that you run here?'

Jim interjects. 'Look, see it's not quite like that. Didn't I explain? Miss Abbott, she's just like a friend round here.'

'You mean they don't work for you?' The captain's voice is disbelieving.

'Ai tray to help out one or two of my friends. If you see?'

'For nothing?'

'Ai think you misunderstand me, captain.'

His large vulgar frame in her tiny tidy sitting-room is beginning to offend her. But her eyes are fastened on the bottle. The captain sees her look, and she knows that he understands too well.

'We saw Biddy on the way,' says Jim. 'She's in.'

'Shee-it,' says the captain. 'That black-eyed cunt? Told you, Jim, I'd have to be hard up.'

'We-ell.' May hesitates. 'Biddy has had a little accident, that's true. Nothing serious you understand, but she's not — quaite herself, shall we say?'

'I don't mind calling in on Biddy,' says Jim. 'She's a cute kid. Said to call in on her any time.' He turns to the captain. 'You see, that's how it is. It's like, well, kinda like a friendship bureau here. I mean being able to drop by any time, right, Miss Abbott?'

May nods.

'But, you see, I thought, well because you're such a friendly sorta lady, Miss Abbott, I thought you might be able to introduce my friend here to — to another of your friends.'

'Well — who knows?' says May. She tries to remember whether Louise on the fifth floor is occupied tonight.

Clara had tried to imagine what Winnie would have thought, if she had told her that she admired a person like Janice. Not that she cared. Well, she hadn't realised that she did. Until now. She supposes that it could be seen as justifying herself to herself. Or trotting out the 'old prostitute with the heart of gold' routine. Were they prostitutes? Hoo-ers, the kids at school used to say. meaning whores. You bloody hoo-er. Fuckin' cunt hoo-er. The kids, and Mrs Mawson.

It doesn't seem like that to her. And she's met some of the ones who pretend, with airs and graces, that they are doing some patriotic duty. They make her sick. Janice has class, some of them don't even have style. She remembers one called Myra. It was actually Janice that introduced them one day up Queen Street, before Clara got too sick to go out. You would have thought that butter wouldn't melt in Myra's mouth.

She had a very bright hard little mouth and masses of frenetic green round her eyes. Janice hadn't seen Myra for a while, they used to usher at the Civic on weekends, before the war, and they still ran into each other now and again.

'Got a boyfriend?' Janice had asked her.

'Boyfriend? Oh my dear, how could you, at a time like this? I mean, it's not really worth it is it, you hardly get to know them and then they're off and dead before you can turn around, you couldn't seriously get involved with anyone, I mean could you? Besides, don't you think we've got a patriotic duty to all those poor lonely Yankee boys?'

'Duty?' Janice exploded. 'Honestly Myra, who's doing who a good turn?'

'Ah doan't think I rightly understand you Janice,' said Myra, her little bright mouth nipping into a tight red line, and Clara thought am I dreaming this, is it really true, that she's trying to talk like an American? 'You're not suggesting for one moment that I would take anything from those poor boys in return for giving them some friendly comfort away from their own homes?'

'Nothing?' said Janice, incredulous. 'They can afford anything.'

'That's not the point.' Myra's voice was injured. 'They are so lonely. Of course it makes them feel better about accepting a little ol' fashioned hospitality if you accept *something* now an' then, but of course I just make sure it's ever such a teeny-weeny little thing. I mean to say, they would feel so bad if you didn't. Especially when you've given them a *meal* in your very own home, because they would feel that they were taking advantage of us poor old rationed New Zealanders if you didn't.'

'You don't say?' Janice was breathy.

'I do say. And I pray for their wives and families on Sunday. They must miss them so much.'

And sweet Jesus Lord, Clara could see that Myra was dripping with diamonds, and that her clothes were silk.

Afterwards, as they walked down Queen Street, Janice said, 'Funny. How it changes people, eh. This war. I mean she was silly, but, oh I dunno. Not like that.'

Clara had mentioned the diamonds, and how they were dripping off her face and fingers.

Janice made a face. 'Probably find she had a dripping undercut too.'

They left it at that. Myra wasn't worth talking about.

So here is this tough beautiful little broad who is her friend, lying stretched over the end of the bed, talking about a padre and looking intense and biting away at her lip and smoking too fast, and Clara can't think of anything to say that isn't self-conscious or smart.

'It's so ridiculous, so crazy, I thought you'd understand.' And because she is Janice and says what she thinks Clara sees herself, not for the first time, but as always, with a renewed shock, as being ridiculous and crazy in that she keeps company with Ambrose. Also, because this is Janice talking, she knows that there is another underlying meaning to her words which is, quite simply, impossible. An impossible relationship with no future except the possibility, if they are lucky, of tomorrow.

'Try me,' says Clara.

Janice lights another cigarette from the end of the first one and squashes the first out on the saucer. 'I was in the library,' she begins.

'Why?'

She looks pained. 'I'm studying Shakespeare's monumental work 'Fatheads I Have Known'. Are you listening or not?'

Clara nods, still not quite able to take her seriously, and knowing now that she must. At least she has decided that it will be a help if she keeps her mouth shut.

'It was raining,' Janice says and her face is shining, and her green-blue eyes with the thick black lashes are very soft. 'I was going to catch a tram but it started to rain and the streets were full of people so that when I came to the library I thought I'd just go in and wait. It was nice inside, have you ever been in there?'

'Only looking for the lavs.'

'They've got a nice room full of books about old paintings and tapestries and things. Very quiet. I wanted a fag but of course you can't in there, smoke I mean. And it struck me as being a very peaceful kind of place. Big. Yes, but without people trying to fill the space up. It sort of flowed around you, all this bigness. I sat down. I did sort of try to look at the books but they didn't mean much to me. They had some opened out on display in glass cases and I could see they were beautiful and I wished I could have understood what they were about but I couldn't so, like I said, I just sat and let it soak in, and thought a bit. Nothing deep you understand, not all of m'past flashing before me or anything like that. Lord they'd have needed another room to put that by itself if it was written down, but just thought, you know.'

'Tell me. You must know some of the things you thought.' For now Clara really needs to know.

'Oh I don't know. What it'll be like when this lot's all over, will we get bombed, will we ever see the end of it, things like that.' She glances sideways at Clara and she knows what she is thinking. Janice is the only person who's ever come right out and asked her what she would like done about her funeral. 'Deep enough I suppose.'

'Then what?'

'He came along. This man, Ron, his name's Ron. I could see right away that he was an American of course. He was in uniform, but he had his coat done right up, the collar up round his face. He asked me what I thought of the collection. I said it was very nice but I didn't understand much of it.'

Clara can hear her saying it, without artifice, not as if she knew more than she really did.

'I told him I'd just come in out of the rain but I liked it so much I wanted to stay. He said it was a bit like that wasn't it, and he came here often because it was a particularly fine collection, as good as many in the States, even though a lot of it had been taken out of Auckland and put in safekeeping somewhere in the country while the war was on, in case it all got bombed in, but it made him feel at home having such good material on hand. He said he often didn't want to go back out into the streets again once he got in there. I said it was funny but that was how it was for me too, at least right now it was, even though this was the first time I'd been in there. So then he said they'd be closing soon and we didn't have much choice because they'd throw us out anyway. Then all in a rush, he asked me where I'd be going next and I said, "Well I might do my cabaret number or if they aren't busy there tonight I might pack my bag and leave for a week in London though I've heard the food isn't up to much there this week, and that being the case I'll probably settle for sixpenn'orth of fish and chips and the next bus to Newmarket." At first his mouth just dropped open but he picked up real fast that I'm stringing him along and in a minute I could see he was just enjoying the ride. "D'you like good food?" he says. "Does a cow like hay?" I say. "It's been a long winter," he says, humouring me, and then he says that I'm to come with him and we'll go to some place he knows.'

She pauses. The cigarette has burned right down and is

scorching her already nicotine-stained fingers. She is too dreamy and still for Clara to interrupt, but she notices the long ash and the stub of her cigarette anyway. She adds it to the pile in the saucer and takes another one. This time her hands are shaking slightly.

'You wouldn't know the place I suppose?' She gives a French-sounding name.

Clara shakes her head. 'I've heard of it, it might be new, but it's a while since we ate out now, you know.'

'Yes, I was forgetting. I don't know whether it's new, it was kind of hard to tell, because it looked as if it had been there forever. It was in an old building down one of those little streets round Stout Street way, and the door was just a kind of hole in the wall, but when you got into the restaurant, well it could have been there forever, or the day before. If it was new it was clever because it looked like . . . like the Savoy . . . well maybe not the Savoy . . . you know what I mean though, established.'

Clara has a vague idea. She hasn't watched Gloria Swanson and Greta Garbo reclining around in a touch of the old luxury often enough from the back rows of the Roxy not to guess the effect Janice is trying to describe, though she can't quite imagine it in Auckland.

'Crimson walls,' she is saying. 'And curly varnished wood, hanging plants, real good white tablecloths and silver.'

'Honest?'

'Cross my heart. It's true. It wasn't very full, but everyone there, well you could see they had money, and there were a few Americans there amongst the civvies, but they were top brass. It was different.'

Janice's descriptive powers are waning. Her eyes are dilated and almost wild. Clara is filled with longing, and something close to envy.

'What did you have to eat?'

She makes an effort. 'Pate and then some ham, they were lovely, can you imagine it, real ham, and brandied peaches, and French wine. Other things. I can't remember now.' She shakes her head wonderingly. 'I just can't remember.'

Clara can't imagine the food she is describing, and even her images of the restaurant are without real substance. She supposes that it is so long since she went anywhere, but the really vivid picture she has is of sausages and chips, or maybe a bit of roast and veg at the Karangahape Road cafe and getting her ration book clipped. She knows that is no trick of memory. She almost wonders if Janice has made it all up.

'There was something strange about it though,' she is saying.
'I knew there had to be a catch.'
'It was his clothes.'
'Don't tell me. He was in disguise.'
'He wouldn't take his coat off.'
'A female impersonator!'
Janice pretends she hasn't heard her. 'Not in an obvious way.
The waitress knew him. She said "Take your coat Major?" . . .
Major . . . you hear . . . and he said, "No, no thank you very much,
it's a cold evening and I'm comfortable. If it's all the same to you
I'll keep it on." It should have looked funny, you know, queer,
amongst all those smart people, but he did it very easily, no fuss,
and he stayed wrapped up right through the meal.'
'When did the violins start?'
'Afterwards I was drunk. Not badly, but badly enough. It'd
stopped raining and we started to walk. We walked down Queen
Street, me holding his arm and trying to walk very nicely and not
talk too much because I was just on that fine line when you can
still say yow, steady baby, and maybe he won't notice if I'm
careful. Of course he did know, but he didn't seem to mind. We
walked down to the Ferry Terminal and I said look I beg your
pardon but I've simply got to go to the little girl's room. He said he
was sorry too, he should have thought of that before. I looked at
myself in a mirror while I was in there. I looked like hell and there
were two girls having a fight on the floor. I thought one of them
was going to kill the other. I didn't know what to do. I thought of
getting Ron, and it seemed an awful thing to have to do, but then
one, the littler one, got free and she had some money and she took
off and the big one seemed to be hurt the worse of the two. I said to
her, did she take your money, shall I get the police, are you hurt
bad, and she climbed up on the dunny and bawled and said she'd
kill the other one some day, she was always hitting her, and went
on about how much she'd done for her and all this. They were,
like, you know, women who do things together, it hadn't occurred
to me. I left her sitting on the dunny and I didn't say anything to
Ron, but I was sober, I can tell you. He looked at me and he didn't
ask me anything, just said he had some tickets for the ferry.'
'The ferry? What time was it?'
'Gone nine. We rode over to the shore. It was cold and salty and
damp but it was beaut. You know?'
'And then you came back?'
'And then we came back. He said he'd see me home.'
'Had to happen didn't it? I mean it took you long enough.'

135

'I said it was a scungy place, though God knows I was glad I wasn't still in this place. Not for him. I wouldn't have wanted to bring him here. He said it didn't matter and we got a taxi of course, and he walked me to the door.'

'Was that all?'

'No, not quite.'

'After all that?'

'He leaned over and kissed me and his coat opened up. He meant it to. I think everything he does he means, well almost, for he can't have meant to meet me.'

'Don't tell. The Green Hornet strikes again. You went glassy-eyed round the picture gallery, ate up at a posh restaurant, rode around the ferries like a couple of loonies, and all the time he was getting ready to go zzz.'

'No.'

'All right, I give up.'

'He had a dog collar.' Suddenly she looks tired and much older than she is.

'So that was that?' Though Clara knows this is not so, because of the new clothes.

'That night. He asked me if he could come back. I said how could he, and he said, that was for him to work out, I had to leave that to him because I probably didn't have the same problems as he did. I said more likely than not, and he smiled and said it was just as well I wasn't the sort who apologised, now how did he know that, eh? And if he could come back the next night he would, that is if it was all right by me.'

'And he did?'

'Four nights now.'

This surprises Clara. Janice has flown in two nights out of the last four in her usual manner without letting on anything to her.

'Tell me more.'

But she has done with it, or has gone as far as she means to. But she does smile a secret soft smile and she says, 'I've got a boyfriend Clara, a real boyfriend.'

'I'm glad, so glad,' says her friend, touching her hand.

'Are you?' Janice says, and there is an acid note.

She pulls back. 'I said I was.'

'For what? Me getting myself in a mess?'

'Why don't we put the gramophone on,' says Clara quickly. 'And there's some brandy in the back of the pot cupboard, we'll have some eh?'

And they do that. The brandy is good quality, off the base, and they put on a record of 'Smoke Gets in Your Eyes', Janice winding up the gramophone. She sings along with it in a curious voice, both flat and husky at the same time but appealing, and when that finishes she pulls out 'Every Cloud Has a Silver Lining' which Biddy had given Clara after a client left it at her place, still wrapped up in the paper from the shop where he'd bought it on the way round to see her.

They drink more brandy and start to feel patriotic and merry.

May and the captain are drinking together too. She has decided he is more of a gentleman that she first gave him credit. He pours Scotch regularly and generously for her. And he has always been a military man, understands her background. It's a pleasure to talk with him.

Now he shakes his head and laughs. 'Not a madam eh?'

'Oh no, not at all.'

'They must give you something though, eh?' He refrains from commenting, as well as, and she thinks that he really has quite good breeding.

'Well of course my friends look after me, see Ai don't go without things. But really. It's a quiet life for me. Ai'm just a little better connected, shall we say, than some of them.'

There is a tapping at the door. She opens it a fraction, recognising the knock, and a hasty conversation ensues through the crack. She closes it and looks down at the captain with real regret.

'Ai'm afraid that Louise is — otherwise engaged this evening. Ai did warn you that it could be difficult. She has a very regular gentleman friend at the present taime.'

'Ah shee-it, lady.' The captain graps the top of the whisky bottle. 'You mean the only thing left for me is to climb in on top of old Jimmy? I thought you coulda done better than that? I mean here I've been sittin' an' waitin' patiently while he enjoys himself, more than half an hour, screwing into this Biddy. I want me a fresh, tidy bit of snatch, not old Jimmy's leftovers.'

She sees then that she has not drunk him under the table at all, as she had hoped. Though he is very drunk, he has come to the Puzzle to have sex. She sighs. There must be easier ways to come by a few of life's little luxuries. She has another quick conference with the shadowy figure outside her door. When she comes back, she offers him hope, though personally she has little confidence. She stumbles, feels the age that no one knows.

'Biddy has class. Really. She trained in opera.'

'I'm sorry I couldn't bring round any stuff this evening,' Janice says.

Clara starts. She has almost forgotten that Winnie is coming tomorrow and that is partly why Janice is here. Ambrose, having missed her at the factory, had called all the way over to Newmarket to tell her what was happening, and about the panic that Clara is in.

'It'll be all right,' she says.

'No it won't, I'll get you some stuff in the morning if I can get over. They're doing checks at the factory at the moment though; you know how it is.'

Clara knows all right. None of them have ever forgotten the night Annie Walmsley was walking down the stairs and the elastic in her knickers had broken just as they were all leaving the factory.

The chocolates had come cascading down round her ankles in a great shower of red and gold paper. At first they thought it was funny and there were a few hysterical giggles and then, uneasily, they'd fallen silent, not knowing what to do, wishing they could help because it could have been any of them at some time or another, and yet knowing that they compromised themselves forever if they made one move in her direction. She'd needed that job too.

'Don't get caught for God's sake, Janice.'

'Not even for you kid. But I reckon the boss'll be out tomorrow, quite early. I heard him say. I'll see what I can do.'

'It's just that she'll smell a rat if I'm broke.'

'At least you're all right for food.'

'As long as it holds out. That's the trouble, Ambrose won't be able to help out and then I'll have to get some in. I'm hoping she'll only stay a day or so.'

'What exactly are you planning on?'

Clara explains and Janice listens as if she's soft in the head, but she says she understands.

'You can see how well I am tonight,' Clara says. 'I'll be fine. I mean if I'm like this she'll never guess will she?'

Janice looks at her hard. 'Is she thick or something?'

'You sound just like Ambrose. And you're supposed to be making me feel good.'

'Am I?'

'Knowing you . . . . I guess not.'

'Ambrose said he'd come over and leave some stuff with me for you to sell, too, if he can't bring it round himself. He said he thought he could get some more stockings and Camels.'

'Good. I'll get you a cut and you can have some Camels, or does your Ron get them for you?'

She blushes. 'I don't like asking him . . . I mean . . . '

'You mean he's a Holy Roller. I dunno what's got into you Janice.'

'It'd put him in an awkward situation, wouldn't it? It'd be out of character. Well, they'd guess he was up to something,' she says defensively.

'You've got it bad haven't you?'

'I'd sure appreciate some of the Camels,' she says, changing the subject.

'Will do. I'll just have to hope it comes together in the morning before Winnie turns up, that's all.'

'All this trouble. I don't know why you don't just take the money from Ambrose. He wouldn't mind and I guess it'd be easier on him too.'

'You know he spends a packet here as it is. Besides, you know how it is between Ambrose and me.'

'Yes. Well . . . I suppose that's why I told you about Ron. Only this is sort of different.' She shrugs. 'Be more practical for you. Oh, I dunno, you're a queer one.'

'Maybe I am.' Indeed, she has often wondered if that is just what she is, for so often she has wanted everything that was different from that which was expected of her. Still, she can see Janice's point. 'Funny how it goes isn't it?' she says. 'When I thought about knocking off at the factory I believed I was going to make a packet out of the Ambroses of this world.'

'Didn't work did it?'

'Nope. God was I scared when you brought him in that night.'

'He was all I could find.'

'I said to myself, well Clara my girl, take a look at him, he's for your learning, if I can cope with him I can cope with anything that comes my way.'

'Did you take money off him that night? You never did tell me.'

'Only that once.' Now it is her turn to withdraw. To go further will involve a review of all her history with Ambrose, and she can't do that, not tonight anyway. She is too tired, and with the brandy she knows that she will have to go to bed soon if she is to be all right for the morning and what promises to be a busy day.

Biddy remembers that she was trained in opera. The captain has

139

reminded her. Once she had actually got to sing a bit part in 'New Moon'. The local reviewer had been very nice about it. Oh those were the days.

Ma is worried and distracted. The night before, Billy has put the meat skewer through his doll. He was very excited about what he had done, and swung the doll aloft over his head, still attached to the skewer. When she protested, he told her that he was practising to be a soldier just like his dad. 'Everyone should practise for the war,' he told her importantly. She supposed it was fair enough. All the kids played war games. But she thinks it would be better if he played cards with her and tonight she can't get him interested for long.

'No lead in the old pencil?' says Biddy. She is fed up. The captain has fumbled with her for longer than she can bear, and he is chewing at her tit now in desperation. It hurts and she's had enough.

But she has said the wrong thing to her visitor. In the next room her child stirs.

She hits a high note as he begins to attack her.

Janice eases her feet into her shoes.

'Hey, if you should run into sister Winnie, would you say that we work in armaments, next door at Mason's?'

She gapes. 'Why?'

'I dunno. It sounds better. People like her, they only have to hear the word chocolate and they think black market.'

'Well some of it is and some of it isn't. We do and we don't.'

There is a small cold moment between them. Janice will lie and steal if it will do what she sees as good, but she doesn't go in for what some would describe as hypocrisy, though it has never occurred to her to work it out in such terms. She doesn't dwell on ideas like that.

'Just to keep her off the scent,' Clara mumbles. 'She'd die of the shame.'

'Keeps her legs crossed eh?' says Janice, her words conveying more than the obvious inference.

'All of that. People do change. I reckon she might have done some pretty crummy things in the depression to keep things going, just like Mumma did. People just forget . . . '

'Okay,' says Janice. Her manner is careless and still a bit distant

140

but Clara knows that if she says it will be all right then it will. Anyway, the chances are against her meeting Winnie. It doesn't seem like a good idea which is obvious to them both, so she is hardly likely to show up without checking to make sure Winnie is out.

Janice is putting her coat on when things begin to happen. It seems that the world is flying at them in all directions.

The door opens just long enough to admit Ambrose and the rank smell of Ma Hollis's puha and fish heads that she and Billy had for their dinner. Clara can recognise their whole meal in one whiff. She has seen them sucking the eyeballs out of the fish heads like boiled lollies and even shared them herself when times had been leaner and before her tastes had been so finicky.

Ambrose slams the door behind him and leans against it. His eyes and teeth are shining and he breathes fast. 'There's trouble out there,' he says. 'I jes' bring you these.'

He dumps a parcel down on the table. Clara moves to open it.

'You can do that after, 's only soap and some cups.'

'You came all that way just to bring me these?'

'I got them along the way.'

There is no point in asking him where, nor does it really matter. He is jumpy and agitated and as they listen they can hear a row going on outside. It may have been going for a while. Janice and Clara have been wrapped in their own conversation and the music, and so much goes on in the Puzzle all the time, that things happening outside can often go unnoticed, unless they get really bad.

Someone outside starts pounding on the door behind Ambrose's shoulder blades.

'Don't answer it,' he says.

A voice screams: 'Clara. Clara, let me in.' It is Biddy Chisholm.

'Let her in Ambrose.'

'I tell you, they make trouble for you.' His dark hands are splayed out nervously across the door at his sides.

'For Chrissake Clara, let me in,' Biddy shrieks. There is a man's voice and a blow.

Clara tears at Ambrose, pushing him away from the door with a strength that surprises herself, and pulls the door open. Biddy collapses through it and Janice springs to close it in the face of the man who is pursuing her. Ambrose catches Biddy as she falls and rights her.

Outside, the man continues to bang.

Biddy is a sight. Her blonde straw-like hair falls to her shoulders

141

in a matted tangle and blood shows through near the crown as if a piece of hair has been torn out, and there is black kohl running down her face, incongruous in itself, for already her eye and the cheekbone beneath are a violent blue-black. She is wearing a skimpy scarlet chiffon robe, only it is torn from her shoulder. She isn't a beauty at the best of times but now she looks horrifying, and she babbles incoherently.

Ambrose leans across and smacks her on the side of her face. Clara opens her mouth to scream at him but when she looks at his face she changes her mind. There is a look of grey fear in it, such as she hasn't seen before.

'Shut up you goddam bitch. You wanna bring the M.P's roun' here like a swarm of locusts woman? What say you shut up your mouth and let all of us off eh?'

'I thought he was going to kill me,' she whimpers.

'He still might. Don't you see woman, no matter what he done to you, you must keep quiet,' he hisses.

And Clara can see what he is getting at. If the M.P's turn up now anything can happen. And if the man thinks they are going to find a woman screaming he will try to stop her mouth for good before they get to her.

'There's two of them,' says Biddy. 'The first one was all right but the second one, he did me over.'

'Why? What did you do to him?'

'Nothing. Honest. It was my black eye, he reckoned he'd been done. He was plain nasty from the minute he walked in and then there was no stopping him.'

'Where's Kathie?' says Janice sharply.

'She's run down to Ma's. He's shickered, that's half the trouble, or he'd have stopped by now.'

'Can you stop him?' Clara asks Ambrose.

But even as they listen the noise drops. The quiet is worse than the noise. Ambrose balances on the balls of his feet, rocking backwards and forwards. 'How do I know eh? Maybe, maybe not.' His drawl has changed. He is the man of the streets, not seen before, and he has a subtle menace, a stillness of presence, even as he moves. 'Depen's whether the ma-an has rank, or whether he is like me. It depend whether he is too drunk to know he is in trouble bad, or whether he wants to move his arse out of it for himself. It is a matter too, of whether the man is — white or black.'

'I think he's a captain,' says Biddy. 'And he's white.'

'Go,' Clara tells Ambrose. 'Get away from here and — and

phone the police, get one of our bobbies, we'll look after Biddy.'

It makes sense and he's tempted, but he says, 'I won't leave you with trouble.' He looks around the three of them and sees that they are confident that everything will be all right. He begins to back towards the door, still tense and ready for whatever might be beyond, and she knows that in less than a minute he can be out across the roof where all the chimney pots and broken timber on top of Paddy's Puzzle stand up in the blacked-out night. That is where she wants him, away from them, and danger. She doesn't want him caught like an animal, here in the sewerlike corridors of the Puzzle, beaten by the M.P's and thrown in a jeep and not to see him for days, or weeks, or ever, as the case may be.

But it is too late. Even as his hand touches the door there is a wild cry from the flat across the passage, Ma Hollis's voice and a child's thin scream, and that same instant they hear the jeeps pull to a halt outside and feet running. Ambrose opens the door; the American outside has Ma's kitchen knife at the little girl's throat. The captain is a white doughy man, with more chins than are good for him and sweat stands out on his forehead.

'Man,' says Ambrose, standing very still, 'You must drop that knife.'

The captain looks at him and all of them. His face curls like a sea anemone's that has been touched, and it is full of contempt.

'You telling me what to do, boy?'

Inside of her, Clara wants to shout again to Ambrose to go, to leave as fast as he can; a part of her wants that even more than she cares about Kathie, slithering now in the soldier's grasp like a little wounded pink piglet, not understanding, as Ambrose does, that her salvation is in stillness. 'Mum,' she shrieks, and Janice's arm shoots out like a steel band holding Biddy back. Ma's and Billy's faces are glazed masks.

Downstairs, two flights, there are raised voices. The M.P's don't come in unless there is a complaint; usually they just throw a cordon around the place. Somewhere in the building someone has got scared maybe, or perhaps it was the captain's mate.

No one can tell what goes through a man's mind when he is as crazed as this one. For an instant more he and Ambrose look at each other with the hate they both understand from far back in time.

'I know a way outa here, man,' says Ambrose softly.

Even the captain who wants to kill the world and is planning to start with Kathie, and then move on to Ambrose and whoever might get in his way after that, can hear the police now. He starts shuddering.

'C'mon man,' says Ambrose urgently. 'You want them to take you? I sure ain't waiting round for them to take me.'

The fog lifts from the man's brain. He doesn't just drop the knife, he has the presence of mind to whip out his handkerchief and wipe the handle, then put it on the floor and kick it backwards with his foot into Ma's flat.

He drops Kathie, and she collapses on the passage floor in a huddle. 'Show me boy,' he orders Ambrose, turning on his heel.

'Ambrose,' Clara whispers. 'Leave him.' For she knows what a man like the captain might do to her lover once he has helped him free. He has a big wet plasticine mouth. She knows he will use it against Ambrose.

But they are away down the passage without a backward glance and in seconds they disappear into the shadows. The police emerge at the end of the passage moments later. Kathie is still on the floor crying and Biddy has her arms around her, her big raw-boned face presses against the child's, rocking her to and fro, whispering endearments in her ear.

The police come up then, with their batons on the ready and walking wide-legged like they do in 'The March of Time' at the movies before the main picture starts, and the one up front says, just like in the pictures too, 'Well, what's it all about?'

They look from one to another. 'Nothing,' says Ma Hollis.

'There ain't nothing wrong with this kid?' says the cop. It would seem that he means Kathie, but it is to Biddy that he looks.

'Nothing,' says Biddy, looking up from the floor. 'There's nothing wrong. My little girl's highly strung.'

'She always belt you in the face? I wouldn't stand for that if it were my kid,' says the officer.

'Ah, look now,' says Ma Hollis. 'I can give witness to that. That was a fall the lady had in the street not two days ago. I was there, now I was out pickin' a little bitty puha for mine and the boy's tea here,' she says settling herself comfortably against the doorway, 'and my friend comes along, and she has been doin' the shopping and she has a very full basket, well as full a basket as one can get nowadays . . . '

'All right, all right, we'll take your word for it.' He looks down at Biddy. Jesus, Clara thinks, he can't be so dumb he won't ask Kathie what happened. But he is. He doesn't ask her anything. Well, Jesus wept, she thinks, but that really is how dumb he is.

144

'We'd better take a look round if you ladies don't mind,' says one, and she thinks of the new crockery and the brandy, and gathers up her courage to refuse because she's entitled to, them having no authority over New Zealand citizens, but she is saved.

A man's scream strips the night bare. It lasts only seconds, but it is unearthly while it does. And the sirens start, that long sad note, and overhead the first drone of a Hudson, followed by the high-pitched whine of the Harvards. The night is alive, and no one knows where anything is coming from any more.

'You got to get to the shelter,' says the policeman, distracted.

'We will, we will,' they chorus at him, and outside there is more commotion, and yet another of the M.P's comes up from off the street and shouts that some dumb bastard has jumped off the roof.

It is as well that none of them are watching Clara for her hand flies to her mouth to stifle Ambrose's name; but then, they are dumb, so bloody dumb, as she has already seen. She wonders how it is that they can like any of the Yanks when she sees these dumb oxen waving their batons like they enjoy hitting people, and just not thinking, even though right now that's the last thing the Puzzle people want them to do.

'It's one of our boys,' says the policeman that's come up the stairs. 'A captain, they're just looking out his I.D.'

Now they'll ask us, she thinks, they must. But they don't. They just trundle off muttering and swearing about their fallen comrade and already it sounds as if they are telling it as if their captain is a slain hero and Paddy's Puzzle is the enemy.

Which perhaps it is.

They crowd into Clara's room and drink more brandy. Biddy is very quiet and takes Kathie off to bed in a few minutes and then Clara begins to cough, so Janice and Ma get her into bed. She keeps straining her ears towards the blackout curtain to see if she can hear anything that will let her know that Ambrose is safe but there is only the whine of the sirens. They have all decided, without discussion, that none of them will go to the shelters. Clara takes a last peek under the curtain, and can see by the moonlight that the Military Police are being hampered by the blackout in their clean-up operations, and after scrabbling around in the dark they throw the body of the captain on the back of one of the jeeps and drive off.

None of them in the room have been looking out for Billy, and Ma gives no indication of whether she has noticed him gone or not, but as they are tucking the bedclothes around Clara he comes up the passage and stands in the doorway, his head wobbling; he is licking his lips in a frenzy to get something out.

'The bloody butcher did it, the bloody butcher did it,' he shouts, and begins to laugh hysterically.

'Hush, hush now, don't you see Clara is going to sleep,' Ma soothes him.

'The bloody butcher did it,' he says again, and retreats into the Hollis's flat. His high laughter continues behind the door.

They put out Clara's light and leave her. She is tempted to get up and put the gas light on again but she is too tired. It is just that she would like to be able to see things solid and real, even if it is the contents of this room in Paddy's Puzzle.

May sits upright in her tidy sitting room. Her eyes don't seem to be focusing properly even with the help of her spectacles. That silly old fool, Ma Hollis, had shrieked and yelled at her before to come out and show herself. As if there was anything she could have done. The novel had been giving her such pleasure, a real delight, with the heroine walking through primroses to meet her lover. Now it is all spoilt. She has had a bad evening and she is not as young as she was. They ought to know better than to pester her like this.

The all clear sounds. Clara wonders about the butcher.

CHAPTER NINE

A night full of dreams, more dreams. Not of blood and violence as Clara might expect from a violent night of sudden death and strange happenings. Here in this maze a child has been threatened with her life, a woman terrorised; on the rooftops a man has died. The war. Maybe nobody has any sensibilities left. For all they sing 'Roll Out The Barrel' in the lunch hours down at the Town Hall and the smoke drifts amongst the people and they smile and nod to each other as if they have known each other all their lives, Auckland is a hard place these days. She knows this better than most. It is a reality that can be lived any day or night. But in her sleep she dreams of Winnie and their lives together. Of Hamilton. And of Mumma. Beginnings. Roots. But they are only half-dreams in a way, for she wakes and sleeps fitfully and the dream will begin in her sleep and when she starts out of it she finishes it off for herself, awake.

It seems strange to be nineteen and trying to impose an order on things, a pattern to your life.

Young to be looking back as old men and women do. What was it Ambrose had said to her? Just a child. No Ambrose, she is not a child any more. She is not divided by age from any of them now. At the time of her dying she will be like all the rest of them, like the men who are still boys, like his friends, getting ready to head back up into the Pacific and die. None of them, including her, are children any more.

It might have been easier to forget. Yet she can't. It is tempting to believe in Paddy's Puzzle that the only people who matter are the people who live there, the people she has chosen; Ambrose and Charlie Ambler, Janice and May and Ma Hollis, Billy and Biddy — what a pattern their names make. She had thought that she could cut out all the others and watch the procession of sun

147

and stars across her window until she was well enough to leave or it was all through; either way she could shut them out, those other voices. But it hasn't turned out that way, even though it has taken her so long to admit that this is so. It is Winnie's letter, written by her busy thickening hand, that has finally convinced her.

Winnie has become a physical presence and with her she has brought back the presence of all the others.

Clara opens the windows. She cannot bear the heavy blanket-like material that blocks out the night. It seems safe enough. She won't be lighting the lamp again tonight. Now that she is settled she does not want to move and even if she does have to get up the moon is bright enough for her to pick her way around, although pale clouds scud past from time to time, casting shadows in the room. There is the steady hum of sound. It is difficult to identify the individual noises in the Puzzle but they accumulate, and the building is never really still; as hard to sleep soundly as it is during the day.

Winnie. Mumma. Winnie again. Her childhood unfolds. But it is easier with Winnie. Up to a point, she is a positive figure. Except that point exists, at which she sheers off. She thinks she will come back to it. But Mumma is a shadowy figure who does not add up. Dotty and vague, not quite real, although of course she was. Clara knows that whichever one of them she is going to wrestle with, there are the men in their lives to be considered too. She is forced to confront the fact of her father. She struggles in her dream, half wakes, and knows that of all she has been seeking to forget, he is the most important. He was there at the beginning. The rest is already history. He has never been. She sighs; accepts him into the night.

Her father and Frankton Junction.

He was an engine driver, a great big powerful bull of a man, as handsome as the day, with a ruddy shining brown skin and a mouth full of flashing white teeth. It was from their father that Winnie got her polished look, her shining healthy skin, and it was from their father that Clara got her head of curls, for under his peaked hat there was a mass of tight chestnut locks lying damp against his skull. He had a chest like a barrel and when Gus Bentley laughed from deep down inside of him, you could hear him all over the railway yards. And his eyes would glow, even at the end of the day; or entering the light after he had had come off the line at dead of night, rimmed with soot they still shone like the coals with which the stoker had fired his machine, all through his shift.

Women loved Gus. At the railway socials they flocked around him, and he would lift them up on his arm until they screamed for mercy, laughing themselves sick all the while and begging him in the same breath not to stop. Some of them would look at him with special eyes and Clara would look to see if Mumma was looking, but as far as she could tell she never was. She would be talking away earnestly in a corner to Nellie Potter's handicapped sister, or somebody else's aged mother. She just never seemed to be looking. Clara couldn't take her eyes off her father when he was like that, for there was so much life and vitality about him that she would be almost sick with love for him herself.

Then she would look back to Mumma and creep over to her, not exactly knowing why. Sometimes his eyes would follow her, considering.

There is a rumble like an earthquake that makes her sit bolt upright. She looks out the window and sees three military trucks passing on the street below. They don't seem to have any particular purpose, but her grim thought is that they will give them no peace round here tonight. Before she drifts back to sleep, she thinks how much she likes her name, in spite of everything. Viewed from Winnie's later standpoint that it belonged to her great-aunt it is a curious old-fashioned name; mothers go in for a good modern Claire these days, rather French and considered to be classier, but she likes Clara. It means bright, and it sounds like clear light which is lovely to think about because she has always gone round looking towards the light if she can. Even though it is everywhere, some lights are clearer and brighter and purer than others and those are always the lights that take her by surprise. 'I am Clara,' she says aloud. 'I am Clara. I am Clara.' She laughs at her own silliness and knows that it is a foil for the darkness that has descended.

He was killed when she was eight. The train he was driving was derailed and it was over as quickly as that.

And even though she has dwelled on the others, it is he who has been lurking there all the time. She has always thought that it was Winnie that counted, with Mumma trailing along behind, not to be taken too seriously. But it had never been true. It is Father who has always been there, lurking in the background.

Why has she always left him out, this big handsome man?

149

She watched for him often enough, standing on the overbridge at the Junction, peering into the distance of those ongoing railtracks, waiting for the cloud of steam that heralded his arrival. So why was she at Winnie's so often when she had someone as exciting and splendid as that, there at home?

The answer was simple and the pieces fitted together quite easily.

Father, which is what they always called him, beat Mumma. He beat her regularly and thoroughly. He was not much of a drinker but he was a womaniser; he had at least two women a week and after he had taken a woman he would beat Mumma till she could hardly stand up. He beat her in a methodical and deliberate way so that where he hit her the bruises could not be seen; avoiding her face and her arms and her legs, he would beat her just enough so that she could still walk around and cook and clean for him when it was over. And the other thing, which Clara didn't know then but worked out later, was that he would make love to her too, when he had done with beating her, down on the kitchen floor after she had put Clara to bed. She would whimper away softly down inside her throat, believing that the child could not hear. She never screamed, not once, but in her throat there would be this animal sound and she would hear it always, as long as she thought of Mumma. It would be a relief not to think of Mumma any more, for then she would not have to hear her in her head.

She never told anyone, and Clara supposed that he didn't either. Yet somehow, out there at Frankton Junction, they knew. She didn't know how they knew, but she could understand that they would. In that respect it was like the Puzzle.

The Military Police will not leave the Puzzle alone. They have come back to take measurements of the pavement where the man fell to his death. They do not seem to care that they are disturbing the residents with their loud voices. Somebody shouts at them and is ignored. It is, after all, Paddy's Puzzle.

And Charlie Ambler is curled up on the sofa in May Abbott's room. When he arrived she told him that on no account could he stay, but in his gummy terror she had taken pity on him, though what it was that had frightened him so badly she cannot discover. He has seen something in the night and he is afraid. She supposes she is beholden to him for all the chores he has done for her this evening, running backwards and forwards looking for a woman for the captain.

Before climbing into bed she pours him a shot of her precious whisky and offers him a quilt. He smiles up at her. 'You're a real lady May. You ever had a man?'

'Had a man? Why Charlie Ambler, I was never even engaged to anyone.'

'Why not?'

May blinks, trying to remember. 'My father was an admiral,' she says. Her voice is faraway and half asleep. 'Such a handsome man. They don't make many like that.'

In the furtive dark, she slides a chocolate under her tongue. There is an explosion of pain in her mouth. It has cost her something to keep her own teeth. With care she moves the offending morsel to the other side of her mouth.

There are two things that still make Clara angry. One is that even though he did this awful thing, the people at the Junction still thought Mumma was somehow to blame. She knew they thought that, and she knew that in their heart of hearts they believed that she drove him to it.

They would look at her in her little glasshouse, pottering around talking to her flowering plants, in her dowdy, beribboned but absolutely spotless dresses, peering round from behind her thick spectacles, and they would think that she was odd, and because of that that it had to be her fault. She was odd too, but Clara thought that she had grown that way and that it was giving birth to her that probably made it all happen, though she wasn't quite sure why she believed this. It was a heavy thing to believe about oneself, but she did. It didn't bear thinking about too much, and so she tried not to in order to avoid being hurt.

The other thing was that Mumma loved Father. Clara was not angry because of the love in itself, but because although Mumma loved him he still did this to her.

Then there were times when she thought that he might have been angry with himself too. Again, she wasn't sure why she thought this, except that once or twice, no more, she had caught him standing looking down the railway tracks from the bridge with a look of such sorrow that she would never forget it. One of those days she especially remembered was a Saturday afternoon and there was a big game at Rugby Park. He had had his ticket for a month. In Hamilton they went wild over football. Nothing would keep him away from a game like that. Or so Clara thought. But on the Friday night he had beaten Mumma up worse than usual, and

151

Clara had watched him, and he saw her watching, and he didn't go to the game.

That was the time she particularly remembered him standing on the bridge. His face, and its pain, had stayed with her, like Mumma's unspoken cries.

It was because of these matters that she had started going to stay with Winnie so often when she was small. She knew that now, although she didn't then.

But there was more to it than that. Clara's belief that the beatings started when she was born stemmed from a suspicion that none of the others knew what was happening, and that it had not occurred when they lived at home. She thought Mumma had only told Winnie because she needed somewhere to send her away from this violence, and she thought too that Mumma hated Winnie having to know, that in this endless seamless web she was angry with her, as people are when they owe something to someone. That was probably the hardest part of all, because Winnie, her firstborn, had been her favourite child and this had come between them. It occured to Clara that Winnie too had secretly wondered what Mumma had done to make their father as he was. Although she didn't know it when she was small, Clara realised later that even if the violence had begun after her birth that Father's women had begun much earlier, and looking back she could not see how Winnie could really blame Mumma.

Seven was the number of children to whom Mumma had given birth. Father had several more, so that she and Winnie and the others had half-brothers and sisters in Frankton Junction. Perhaps, after all, it was not so hard to understand why the Hoggards were stuffy about Reg's marriage to Winnie. Perhaps, Clara thought, you can expect too much of people. But even so she sometimes thought that Winnie looked at Mumma with cool critical eyes and wondered what it was all really about.

Until Winnie met Albie.

Then Clara never heard her mention their father again and in time she almost forgot that he had existed. But she supposed that it must have weighed heavily on Winnie, a father like that. Perhaps it was not so surprising that poor Albie never consummated his love. Winnie lived with the guilt of others' sins lying heavily on her. No wonder she was, as they said, a good woman.

The Yanks are still there. Clara has been shivering but now the

152

sweat breaks out on her skin. It is an old companion, though that could be too friendly a description for the fever that stalks her in the nights. An enemy she cannot shake. She wishes Ambrose was there. She knows she could shut the window but she does not have enough strength for the task. From experience she is certain that if she lies quietly the fever will go. She hears singing:

'Show me the way to go home
I'm tired an' I wanna go to bed
Had a little drink about an hour ago
And it's gone right to my head.
Wherever I may roam,
On land or sea or foam,
You can always hear me singing this song . . .
Show me . . . the way to go . . . home . . .'

Winding down, like her gramophone running out of steam. The police detain the singer. Something to show that they are doing their job. They will know that it was not he who killed their officer. But it is important of course, to do one's job.

In the Rose Gardens a man with a body like a black seal that has emerged from the bay lurks beneath the trees. He is stiff and cold, for he has been crouching under the bank for a long time. Now he unfolds himself and paces backwards and forwards, restoring the circulation in his cramped limbs. He waits for something to happen, as he has waited through the past hours. Nothing does. He flexes his fingers, testing them one by one. He moves his head from side to side. He is in good working order.

Along the path there is a tap of feet. He sniffs the wind, alert for danger, but there is none. It is a girl. She comes close to the spreading pohutukawa where the man stands. He sees her plainly in the moonlight, and in the same moment she sees him. She has gleaming fair hair, down to her shoulders.

'Hullo beautiful,' says Ambrose, out of the corner of his mouth.

There was the way, too, that Clara replaced Winnie in Mumma's affections. That must have been particularly difficult to understand, how Mumma seemed to love her more. It should have been the other way round, one of them the firstborn and wanted, the other the lastborn and not exactly welcomed.

But for all Mumma's strange ways — and Clara, who knew more about those than anyone, recognised that they really were

153

strange — there was some antique strain of wisdom, some knowledge which Clara could not have explained if she had tried to, but was aware of its presence. Whatever it was, Mumma had prepared for the worst.

She loved her man, her engine driver. Yet at the same time she knew she could not have him to herself and so she set up her own defences. Long before he died, and long before Clara was born, she had retreated into her world of flowers.

He had put up the glasshouse for her when she was young, maybe when it still seemed a pretty thing for her to do, and as the years passed she had come to spend more and more of her time out there. It was beautiful. Cool in summer, warm in winter, and always the radiant, icy glow of the cyclamen, so intense and yet so delicate, perfect statements of flowers.

Clara had watched Mumma with her flowers and heard what she had to say about them. Now the scent of roses lay heavily around her. She loved them but it reminded her that Mumma thought roses rather fat and excessive sorts of flowers, greedy in their glory. She liked chrysanthemums, because they were untidy, uncontained creatures, observing no rules in their magnificence. That appealed to her, but it was not enough. She was fond of geraniums and Clara had actually placed one in a pot on her windowsill, because Mumma had recommended them once. Until Billy came in one day and knocked it off (she thought he might have been aiming for Andrew Gourlay's head, for he'd been tormenting Billy all morning about being fat). That was a nice enough flower, and some of the colours were close to those of the cyclamen; but she had to admit that they smelt like cat piss, and that there was a slight flouriness in their texture which put them in a different class.

No, it was the transparency, the absolute perfection of shape, that strange heart that had to be studied if it was to be seen properly, that placed the cyclamen apart and so absorbed Mumma. Clara believed that it said something about Mumma herself. In a way they described her, for they demanded not to be held or touched too closely, held a secret within themselves unless they were examined carefully.

Clara did not think that Mumma was mad, or ever had been. Those flowers had been the expression of a beauty inside someone who longed to be seen as more than her myopic eyes and plain face. If she cultivated flowers that were unruffled by any wind that blew, that sat in a glasshouse, that is how she had decided to present herself to the world.

Yet Clara knew that there was a side of her that would have liked to have got up at the railway socials and danced the feet off all those wild laughing women who thronged around her father.

And she knew this because Mumma danced with her. She had learned to dance a tango with Mumma when she was three.

She touches her pulse. The rate goes up at night. According to her book, it might reach one hundred and twenty beats in the minute, 'performed with a jerk, as if the result of a weakened heart'. She has no way of knowing how long a minute is unless she turns on the gaslight and watches the clock. She does not have the strength to do it so instead she lies there, holding her wrist and counting. One hundred and twenty beats seem to pass very rapidly, yet time itself has slowed right down. Out there, the night is heavy with stars. Ambrose, we share the same sky.

His body is as hard and unyielding as dark obsidian now.

'Move under me, move,' he commands. He is like steel through her core, pinning her to the earth. She moans and seeks to please him, and in doing so, pleases herself.

'White cunt,' he snarls, as the first wave of her response carries them along.

Below, in the bay, the sea breaks on the shoreline. He thinks he will drown.

When she was tiny they would be alone in the house together and Mumma would sing to her, not much of a voice, but fair enough, and the rhythm was there, and they would dance round and around the kitchen. When Clara was very small she would hold her in her arms and swing her this way and that; when she grew a little she would invite her to totter after her, trying to follow her footwork. At first the steps would be careful and correct, then more and more frenzied, dancing, dancing until they both collapsed.

And all the time she would have one ear tuned to the railway line. She knew each engine that passed, the 'K', the De Glehn, the 1274, each had an individual clack of the wheels and her hearing was very sharp; she could hear them far off in the flat frosty Waikato night, and if it was her husband coming home they would stop their dancing and she would hurry Clara off to bed, so that when he came in she would be sitting at the kitchen table with her sewing box out. What happened after that could never be predicted.

Clara supposed it was things like this about Mumma that made her seem mad. But she didn't believe it the way other people did. And she thought that she knew her mother better than other people.

She had never told anyone about her and Mumma, at least not until she met Ambrose. One wet afternoon, not long after she met him, he asked her about her life. For all that he would tell her so little of himself, his past still seemed colourful and strange. Hers was ordinary and lacking in incident by comparison and so she told him of Mumma. She thought he would find it peculiar and was put out when he seemed to find it unexceptional. What he found odd were the things she found the most everyday. He could not understand the quiet town that she tried to describe to him, the farmers coming in to shop, the ordered way of life. It was a happening like Mumma that made sense to him. The rest would choke him to death, he said. In a way she knew what he meant, for in the end it had nearly choked her too, as surely as the damp smoke from the burning land had all but smothered Reg, and all of them, in the wake of what had happened.

Lying very still in Paddy's Puzzle, she remembers the sensation so vividly that the smoke and fog could be around her now. The fever abating. She is afraid that the chill will begin soon. She knows that she must move to close the window. She is even more afraid that when she does she will begin to cough. Easier perhaps to let herself go, for it all to be over in the morning. Then she would not have to see Winnie at all.

But then neither would she see Ambrose, ever again.

'Move cunt, move,' he says, between his teeth. His lips are stretched back over them. They shine above the girl's face. Her pleasure is turning to fear.

After her father died, the dancing stopped. It had been all but over before that. Mumma appeared to have decided that it was dangerous for her, or both of them, to continue their wild gambols. It was that, and her determination to leave her with Winnie as often as she could, that made Clara so certain that her mother had always had a sense of the order of things, whatever might be said of her. In the end she protected Clara simply by sending her away. Clara thought that it must have been hard on her that she turned so avidly to Winnie, treating her as a mother;

none of them really got what they wanted; not her, not Mumma, not Winnie.

She has set out to fill the gaps in her memory about her father. Instead she has ended up thinking about Mumma.

She tries to think back to her father's death; to the pall of gloom which settled over Frankton Junction; to the funeral on a day so dense with river fog that the mourners had to stand right at the edge of the grave to see the coffin lowered; to Mumma shutting the door of the glasshouse firmly between herself and the people outside.

The glasshouse became the centre of her life. Clara was shut out, even if she had wanted to come in. Mumma had tried love and found it wanting. Or perhaps she had tried all there was to try and there was nothing left. Only potting mix and the sprouting plants.

If she missed him, she did not say so. Later she would drink gin. It was not all the time, or even often, but when she did it was a great deal all at once and she wouldn't wake up properly for two or three days afterwards. Clara was frightened the first few times, and then it didn't matter. As with Winnie, she became more interested in herself than in Mumma.

Perhaps her mother noticed things, but if she did she gave little indication. In the evenings she crocheted mats to go around the house; she dusted on Saturdays and if Clara thought about it she would help her; they ate regularly, and she remembered the grandchildren's birthdays; she continued to tuck and pleat her old clothes as she had always done and she scrubbed her solid false teeth like sound railway crockery every other night, and she shaved regularly the little black moustache which had developed on her upper lip. Except for the gin, it might be said that things were more normal than they had ever been. Only none of these activities absorbed her. Her heart's ease was behind the glass door, beyond where any of them could touch her.

Clara supposes she could try to imagine her father's life as a whole, all those years in the belching huffing engines, pulling the trains along through the green centre of the North Island, over the viaducts, through the tunnels, round the spiral at the very heart of the island. But she can't. He had taken her as far as Ohakune once, and back. Her memory, and with it her imagination, stopped there. She could try to think of him with the women, and living here in the Puzzle it is not as difficult to understand him as it had been before. But they are her friends in the Puzzle, while those

157

women of his were people who had disturbed and distressed their lives. She cannot really relate to them.

Or she could try to imagine him in relation to her brothers and sisters and their lives with him. But she had never known any of it; only that it had been better for them, that somehow they had got along then as an ordinary Junction family, bossed by Winnie, looked after by Mumma, fed by Father. It was her life with him, or them, that was different.

She would never get closer to him than the afternoon on the railway bridge. She felt more about that afternoon than about his dying. So that in the end there wasn't much to think about except what happened to Mumma.

She has decided not to shut the window after all. It is so cool, and even though they are down in the gully she can smell the sea, very strong tonight, a sharp gutsy smell of salt. There is an element of danger and recklessness in letting the air spill across her like this. That is how she had always imagined life would be, a great adventure, and somehow different to Mumma's and Winnie's. But there has not been much time to live daringly, or not so that anyone would take it seriously. In small ways, however, she has set her face against the wind. Oh how cool, how clean.

Ambrose has reached his goal and he feels the girl filling with a great pool of his come which seems to have been unspent forever. It is almost unbearably better than he had expected, to the point of pain, and he slaps the girl's yellow head sharply with the flat of his palm. Her neck jerks and cracks and for a moment he thinks he has broken it.

Down below, another wave breaks, and this time he remembers the dark oiliness of the sea at night beneath the ships he has travelled on, and how he has stared into those chill passing waters, thinking with dread how quickly a man would drown beneath them.

He lifts his head, fighting for air. He still has murder in his heart; thinks, once is enough.

The girl rolls out from under him, moaning to herself. They struggle to their feet and her head seems to sit on straight, is intact. She mops futilely at herself and he hands her his handkerchief without speaking. She takes it and wipes the sticky mess from between her thighs.

'What you's crying for?' he asks, as if he doesn't know.

'Nothing.' She wipes her face with the soiled handkerchief. She returns it to him in exchange for a handful of bills.

'Thanks,' she says, and turns and walks back through the gardens, her high heels tapping out a pattern on the path.

'Any time. Any time you need me, beautiful,' he calls, but he does not expect her to hear him, and she is not listening to him anyway.

There was another thing. After her father died, Mumma grew more orchids. Clara thought that said something about her too. Tucked away inside, perhaps there was a longing for the rich and the fabulous. It was as near as her mother would ever get. That and a daughter called Clara. Clara thought that she might know more about the 'It' girl than Winnie guessed, and she did not believe that she ever really sold out to the memory of great-aunt Clara.

It was as good a reason as any not to see Mumma again. She might as well keep her illusions. Whenever she had noticed Clara in those later years, it was to note with pleasure that she was pretty and that her hair curled. Now she would probably have to ask Winnie who she was.

The sky is streaked with light. The dawn is about to break over Paddy's Puzzle and the hard prickle of stars is fading. She is tired now. Winnie will be here today. The night has been long, yet not long enough. There have been so many things that have slipped her by. So many things that she still has to get into focus. Robin for instance. Reg, for she hasn't done with him yet. Her own self. How did she get here? She has never really asked herself that, and even if it does sound like part of an old music hall joke, the answer is important. But now there is no time. She is so tired. There are a few hours left to sleep before Winnie comes. Winnie. Win, how far have we come? She wonders if she can afford the luxury of sleep any more, or if placing some semblance of order on things is not of greater importance.

She sleeps.

In another part of town, her lover is grateful to have survived the night.

CHAPTER TEN

Morning comes hard over Paddy's Puzzle. It is a harsh revelation, a folding up of the night like a fine cloth taken from an old and scarred table. There is no hope of restoration because the Puzzle has never been good. It is as it is. Yet it serves the purpose for which it was intended. It gives shelter.

There are rituals in the streets of Parnell. They are not for the faint-hearted. Down St George's Bay Road which cuts across Cleveland Road, men come out with cages full of fox terriers. The noise is deafening as the small hungry dogs scream rather than bark with hunger and excitement. These are the rat catchers. At a given signal they will be let loose and the street will erupt with them as they fly in all directions, darting, sniffing, making their first kills. Soon the rats will begin to emerge, hounded from where they have sheltered for the night, or if they are in safe houses they will stir and push their way deeper into their cover. The Puzzle is not selective about the creatures it shelters. The inhabitants dislike this time of day for they know that their companions, the rats, are on the move. It is some small comfort that the walls are concrete. But that is their only protection, and still the rats find their way in.

Out in the street they begin to squeal as the terriers attack. It is a sport for some, especially the children. They shout encouragement to the dogs as the first rats appear. These animals could be mistaken for cats, they are so large and sleek, and their fur is often as long as that of a cat. They are driven by their attackers up the street, and as they are cornered a frenzy mounts as the first kills are made. The streets are splashed with blood. On they go, past Paddy's Puzzle and up towards the wool stores. The wool stores are splendid hunting grounds, for the rats much favour those warm and comfortable quarters.

But they have their escape routes too. This, after all, is a regular

160

occurrence. They run across the road in a horde to the open wasteland on the far side of the road, where toi toi and fennel grow in thick clumps; and there they disperse, leaving trails in all directions. The waste ground is piled with litter and stagnating rubbish and it is easy to throw off a scent amongst it and reach the plants with their thick tracks and well-worn burrows. Before long the dogs are called off and they make the most of what they have caught.

It is a sport like cock fighting or bulls. The difference is that the prey of this sport is also an enemy. It adds a separate dimension to the onlookers' glee. There is the element of hate and of fear. There are stories of babies who have been mutilated, of people attacked in their sleep, there are dark mutters of impending plague. Up at Craig's the rats are thrown in drums and left there, two at a time, until they are ready to fight to the death and the victor to devour the loser. It is a deadly game.

This morning the Military Police call again. The dogs have been put in their cages and taken away and the children are looking for new excitement. The M.P's want to take measurements by daylight. Now they are accompanied by the local police. It is a wise precaution, for though the people of the Puzzle like the Yanks to visit here, they do not appreciate them prying beyond a certain point into their lives. The Auckland police rarely bother them. The residents keep themselves to themselves and the police think they drain off trouble rather than cause it. The M.P's know that it needs only one person to complain of harrassment and their troubles will be unlimited. Indeed, with the night behind them, and a new lot on duty, the Americans look as if they would rather be well out of it. It will be all so much easier if they are allowed to send a suitable telegram home to the dead captain's family, bury him with military pomp, and forget that the events of the night had really happened. Whatever it was. Who really wanted to know?

So that when the Auckland bobby knocks on Clara's door she is up and waiting for him.

'Did you see anything last night round ten o'clock?' he asks.

'What should I have seen? What's it all about?'

'Trouble. Was there any trouble here last night?'

'I heard there was trouble with the pipes.'

'There's always trouble with the pipes.'

'Oh. Then nothing special.'

'Nothing special?'

161

'No.'

'Hear anything?'

'You always hear things around here.'

'What sort of things?'

'Listen. Anyone can hear things around here if they listen. The noise comes free, along with the plumbing.'

And as they listen, the children shout to the M.P's, 'Got any souvenirs Yank?' 'Got any gum Yank?' 'Yank. What d'you got Yank?'

Then there is the sound of scuffling as they fight over the spoils. Someone whistles in the passageway. Biddy calls out to Kathie who is quarrelling with Billy over a packet of gum and what happened last night is just that, last night. It is over.

'Plenty to hear round here,' Clara remarks and looks the policeman in the eye.

'Thanks for your help,' he says, and the funny thing is, she really has helped him. He has as much as he wants to know, which is exactly nothing.

When he has gone, Clara applies herself to more important things, like making herself look as nice as she can for Winnie's arrival and distributing the goods Janice had brought her, nipping in fast just after eight, throwing the stuff down on the table and taking off as if it were her the M.P's were after.

Distributing? Selling. She tells herself she is being squeamish because Winnie is coming. It is a trade, and useful for both of them.

But first there is her appearance to consider. It seems important to begin with that for later she might not have the strength. It is weeks since she has been properly dressed and it is hard to decide what to wear. There is a green dress that she has always been fond of and she holds it to herself and wanders into the bathroom to gaze at her reflection. She never looks as she expects when she sees herself in mirrors. For as long as she can remember she has avoided them if she can. She has a secret dread of being accosted in shop mirrors by her own reflection because the figure and the face is so familiar as to be instantly arresting, yet it is like looking at a stranger, of being outside the body but knowing it all too well. And the trouble is, she is never satisfied with what she sees.

The eyes stare back at her relentlessly and the mouth thins, and there is nothing she can do to stop it happening, yet all the time she believes there must be something. She has tried smiling at herself in those sudden confrontations and it is like observing a grinning mask. She supposes ther are clever people who would say that that was the way she saw herself as a human being. The odd thing is when she walks away that apart from a momentary unease she forgets the person almost immediately. It has nothing to do with what is inside of her. And the reflection in other people's eyes has always suggested that she is hard on herself. That is, until she became ill.

This morning she is not going to be let off lightly. The picture she sees is of a girl/woman with a shock of lustreless hair that was curly once but is now matted and untidy with no shape or style to it, and a thin white face. If the face had any vestiges of colour left they have all drained into the green dress. So that dress is no good.

She tries a pinky-coral one, a soft wool with padded shoulders. Ambrose has always liked this dress. When she used to wear it, it seemed to inject a special life of its own into her. She was always gay and laughed a lot when she wore the pink dress. Now it is garish.

Not only does it look hectic and strange on her, but it hangs like a limp rag. She has lost much more weight than she had realised.

In the end she settles for a plain brown skirt and a blue sweater. They are neat and neither garment draws the eye too much. As well as that, she can roll the skirt over and hide the top of it with the sweater, so that it doesn't look too loose. The colours are neutral, which helps, because she can concentrate on making up her face to be quite colourful and not too bright. She wonders if Winnie has accepted lipstick yet. She was always going on about Clara wearing it in the old days, resigned and disapproving. Too bad if she hasn't, Clara thinks, for she certainly needs it today. She is careful though, and makes the rouge soft and puts eyeshadow on just lightly so that with a bit of luck Winnie won't quite notice it, but she'll still look the better for it.

She finishes off the effect with a scarf round her hair, so that only the back of it shows; she has brushed it well so that she thinks she looks quite passable.

When she knocks on Ma Hollis's door and presents herself she can see that it's worked because for a moment Ma doesn't know her; then she calls for Billy to come and look. Clara is not sure that she likes that. It makes her nervous to have Billy look at her, but at least she is pleased with their reaction. Old Charlie Ambler wanders down from the fourth floor and Ma calls out to him as he is going down the stairs and they both look at her again and there is something close to tears in Ma's eyes, as if she had just personally resurrected Clara.

'Doesn't she look beautiful? Eh? Eh? Isn't she just lovely?' she demands of whoever will listen.

'You want some chocolate Charlie?' Clara asks.

He nods and she slips back into her room and gets him a packet. He likes the hard dark blocks to suck while he is drinking tea, and Janice always makes sure of bringing those especially for him. He presses a florin into Clara's hand and she pockets it. A price is never discussed in these transactions, the seller receives what the buyer thinks the goods are worth and usually both are satisfied. The point of course is that if there is a haggle or no fair return for either, both will go elsewhere the next time.

'I'se courting,' he says.

'Yes?'

She waits. Stranger things have happened. She can't imagine who would have Charlie with his weaselly little face and grey stubble of whiskers. She thinks that the lady can't be fussy, but then there is no accounting for taste. And thinks of Ambrose.

'Soft centres. You got any soft centres?'

She tells him she has.

'Lots. Many as you got.'

The foil-wrapped chocolates are hidden under her bed, and she counts out three dozen, leaving a dozen, for she has other customers to consider.

She shows him what she has. He seems satisfied, and gives her a pound, then another ten shilling note, and he grins with such delight that she feels unkind to have taken so much money and not given him the rest of the chocolates. But when she tries to shove the ten bob back he won't have it.

'Her teeth ain't too good, see,' he says, and retreats back up the stairs, chuckling, to hide his booty.

It is a good start. Clara gives Ma Hollis a couple of cakes in return for the loan of the bed. At least that's what she tells her, because Ma wants to pay, and there is no way Clara will take money from her. She always has to think of an excuse to make her accept the goods without paying.

'You gu'n up to May Abbott's?' asks Ma.

'Don't know yet,' says Clara cautiously. She realises that they all carried on some more at each other last night, after they had left her. If there are sides to be taken, obviously she must be on Ma's, but she hopes they leave her out.

But Ma only says, 'Lucky it's not me what's givin' thim to her. Put ars-nick in thim, that's what I'd do.'

So Clara makes her way from one to another of them, the people of the Puzzle. She supposes they must all look pretty much alike to outsiders, a uniform pack of down-and-outs.

But they are the people who have helped her and care whether she feels ill or well. They come to her when she needs them. It has taken no great effort to like them. She thinks it may well be that she is living less of a lie than she has ever done. Since she came to stay here she has done less to impress and been more herself than ever before.

Only this morning she keeps looking at them through Winnie's eyes and that reminds her that she is dressed up and playing a part already, even before Winnie arrives.

By lunchtime she has sold everything and is back in the flat. She has done as much and more in a morning than she has done in weeks, and she is still feeling fine. A kind of excitement is overtaking her. The idea of confronting Winnie on her own territory has a certain appeal. So much has been on Winnie's terms; now it is she, Clara, who is in charge. Or so it seems.

She goes to the window to watch out for her. Winnie would have caught the morning train. Clara thinks that if she had planned things really carefully she would somehow have got to the station to meet her.

But that is beyond her.

She looks around the room again. What will Winnie make of it? The roses. The wall hangings. The mats, and her old patchwork quilt. The cupboard door under the sink hanging on its hinges. What a mixture. Will she see her at last as really being her sister rather than another difficult child in the family? What dark thoughts does she still harbour about her? If any? Perhaps it has all been in her own imagination. For all those years in the exchange of their lives she realises that she still does not know what Winnie thinks, and she has no idea whether this time will be any different from all the rest. No wonder she has been afraid of her, believing that she despised her.

Suddenly she is there. A small black taxi draws up outside and Clara sees Winnie sitting in the back. She and the driver crane their necks looking up at the building and they appear to be engaged in a long conversation. Clara cannot see either of their faces from where she stands and at first she wonders what can be the absorbing topic. It is not like Winnie to sit around being

165

chatted up by strangers, especially when you think what taxi drivers are like, and even Winnie must know that.

Then it occurs to her exactly what they will be talking about and she can almost hear the conversation. She can bet her last quid that the driver is looking over the nice solid dependable looking lady who is her sister and asking her what she is doing going to a place like this, and Winnie busy and chattery, will be telling him that she is going to see her sister, and the driver will be going, 'Uh huh, sister, *your* sister ma'am, are you quite sure this is where she lives?'

At last she gets out and the driver comes round to the door and hands her a little handgrip suitcase. She stands, peering around in the cool wind. She pays him off and Clara can see from her manner that she is distracted. When he has gone she looks up and down. Clara can actually see her wondering how she will get into this building.

In the meantime Clara has the chance to observe her. She looks good in a matronly middle-aged Hamilton kind of way. She has put on weight, not that she has ever been exactly slim, but now she is solid and it has travelled into her chins too. There is quite a little roll above the spotted blue blouse neatly tied in a bow, setting off her navy gaberdine suit. But she isn't without a touch of style, for perched on her head is a jaunty black hat, Robin Hood style, slouching over her eye, with a sporty black feather quivering above. The kids start crowding around her. Clara has to hand it to her, she is impressive; though it gets to her that Winnie looks so middle-aged. It seems crazy, as if she sees her in a new light, has never confronted the prospect that she will age like ordinary mortals.

Clara feels irresolute and rather foolish. Should she go out and meet her or what? Then she remembers that Winnie probably isn't expecting her to be home, so that it is better just to sit and wait. There is no need for her to know that her progress is being watched, the neat lady from Hamilton picking her way through the slums.

The children guide her into the building and in a moment Clara can chart Winnie's progress from their voices: the top of the stairs, along the passageway, and then her voice.

'Are you sure she'll be here?' she asks one of the children.

They all chorus assurances.

'I thought she would have left a key,' she fusses.

'But she's *in* there,' says one of the children patiently.

As Clara moves to open the door she hears Ma Hollis call out.
'Go in luv, she's waitin' fer ya.'

She opens the door as Winnie is stretching out a hesitant hand
to knock.

'Clara! I didn't think you'd be here.'

And, 'Winnie, you're looking marvellous,' Clara says in the
same breath as if she has just set eyes on her. She pulls her inside,
shutting the door firmly behind them, and grabs at the handbag
and grip, chattering on about her appearance.

'Take off your hat, it's a lovely hat, you really do look nice, you
must be dying for a cup of tea, now do sit over here, what sort of
trip did you have? How are the girls? Where did you get that outfit
Win?'

'In Victoria Street, you know the shop, the one along from the
Post Office, cup of tea, yes please, that'd be lovely . . . '

'And the girls?'

'Give me a chance, what a tongue you've got Clara, you don't
change do you?'

Clara can tell that Winnie is awake to the fact that she is trying
to divert attention from herself and the place because she slows
down all her movements, becomes very deliberate. Clara knows
she won't budge until she's ready.

'I thought you'd be at work,' she says, and walks around the
room.

Clara knows what she is going to be like then and feels helpless,
just as she has always done with Win. She is going to look things
over bit by bit and talk about something else at the same time and
each will be an important and nosey thing, so that Clara can't
concentrate on both at once.

'Well I'm here aren't I?' She addresses herself to Winnie's last
remark.

Her shiny skin, the lovely polished apple skin, has gone doughy
and Clara thinks she can see the suspicion of a whisker on her too-
round chin. She thinks of Mumma. But it is still Winnie all right.
She counts back. Two years since she's seen her. She wonders if
Winnie's noticed that that's how long it is since Clara left
Hamilton too, or whether it seems important to her.

Clara waits for her to say something about the place.
Maddeningly, Winnie just keeps on looking without saying
anything.

'What d'you think of my place?' Clara asks, giving in.

'It's plain, isn't it? Still I expect it's all you can get these days.

You keep it nicely. I never thought we'd make a housekeeper out of you.' As if she had had a hand in it. Perhaps she had.

'I used to help you enough.'

'Oh yes. True.'

She plumps herself down on one of the plain hard chairs, and leans down to rub one of her ankles. It is swelling a little round the top of her smart but sensible brogues.

'I'll make that cup of tea.'

'Thanks,' as if she had thought it was never coming.

As Clara fills the kettle she says, 'What did the taxi driver say then?' She could bite off her tongue the moment the words are out.

'You saw me coming?'

'I wasn't sure it was you,' she mumbles. The match goes out as she tries to light the gas. She strikes another.

'You might have helped me with my stuff,' Winnie complains, only that is not exactly what she means for there is nothing to her luggage.

'Well. What did he say? You were there long enough. That's why I thought it couldn't be you.'

'He thought it might be the wrong place.'

'He didn't?'

'Well he just wondered,' she says.

'It's a bit rough. It's what you make of it.'

'I can see that. It's nice Clara. Honestly. I'm just not used to the city.'

She sounds so warm and kind, it makes Clara feel as if she has been bitchy. It takes her back a long time to when Winnie had been the centre of everything.

'We started talking about things.'

'What sort of things?' Clara asks. She really wants to know.

'He'd been in the depression. Like Reg.'

'Well so had lots of men. Thousands. I mean . . . thousands and thousands.' She doesn't mean to sound hard but it comes out wrong.

'Yes. Of course there were. Forget it.'

'No. I'm sorry Win. It's been a long time. Forgive me. I do want to know.' She wants to say other things. She wants to tell her how sorry she is about Reg, and her being on her own, but she can't find the words. 'Tell me what he said.'

'Oh . . . nothing really,' she says, softening. 'Just that he wondered if it had been worth it. The hunger, the queuing, all that sort of thing.'

'I used to queue up with you. Remember?'

'Did you?'

'Of course I did. You must remember.'

'I suppose so. Like you said, a long time.'

'But you said . . . what about Cora and Ellen? You must remember them?'

'Yes. Of course I do.' Only Clara can see that she doesn't. She goes on to some private chord of memory that the taxi driver has struck. 'He'd been on the tussock. Same time as Reg was on the goldfields . . . '

The kettle is whistling away and Clara pours the water into the teapot.

'He says this place is full of Yanks.'

'Well of course it is,' Clara says shortly. 'Hadn't you heard, there's a war on?'

'Clara!'

'I'm sorry. Again.'

Winnie sits in awkward silence as the tea is poured. It hasn't drawn properly but Clara can't think what else to do.

'About Reg.' The words hurt in her throat. 'I'm sorry about Reg.'

'Yes. You wrote. A nice letter. Thank you.'

Clara wonders if she knew what the letter had cost her. It seems unlikely. Winnie looks very tired all of a sudden, and Clara is ashamed that she is behaving so badly. The silly part is she is behaving as well as she humanly can. Winnie can't know how hard she is trying, and still it is all coming out wrong.

'He said that they get the best of everything.'

'The Americans?'

'The Yanks. Yes.'

'I expect they do all right.'

'He said I was very lucky to get a taxi, they're always at the head of every queue as a rule, and they pay better. He says some of them will get their desserts though. There's some people waking up to them. He said he wouldn't take them first off every time.'

'They have to get round like everybody else.'

'Don't tell me you like them?'

'Well why shouldn't I? It's not their fault they're here to do a job.'

'We don't need them,' she cries. 'We had our own forces, why couldn't they have stayed here and defended New Zealanders, instead of bringing foreigners in?'

'I don't know.'

'Well you think about it my girl.'

'I'm sorry, Win. I don't know how wars are fought.'

'They're alive. Reg isn't. He should never have gone, you know. He didn't have to go, d'you realise that? He was past the age but he volunteered. Did you know that?'

'Yes Win. I knew. You told me at the time.'

'Well then.' She sips her tea, her face set, as if what she has said resolves everything.

'You really hate them then?'

'Who?' Her eyes have a fixed, slightly glazed appearance.

'The Americans. Yanks.'

'They get everything,' she says again. 'Look at the way girls are selling themselves for them. They're overpaid, they're oversexed and they're over here.'

There is a silence and Winnie looks a bit uncomfortable as if she can suddenly hear her own voice in the room and hadn't meant to say all that she has, but there is no way she can go back on it.

'How's Mumma?' Clara asks.

'She doesn't keep so well. You really should get down to see her. She misses you a lot.'

'She's got all you lot.'

'You're still her baby, you know.' She says it without rancour.

'Me? That's a laugh. I'm no baby.'

'You mightn't think so.' She is bossy again, and there is another silence. They don't seem to be getting far.

As Clara tries to think of something to say that will help her out, Winnie says, 'Anyway, you still haven't told me why you're not at work.'

'They gave me a couple of days off, what with you coming and all.'

'Really!' Her face brightens. 'That was generous of them. I didn't think they could afford to give people time off, especially if they were in munitions.'

'Oh . . . Mason's isn't quite like that,' Clara says. 'It's not essential war work. I mean they just make some of the bits.' She thinks she has done rather well. She hasn't actually said that she works at Mason's, or whether she works at all, except maybe the bit about the days off. The effort has drained her though, and she is suddenly giddy. She sits down quickly and carefully.

'See, I've got a bit of a cold too.'

'Is that what it is? I thought you didn't sound quite yourself.'

'Oh I'm all right. Honestly. But there's no point in spreading my

170

germs around is there? I mean that's more damaging than being one short for a day or so. You better watch out too. You don't want to catch anything.'

'You're not really sick are you?'

'Me. Good heavens no, what d'you take me for? You couldn't ever keep me down for long.'

'Can I do some shopping for you then?' Clara sees her face brighten, though Winnie doesn't mean her to see, at the prospect of getting on with something outside of the flat but she can't think of anything quickly enough.

'I got everything before you came. We'll be all right. So you've come to fix up Reg's things have you?'

'There's still some forms to fill in with the War Office. I got sick of writing letters so I decided to come on up. Besides — I wanted to see you.'

'Give over.'

'I did. And Mumma, she wanted me to see you. You write so little.'

'Yes, well I never was much for reading and writing like you lot, was I?'

'That's only because you liked having a good time at school too much to bother.'

'I'll bet Jeannie's doing well.'

'Top of her class in pretty near everything,' says Winnie. Her face lights up. 'They say she'll go to university. I mean — university, Clara. Can you imagine it? She'll have to work hard. It is hard work for Jeannie you know, she's not a natural talent, that's what makes me so proud in a way.'

'And Caroline?'

'Well there you are, you see. She could do better than Jeannie if she wanted to, but she doesn't try. Got a bit of you in her if you ask me.'

'God help her. She got a boyfriend?'

'Don't be silly. She's only thirteen. Still a baby.'

'I was less than fourteen when I started with Robin.'

'He's back you know,' she says sharply.

Clara had started to relax. She had thought they were getting somewhere. Now she raises her head, guarding herself. There is something about Winnie's tone.

'Back?' she repeats stupidly. 'Robin?'

Winnie fiddles with the handle of her teacup, not looking at her. 'They sent some of the men home on furlough. He had a small injury. Nothing much. They'll probably send him back, though some of the men who're back say they won't be going again. They say they've had enough.'

'They won't let them get away with that.'

'Most of them are pretty tired. Nobody seems to care much whether they go back or not. We'll see.'

'But there's a war on. Like I said. No, I'm serious now. You can't just walk out of a war.'

'Why not? It's better than getting killed isn't it? Well, isn't it?'

They sit staring at each other.

'What about Robin then?' asks Clara.

Winnie gets up and pours herself another cup of tea. Clara thinks that she might have asked her. It is her place. Even if it is plain.

'He's been gone two years. It's enough.'

'If you say so. But — what about him?' she insists.

'What do you care?'

'Nothing. I don't know. What do you want me to care? I just wondered about him.'

'Yes. Sorry.' It seems to be all they are able to say to each other. 'He looks well now. He didn't when he came back, but he's good. He's got a girl.'

'Who?'

'I don't know whether you'd remember her. Sally Carver.'

'Her!' Clara bursts out laughing. 'Robin used to throw peanuts at her from the back of the Roxy every Saturday afternoon.'

'The Roxy. What were you doing at the Roxy? You always said you were going to the Strand . . . or the Embassy.'

'What's it matter?'

'But the Roxy was rough, Clara.'

'Don't be silly. The pictures weren't any different.'

'Well you told lies.'

'I often told lies. You made me.'

'You're blaming me?'

'Winnie, don't be stupid. Who cares? Everybody tells lies. I'll bet Jeannie tells you dozens . . . '

'She wouldn't.'

'Caroline then.'

'Well . . . '

'Well. Sally Carver, eh? What a laugh. You know she had amazing tits. I remember when we were going swimming at school and we were getting changed. She looked as if she had these really enormous tits but when she took her clothes off they were really skinny and they hung down. She used to roll them up like a skein of wool. I told Robin but he never believed me. Ha, I'll bet he does now.'

'That's disgusting.'

'Is it? It's true.'

'They're talking about getting married. Sally's mother thinks they're too young.'

'I seem to have heard that one before.'

'They're afraid Robin'll have to go back overseas though.'

'And so they want to get married before he goes. Right?'

'Yes . . . '

'Boring. I mean, that's Robin's favourite line.'

'But he doesn't want to go back overseas.'

'That's his business.'

'It was always you Clara.'

'We were kids.'

'So I recall.'

'He's still only . . . I don't know Winnie, what is he, twenty I suppose?'

'Don't you remember?'

'Of course not. Well . . . not necessarily. You soon forget these things, don't you.'

'I'm sure he'd like to see you again,' Winnie says with an effort.

'See me? Winnie.' Clara looks at her, trying to probe inside her mind. It is impossible, for her at any rate. 'Is that what you came for? To tell me to go back to Hamilton and see Robin so he could pick between me and Sally Carver? Win, he can pick her teeth for all I care. Or her nose. She's got enough for two.'

'I simply mentioned it.'

'Yes. Well thank you.' She can feel herself getting hot and knows she is going to start coughing. She tries to stifle it, sitting on her breath, tightening her ribs and diaphragm, but it is no good. The wheeze swells up. She takes shallow, rapid breaths, hoping to keep it under till she can get through to the bathroom.

'Clara.' Winnie's round face is alarmed. 'Clara, are you all right?'

Clara slams the bathroom door and pulls the chain of the lavatory as she starts to cough. It flushes bright purple.

When she has stopped coughing she doesn't know whether to laugh or cry. The Puzzle, showing its colours again.

She stays in the bathroom for nearly five minutes and would

stay longer only she knows that the sound of the water flushing over and again must sound odd. She is afraid it might spill over onto the floor if she pulls the chain too often. Besides, she guesses that Winnie must be able to hear something of what's going on. When she goes through to the living room again she is standing at the sink with her back turned. She jumps as Clara goes through and tries to hide the medicine bottle which she has taken from the cupboard. When she sees that she is caught she straightens up and looks her in the eye, the old Winnie in charge.

'What's this for, Clara?'

'Leave it,' she says, and sits on the bed.

'It's some sort of medicine.'

'Just leave it. Can't you leave things Winnie?'

'What is it? What's wrong with you Clara?'

Clara feels anger rising like bile in her mouth, and tries to stem it the same way she tried to stem her cough. 'I've got bronchitis a bit this winter, that's all,' she says. 'This place leaks a bit. My cold's brought it on again.'

'You didn't tell me that before.'

'Why should I? I hate people who go on about being sick.'

'Then you are sick?'

'No. No, I'm not.' Like the cough she can't suppress her anger, but the way it overwhelms her surprises even her. It is like illness itself, a boiling over, and it comes from deep inside her, as if some old pain has suddenly been thrust to the surface. 'You put that down Winnie,' she hears herself say. 'You hear me? This is my place. I'm on my own now. I don't come nosing down to Hamilton to see what you're doing. I keep out of your place, you'd have fixed me all right if I hadn't minded my own business in your place wouldn't you? Eh? Well I'm grown up now, this is my place, and I don't want you into my things.'

She couldn't get off the bed even if she tried. She sits, half-collapsed, panting, and can't believe that she has said what she has. Winnie stands there looking at her.

'I see.' She puts the bottle back in the cupboard and closes the door.

'No you don't. You come barging in here like it's your place, like I'm still your kid sister, but it's not like that any more.' There is little fight left in her but she knows she can't give in now. She's gone this far and she won't make it there again.

'Why don't you have a bit of a rest if your bronchitis is troubling you and I'll hot up the pot,' says Winnie quietly.

174

It is over. Clara leans back against the wall, and closes her eyes. There is a hot line of pain behind them. Why is she so angry with her, she wonders. Guilt? Regrets? She is too tired to try and work it out.

'I'm sorry,' she says. 'Things sort of get to you.'

'I know.'

'The war . . . everything.'

'Don't worry. I blow my stack too.'

'You? I can't imagine that. You were always so calm.' Had she been, Clara wonders. From this distance it seems that she had, but she could have been wrong. Though somewhere far in the past, before memory had properly formed, she remembers something.

'Not now. Not any more,' Winnie says.

Clara is breathing deeply again. It is all right. Winnie talks as if nothing had happened and her own anger, trapped like an angry wasp in the room, has gone, as though she had opened a window and let it out. She wonders if she has exaggerated what has happened between them. Perhaps she has suffered more from the outburst than Winnie.

Winnie goes to the window, lifts the curtain and looks out. The hot heavy smell of chocolate floods the room. She sniffs the air.

'Nobody can afford stuff like that nowadays.'

'I suppose not.'

'How could they? It's black-market stuff in Hamilton. I suppose they feed the Yanks on it. D'you know we haven't been allowed pork in Hamilton this year? No bacon, no nothing, and there it is being produced right on our back doorsteps. Frank was going to bring some in to Mumma a few weeks back but it was more than his life was worth to get caught. Not that Mumma would have told anyone, but they have to account for their production, you know.'

'Will things ever come right again?' Clara asks. 'For people I mean? Not just — food.' It makes her uneasy, Winnie looking out at the chocolate factory like that and talking about black marketeering. It actually makes her sweat again, and it isn't fever this time.

'I don't know, Clara.' She lets the curtain drop. 'Before the war — after Reg had come back from the goldfields . . . he was a good sort, you know. Well I know you didn't see much of him, but he was a good sort.'

Clara nods.

'I tried to shut out the world, just make a little space for him and

175

me to live in. Him and me and the kids. It was harder than you might think.'

To which Clara thinks 'amen to that', but she lets her go on.

'We tried to keep up with the Labour movement at first but it didn't seem worth it after a while. I mean things are changing in Hamilton. Times aren't as hard like they were, and we had things. You know, things. We could buy things. It changed us. Well I suppose that was what changed us, I don't know.' She is quiet. Clara thinks, it's strange, she really hasn't seen me as a sister, just as a kid, she really thinks I never saw anything. 'It's easy to let things drift,' Winnie says. 'Easy to fool yourself.'

'Yeah. I know how easy it is.' Why has she said that, Clara wonders; she feels the treacherous rattle in her chest and wills it away. This time it obeys her.

'You? You haven't even begun to live yet.'

This is where we should leave it, she thinks. They have said enough to each other. Later Winnie will regret that she has not said more, but for her part she is sure that they need go no further.

Later in the afternoon Winnie goes for a walk on Clara's urging to look at the gardens, though there is precious little to see at this time of year. Clara thinks Winnie might like a glimpse of the sea down at Judge's Bay. It is a still kind of day and she has warm clothes. Clara had wanted her to go very much so that she could rest a while before she prepared a meal; and so that she could perform that task, at least in part, without Winnie watching.

She is gone for a long time, and when she returns the meal is ready and her cheeks are brighter and fresher than when she arrived. She looks more like the Winnie of old.

They eat and their conversation is more companionable, gossip less barbed. They both skirt dangerous topics, although Winnie asks about Clara's work, not that she is to know what an unwelcome subject that is. But Clara is able to look suitably hazy, and Winnie obviously believes, as Clara intends to convey, that what she does is secret. She respects that, even though she says she has had enough of war. It is strange in a way, because although Winnie is older, and conservative, and from Hamilton, Clara realises that she is the one who cares more about the war effort and winning. She can see Winnie's point of view, that enough is enough, and of course she knows too that her own interests in the war are different. Her man is still alive and Winnie's is not. It's still going on for her; for Winnie it is all over. But she can't tell her that.

They manage to skate over the surface of things until bedtime and Clara is grateful that it is a quiet night. With all the M.P's and the carry-on of the previous night and this morning, it looks as if everyone is keeping a low profile. To be sure, round ten there is one of the usual scuffles and some shouting but it changes to singing and the argument falls apart in a few minutes. She turns off the gas and the room splutters into darkness.

As she is on the edge of sleep she thinks to ask Winnie how Mumma's glasshouse is these days, and if she still keeps her blooms in order.

'She kept them right up to the end,' she says. 'Though they'd got pretty run down. I think the new people'll probably demolish the glasshouse. They don't look the types anyway.' She sniffs.

'What d'you mean, the end?'

'I told you didn't I, she went into the old people's home last week, same one as Mrs Hoggard. Now there's a laugh for you.'

Only she hadn't told her. Of course she thinks she has. Clara can see that people do believe they have told you things, and if they are very close to events and caught up in them as they happen, they forget that other people don't know. Clara listens to her sister's quiet breathing. She feels the wooden ribs of the camp stretcher under her shoulders. She lies and thinks about Mumma. She badly needs to sleep but again she lies wide-eyed, with grainy lids.

CHAPTER ELEVEN

It costs Clara something in the morning, getting up to make Winnie a cup of tea. She has slept badly on the stretcher and for a long time she had lain awake continuing to think not only about Mumma, but about Reg and Robin and all the people from the past who have come crowding back into her life, with the presence of Winnie.

There were so many ifs and buts about it all. If she had been older. If there had been no war. If Reg and Winnie had stayed happy together and he had not sought his consolation with her. If the past was not so full of regrets and she had gone home to see them again.

If all these things had been so, her life, even now, might be different. She might not be here in Paddy's Puzzle, wishing away her sister and lying in wait for the black soldier who is her last love.

To think that Robin is back and he could love her again. But that is not so. He could never love her again, nor she him. That is some fond figment of Winnie's imagination.

Her mind would run on and on if she let it but she is determined to get some sleep; the night before has been such a bad one and she is no good without sleep. She listens to Winnie's even breathing and tries to match hers alongside of it, a trick that has often worked when she has been with Ambrose. In the end it succeeds, though it takes longer for she does not have Winnie so close. Nor are they sharing the rhythm of their bodies. But at least there is the sound to measure herself by and remind her that she is still alive. Again she imagines letting go of her breath, so that it just stops. Of course it is not that simple. When it comes to the point she finds she cannot let go like that and the next breath is still more difficult and painful; yet in spite of herself she has to go through with it. So

178

it is important all the time to keep on going, in and out, slow and easy, easy, but not stopping. That is the secret.

Every now and then Win gives a disconcerting old woman's snuffle, or something approaching a snore; indrawn oinks, and that doesn't help either. She seems deep under though, and still is when morning comes round again.

The weather has turned and a slow Auckland rain is falling. Not teeming or lashing at the windows, just steady, solid rain. Clara doesn't think Winnie will have much of a day in the city. She forces herself out of bed. Uncomfortable as it is, she wouldn't mind staying there. It is a day for staying in bed.

She wakes Winnie with tea, comforted by the ordinariness of her face on the pillow, pleased in an odd way that she is there, but at the same time thinking that she has been there long enough.

Winnie opens her eyes almost immediately and smiles. 'Doing quite well for my kid sister, aren't you?'

'You sleep well,' Clara says by way of reply.

'Not bad, but you know what it's like in a strange bed.' Her face does look crumpled too, now that she is awake. She pulls herself up and lumbers out of bed, pulling on her wrap. She goes to the window and looks out.

'It's just as well I brought spare shoes.'

'You'll need them.'

'You were restless,' she says, without turning.

'Ma Hollis's camp stretcher. You would have been too.' Clara is annoyed. It means that Winnie has been awake while she was asleep at some stage. It is like being spied upon.

'You coughed.'

'I told you . . . '

'Yes, I know, it's all right.'

'It's been a lousy winter.'

'I can see.'

She sips her tea. Clara sees she is being careful and doesn't want another row.

'The chocolate smells strong doesn't it? You'd think in the rain . . . you'd think it wouldn't be so strong.'

'There's no wind so it's just the same either way.'

'It gets to you. Doesn't it get to you?'

'I can take it or leave it. You get used to it.'

'Strange. You'd think it'd lift.'

'Smells can hang on in this gully for weeks. They say when the stables burnt down, up there at Craig's where the wool stores are now, they say you could smell burnt horseflesh for weeks. That's what they say.'

She looks shocked, as Clara had intended.

'That's horrible.' She turns back to the window. Clara doesn't know whether she is thinking about the horses or what. Clara often thinks about them, for though it had been years before, people still talk about it as if it had happened yesterday, the beautiful animals screaming and screaming and the terrible stench which came and would not go away. One of the crazy old women round Parnell still gives away vegetables in the street to anyone who will take them, rather than have them go home and cook meat. Nobody should ever have to live with the smell of burnt flesh again, she says. Clara thinks that if she had lived here then, when the fire happened, then maybe she would take her vegetables too.

'Why don't you come home with me, Clara,' says Winnie quietly. 'I reckon you're run down.'

It is what she has expected.

'And lose my job? Not likely.'

'I can afford to look after you now,' she says. 'Nothing marvellous, but we get by all right these days. It'd just be till you were stronger.'

'No, you don't understand.' Clara tries to sound matter-of-fact, casual even, but it doesn't work. It comes out tense and edgy.

'It's all right about Robin. I'm sorry I said what I did. Truly. It's your business. I didn't realise you'd grown up. I mean, I suppose I just hadn't thought about it.'

'It had to happen some day.' She tries to be flippant but Winnie will go on in this serious awkward way.

'I know. At least I do now. But growing up's something that happens to other people. Not baby sisters. Please Clara, can't you see I'm trying really hard not to tell you what to do. I know that's what you think I'm doing but I'm not. I've got to make you understand that or I can't help.'

'I don't want help Winnie. I don't need it.'

'Are you sure?'

They stand looking at each other. Clara turns to the sink. She thinks that she will have to get the top of it fixed if she is going to be here much longer. It is getting so cracked and worn; it can't be very healthy like that. She wonders if Ambrose might be able to find a piece of red lino somewhere and they could lay that over it. It would polish up nicely.

And that is her answer she supposes, because just for a moment there she had been tempted. It had flicked through her mind that it would be sweet and easy not to have to get up in the mornings at all, just to have things brought in to her on a tray and have a bedjacket tucked round her shoulders when she got cold, and her sheets changed when she had a fever. Only of course it wouldn't be like that. Winnie would see her illness for what it really was and she would have her out of her germ-free Hamilton house, away from her healthy spruced-up daughters with their brains and their promise of university, within a week. She would wake up one morning and find herself in a sanitorium on some high and windy hill where the frightful fresh air would sweep through and make some last-ditch desperate attempt to clean out her diseased lungs. Of course it might work, but did she want it to? And if it didn't, what might she miss in the meantime?

'I reckon I've got a duty to the war effort,' she says. She looks Winnie straight in the eye and doesn't waver.

After a moment or so, Winnie says, 'Think about it then. If you change your mind . . . you just have to say.'

'Thanks. I'll keep it in mind.'

Winnie leaves soon after, with her spare shoes wrapped in newspaper and tucked in her shopping bag. Neat methodical Winnie. As Clara watches her trudging off up Cleveland Road in search of a tram she almost thinks she loves her again. If she was in Hamilton, where she belonged, it might even be true.

Clara had come to Auckland to grow, and to learn about things. Also to change her life. She had done all of those.

Sometimes it seemed like a long way from Hamilton to Ambrose. She didn't see it that way.

When she got sick some of the girls from the factory, Janice in particular, started taking care of her. They covered for her for a while. Then Janice, who lived across in the Puzzle then, got the chance of a better flat up in Newmarket and she took it. She said the rats were getting to her. She offered Clara her place in the Puzzle because it was so close to work and she might be able to keep going a bit longer. She said that in one way she felt like a rat herself, offering it to her, but it made good sense if you looked at it the other way. The place Clara was living in wasn't up to much so she was pleased to take it.

All the time they were at her to go to a doctor. She hadn't had much luck with doctors and she kept putting it off. She didn't really believe she was ill anyway. She was having too good a time. The pink silk dress had done its turn so many times that she had had to get some more dresses to give it a rest some Saturday nights. One of the girls at the factory gave her her old diaphragm when she got pregnant, and she swore it wasn't because there was anything wrong with it, just that she'd been careless. Clara washed it out carefully and let it dry on the window-sill and took to poking it up. Janice said she was mad, that you had to have them properly fitted, which Clara said was all very well for her, because she went to doctors about that sort of thing and had a record of babies, but they weren't likely to give her one if she wasn't married. Janice got a bit impatient with her then, and pointed out that that could be arranged. If she had a ring no doctor was going to ask many questions these days, but Clara thought of Doctor Mawson's long bony fingers prodding around inside her and decided to take a chance.

Not that she slept out often anyway. It was the dancing she went for and getting hepped on music. The laughter of guys, kids like Robin on their last leaves. She wondered if he'd done Auckland over, the way some of them did, after she had told him they weren't going to get married. Sometimes though, after a taxi-ride home on a wet night, or if she got a particularly sweet young chap (the scared ones really brought out the worst — or was it the best? — in her) she couldn't say no.

Being sick caught up with her. One of the supervisors had his eye on her and he saw her coughing one day and demanded to see her handkerchief. She had just brought up a whole lot of rubbish out of her chest. He held the handkerchief away from him with a disgusted look, but afterwards he and the boss were very nice when they took her into the office. They gave her the name of a doctor, told her what benefits she was entitled to and gave her three weeks' pay which they didn't have to. She asked if she could come back when she was better. She saw them glance sideways at each other. The supervisor shrugged. 'If you get a clean bill of health,' he said. There was nothing else he could say, she supposed.

When she told Janice she gave a sigh of relief. 'I'm glad someone's talked some sense into you,' she said.

'I'll be all right,' Clara told her.

'Oh for Chrissake Clara,' she snapped, with a real edge of temper.

182

That was when Clara told her about the Mawsons and why she didn't want to go back to Hamilton. She listened quietly and didn't say anything for a while, then told her about her own babies. They went out and bought some beer and got weepy drunk. She asked Clara if she wanted to go on the game for a bit while she sorted herself out. Obviously she would have to have something to tide her over, and the Marines were nice clean boys who took their own precautions so she'd probably be all right for clap so long as she didn't go picking up any dirty old local grubbers. She took in a few Marines herself at the weekends but she still had the devil's own job with birth control and seeing as she fell so easily she wasn't prepared to take the risk, except when she knew she was safe. Which brought her to the point, that she wouldn't be responsible for anything that happened to Clara.

What did she get out of it, Clara asked. Janice gave her a list. Cigarettes, gum, stockings, perfume. You could make the money go round, she should know that by now. She did of course. She had been selling chocolates for months in the Puzzle, largely because Janice had before her and her regulars wanted their supply kept up. For a cut she would make sure they didn't go short now.

Clara wanted to know why she was doing all this for her. 'Call it soft-hearted,' she said.

Clara knew now that it was because she didn't like her chances and, being Janice, she couldn't think of anything else to do. That was the evening that Clara took the *Homeopathic Vade Mecum* with her and read up the symptoms of tuberculosis, though she had trouble finding it because it was listed under Phthisis Pulmonalis. She had an idea Doctor Mawson wouldn't approve of her reference source but she kept seeing words on the page with which she identified. Thirst, plenty of that, she could outdrink any bloke these days; heightened temperature, but it was summer at the time; then she got onto the blood-streaked sputa and she knew that that was what the supervisor had seen that morning, and she couldn't fool herself any longer.

She got out the name of the doctor that he had written down for her and studied it. She decided that the following morning she would make an appointment.

But it was a wet day, a sticky Auckland day, thick as a vat of chocolate, one of those close humid days with the rain pouring down, just like it was today, only hot. She ran a temperature and slept till round four. When she woke the rain had stopped and a cool clean breeze was eddying in through the window. She felt better than she had done in months, now that she was prepared to admit she hadn't been feeling well. It seemed clear to her then that all she needed was rest. She was buoyant as she dressed, and she walked up to the village in Parnell to get a meal. There was a little dining room where you could get a roast dinner for two-and-threepence.

It was only afterwards that she felt uneasy. In spite of the generous pay-off from the factory there wasn't an inexhaustible supply of two-and-threepences. She cheered herself with the thought that at the rate she was going she would soon be back at work.

On the way back to Paddy's Puzzle she felt so faint she had to hang on to a paling fence, and when she got inside she brought up more phlegm. She decided then that she would have to be more organised about her rest and get some of the girls to shop for her for a week or two.

That night Janice brought her Ambrose. Clara told her afterwards that she was afraid, and it was true. He looked as if he could not bear the sight of her white face and got up to turn out the light. That made her angry and she tried to stop him coming in again, but he did and they stormed their way through their love-making, a mutual and terrible anger about themselves; for him, she thought, the matter of blackness and whiteness; for her, her illness. When this battering was over, they were calm and quiet for a long while, then he put on the light again, so that they could study each other. She wept then, and he traced the tears on her face with his finger, as if they were comment enough for both of them.

In the morning he stayed with her. He was her protector after that, and they treated each other gently in the dark. She took no money from him, nor from anyone else. That was good fortune. She could easily have done so, and unlike Winnie and her Albie, she didn't claim to be better than those who had fallen from the paths they claimed were righteous. There had been a number of times when she had to admit that it would have been easier than keeping all the complicated deals she and Janice and the others had on the go. Some called it black market. She shied away from that but if she was honest that was its name. Not to admit it was as bad as slinging off at Winnie.

For a while, after she met Ambrose, she really did seem to be better. They went out a lot, exploring Auckland like children together, as if she was a newcomer to the place. In a way she was.

They rode the ferryboats round and they went to the zoo. When she got tired walking up the hills he would make her watch her feet, because that way the ground looked as if it was flat. At first she didn't believe him but when she tried it was true and thinking she was walking on flat ground made her forget she was tired.

Sometimes when he could get a stretch of leave they would stay in for days at a time, or she would, for he would venture out to get food and drink, and then they would talk and make love and sleep when it suited them, day and night sometimes turning into each other without them noticing.

On other days they walked in the Domain and took picnics. Ambrose developed the same passion for roses that Clara had, and the Rose Gardens were so splendid that they could indulge themselves to their hearts' content. She remembered Mumma's cool cage of cyclamens, but because she was in love with the world she turned hungrily to the fat voluptuousness of the roses. She had been brought up with the clean scent of leaves and earth, and frosty petalled flowers; now she wanted them sensual and overstated, not icy and detached like Mumma's.

Sometimes as they walked back down Cleveland Road from the Gardens, the toffee-nosed people who lived in the nice houses at the top end of the road would stare at them over their gates with hostile eyes, worse at her than at Ambrose. They wouldn't put their trash out in the same can. The thought intrigued her. The war would make a lot of difference to the people who survived it. The whole way they talked would change. She wondered whether people would talk about rubbish tins still in ten years time, or whether they would say trash, like she did. And dates. Maybe everyone would go on dates like the girls who were going with the marines did. Perhaps Paddy's Puzzle would have a janitor — that was a laugh — and maybe pigs would fly. She was changed. It must show. The people in Cleveland Road knew she had changed, even though they had not known her before she walked past their gates.

Ambrose was sent away and she thought she would never see him again. For days she imagined she would die of longing for him, and then she resigned herself. She might still have been saved from herself, might have turned back towards home and a chance to get better — if such a possibility still existed — but they brought him back. The expected push into the Pacific had not begun. He need not have come back to her. She would not have known of his

185

return unless he chose to tell her. But he did, and after that there was no turning back.

She didn't know why he loved her, although it seemed that he must. It was clear to her that a white woman could not tell a black man's story, any more than he could tell hers. In time he might have difficulty in recalling it himself. She didn't know what he had to go back to, because he didn't tell her what it was like, and she suspected that even if he had, she would not have recognised it through his eyes. But at least it was somewhere. If he got back. If the war didn't get him. Whatever it was, it might not include the memory of her for very long. Whereas in the clear light of each day that remained, she would know him.

For she had an advantage. She would never forget Ambrose. In finding a love so improbable, so certain to end, she had satisfied her own requirements and those of anyone who might be interested in what became of her, of a last and ultimate love. She would not have to experience love wearing out.

It is still raining over Paddy's Puzzle. Outside, the gutters are overflowing with water and an accumulation of garbage.

Janice's voice is in the stairwell. Clara has not expected her today.

CHAPTER TWELVE

'There's a stink out there,' says Janice as she rushes in. She has rain in her hair and water drips from her mackintosh.

'There's always a stink around here,' replies Clara. 'You must have forgotten.'

Janice dumps a small carton on the table. 'A few extras.'

'Extras? You mean goods?'

'Yes.' Her back is turned to Clara, as she unloads chocolate, laying it out for inspection. She shakes her blonde hair like a dog drying itself.

'I can't have that stuff here. Not now.'

'Oh for Chrissake Clara,' she snaps. 'You can't always have things when you want them.'

'Then you'd better take them back,' she says flatly.

'All right then.' She starts scooping the chocolate back in the carton.

'Janice, what's the matter?'

She keeps on with what she is doing. Keeping on and on and when she has finished, rearranging the packets in meaningless patterns. 'I'll be going along then,' she says, and picks up the carton.

'Janice, please tell me what's wrong.' Clara is overwhelmed with panic.

Janice stands as if deciding whether to go or not but when she turns back to her, Clara sees that she has been going to stay all the time. Her face is haggard and there are deep lines around her mouth. The skin on her neck is like crepe. The rush and bustle has drained away. She puts the carton down again. It is like one of those games of drop the parcel that children play at birthday parties.

'It's Ron,' she says, in a hard strained voice. 'He's gone.'

187

'Gone? Back to the war?' She feels her own lurch of fear. They are on the move again.

But then she says no, that it isn't it.

'Then what? He can't just go.' Which is true. It is not exactly one of those situations where you can up and say, 'I'm going for a holiday,' or, 'See you next week, I'm doing a business trip.'

'They've sent him down south. To McKay's Crossing near Wellington.'

'Janice.' They stare at each other. 'I'm sorry,' Clara says, and knows how weak it sounds. 'Honestly. I really am. How come it was so sudden?'

'It wasn't. He knew.'

Clara looks at her and knows that she isn't lying or imagining it. However she has come by this information, it is true.

'I was to have met him last night outside the library. He told me to wait there because I could keep warm if he was late. I waited, and I looked at all those books of paintings, you know, like we looked at before. And he didn't come, and he didn't. I found out, I know someone who knows someone else . . . Ron didn't think I'd be able to find out. He went yesterday morning. Known for three weeks. Before he met me.'

'He could have told you.'

'Yes. He could have.' She bows her head. Clara thinks then that it will always be like this for Janice. She will always arrive with hope and leave empty. She will walk around in the dark sucking on a cigarette like a drink through a straw, seeing through windows, seeing the lights. All those houses, all those lights. She will try the doors and someone will open one for her and let her in. Then, when the party is over, they will turn her out. Nobody ever asks her to stay on. And it isn't fair because she deserves more and gets less than anybody else she can think of.

She wonders why women bow their heads like that when they are having things taken away from them. She wonders why they don't fight.

'Well, he didn't, did he?' she says and shakes herself. 'I wanted to tell you. That's all. I wanted to tell someone. It's all right, you don't have to do anything. There isn't anything to do, is there?'

'He might come back.'

'He needn't bother.'

'But I thought . . . . '

'When the flame goes out, boy, it goes right off at the gas meter

188

for this lady,' she says. She tries a smile and it nearly works. But she looks weary as she stands up.

'Leave the stuff,' says Clara. 'I'll put it in a suitcase in the wardrobe. She won't think of looking in there.'

'You sure? It was just an excuse to come over really.'

'Yes, of course I'm sure. Go on, you can't go carrying it back over there.'

As they stuff it in the suitcase Clara tells her about Winnie. Janice says that Ambrose had been in the day before to see if the coast was clear.

'He's all right then?'

'Of course he's all right. Why shouldn't he be?'

Until that moment Clara has not been consciously aware of being worried about him but now that she knows he is safe she realises that since the moment when he disappeared into the alleys and byways of dark Paddy's Puzzle, the night before last, she has been afraid. But she does not say this to Janice. Instead, she says,

'He was a bit hopeful. She only came yesterday.'

'Of course he's hopeful. I expect he'll be back this afternoon.' She sounds envious and Clara wishes that there could be some other way of letting him know, but only to spare Janice, not because her envy holds malice.

'I don't think she'll go today,' says Clara.

'D'you mind?'

'It was good to see her. But I've had enough. I'd rather Ambrose was here.'

'He's really keen to see you. Like, extra. Well that's what I thought.'

'He'll just have to wait. Do him good.'

'Some people don't know when they're lucky.'

'Don't they?' For a moment there is hostility in the look they exchange, but as if on signal, they shrug it off.

'Life's a bitch,' says Janice.

'Janice.'

'Yes?' She stands at the door, the damp hair clinging to her head like a skullcap, the green-grey eyes sombre.

'There'll be someone else.' She feels silly the moment she says it. Janice looks at her pityingly.

'I don't believe in miracles, you know.' She shuts the door behind her, leaving Clara sitting there, watching the rain and wishing it would stop, even though she doesn't have to go out in it.

189

She thinks about Janice and what she said to her, and knows that it is true and not true at the same time. There will be someone else, like at the imaginary party in the lighted house. That isn't the problem. It is the matter of them staying with her, or worse, allowing her to stay with them.

She wonders why she has been let off, and thinks about Janice saying she was lucky. She had regretted saying that, yet in a way, Clara agrees that she is the one who has got off more lightly in the matter of luck. No one could say Janice has much of it.

Like Mumma or Winnie or her niece Jeannie. Now there was one who wasn't going to have much luck. You could pick it a mile off.

Janice hasn't been gone ten minutes when there is another sharp rap at the door. It opens before she can get to it so she knows immediately it is Ambrose. It's crazy but she is overcome with relief at the sight of him. Now there can be no doubt that he is safe. He is here in the flesh when he is least supposed to be and she wants to cry with happiness.

'What the hell are you doing here?' she snarls.

He backs off, even though he hasn't touched her yet.

'Janice said she wasn't here. I met her outside the factory.'

He is wet too, only the rain nests in drops in his wiry hair.

'Winnie could come back any minute.'

'Yo' sure as hell still her little sister ain't you?' His voice is deliberately heavy and mocking.

'Piss off,' she screams. 'Goddam you Ambrose, I can't take much more of you. None of you give a goddam about what happens to me.'

He stands looking at her, a sullen mutiny in his eyes. She begins to cry, afraid that he will walk out the door and she doesn't have the strength to ask him to stay. It is not just pride, it is worse than that. It is giving up, like Janice.

If he goes, I really will die, she thinks. It will be easy. She need only stop breathing. She has thought about it often enough. No more effort. Just stop.

He puts his arms around her and says, 'Don't you think that no more.' His wet face is against hers and she reaches to brush it dry and sees that it is tears too, not just the rain.

'You don't know what I was thinking?' she says.

'Yes ma'am. I know what you thinking.'

'I love you. Ambrose, I love you so much.'

190

'I know. Hush little girl, hush. You don't need to tell me.'

'You're my black man. You keep off the spirits.'

'Yes, yes, Lordy, Lordy.'

'You're my love. I've got no other.'

'Yu-uss Lordy.'

'You're my bullshit artist. The biggest in the world.'

'Oh yu-uss Lordy.' Sending himself so far up the line and her with him. The images overlap. She has not had time to learn any new language for her loving, will never have time now, yet it is serviceable in its way. She is shy because it is not original, has been said so many times before, but it is he who makes it funny for both of them when they run short of the right words; and it in no way disgraces what they are trying to say.

'It doesn't matter if she finds you here Ambrose. I don't care. You're more important than she is. Than anyone.'

'I know. But you listen to me. I don't want her to find me here.'

'You're not getting scared of her too, are you?'

'I'm not scared of her Clara baby. No, it takes more than a honky lady to make me scared.'

She believes him. She has seen him when he is afraid. But he hasn't been scared, which is different.

'Come on, sit down.' They sit on the edge of the bed, awkward, because usually they would have wrapped their arms around each other but he is trying to fasten all her attention on what he wants to say and he has one eye on the door at the same time. 'I had to see you,' he says.

'Janice said. She came in here, just a few minutes ago.'

'I know.'

'Yes, of course you do. I forget. I'm so muddled this morning. She brought me more stuff. I haven't got time to sell it this morning though.'

'I brought you this.' He puts some tea and a half-bottle of brandy on the bed.

'More! I'll have to put it away.'

'You need tea, all you drink.'

'I get such a dry mouth. Shall I make some now?'

'No. Listen. I don't want her to find me here, because she mustn't be angry with you.'

'I don't want that either, but why . . . you teased me about it before? What does it matter really? I thought it did but, you know, she's nothing much to me now. We're different, Winnie and me. I used to think, that's what I'll be like some day, when I was a kid,

that's what I used to think. But I never will be now. Even if ... '
She looks at him. 'Doesn't matter what happens, I'd never be like
Winnie. She's all right but she doesn't know anything. I thought
she did. She's just ... ' She stops once more. She has been going to
say different again, but it is she who is different. 'Ordinary,' she
says. 'She's pretty ordinary is Winnie. Makes no difference really.
I'm glad she came. I'm glad I found out.'

'You're not listening little girl,' he says softly. 'You're talking to
yourself and you ain't listening to me at all.'

She sighs. She suspects she doesn't want to hear what he is going
to say. 'I'm listening. What is it then?' she asks.

He answers her with a question. 'Did she say anything about
you going home with her?'

'Yes,' she says cautiously.

'She guess you sick?'

'Ye-es. But she doesn't know how much.'

'I want you to go with her.'

'Ambrose. No.'

'Please. Please little girl, let her take you with her.'

Fear engulfs her. She sees Janice's wan face again. 'You don't
want me any more?'

'I want you.'

'You don't.' Her voice is rising. 'You got another girl ... ' She
starts to cry hysterically, ashamed of herself because she is sure in
one way that she is talking nonsense, and not knowing what is
happening to them, in another. 'Janice, Janice,' she says over and
again, through snuffling and screeching at him.

'You all right Clara?' Ma Hollis shouts through the door.

'She's all right Missus Hollis,' he calls.

'You sure Clara?' she calls back suspiciously, waiting on her
answer.

'Yes, yes, it's all right Ma. Honest.'

They listen to her retreat, grumbling, back into her room.

'See what you're doing? You'll get everyone going if you're not
careful.'

He waits until she stops crying and wipes her face with his
handkerchief. 'Listen,' he says gently, as before, 'That man of
Janice's, I heard what happened. Very silly man. Vain. Selfish.
Frightened. Easy way out.'

'She loved him,' Clara says.

'She didn't know him too well.'

192

'She still loved him. How d'you know he was like that — those things you said?'

He circles his throat with his fingers and thumb, indicating a clerical collar. 'I've seen men say they love the Lord God. They think, some of them, that they're better than others. That's vain. They fall from the Lord's grace a little because they are like all men, okay?'

'Okay.'

'So they must get back on the right side of the good Lord. Frightened. They will take any easy way they see. They think they will please their good Lord even if they are unkind along the way. That is selfish. I think.'

'Poor Janice,' she says. 'I hope the Lord's pleased with Ron now.'

'The Lord. Pah.' He makes a dismissive disgusted noise. She wonders afresh if he has someone waiting for him at home, and if he has made his own peace. But she does not ask him that. Instead she says, 'But you thought He was okay?'

'The Lord?' He shrugs. 'I thought. Never mind. It doesn't matter.'

'What did you think?'

'Oh. That it makes some kind of diff'rence. When we sing and clap and shout Hallelujah to the Lord on Sunday, then I think it makes some kind of diff'rence to the rest of the week. And it does. It does. If you never know no diff'rent.'

'You do?'

His damson-coloured eyes, protruding slightly. Their gaze rests on her.

'I want you to go with your sister, little girl. Not for any other girl I know . . . '

'Not for one that you could step out pretty with in the streets?'

'No.' He shifts slightly. 'You know that ain't true Clara. Eh?'

'I know. But why then?'

'I ain't supposed to know, but I reckon it's right, what I've heard. The ship's due to sail, maybe next week, maybe two weeks, no longer than that.'

She has known all along that her fears are not misplaced.

'So you see,' he goes on, 'I could go, knowing that you were being looked after real good. I'd sure like that Clara.'

'No.' She says it with such fierceness she surprises herself. This is what it is about then, fighting to keep what you want. How like

193

her, she thinks, that she is prepared at last to fight an impossible enemy outside and beyond her, when her will, however strong, cannot change things.

'Please.'

'No.'

'For me.' She has forgotten, temporarily, that he is asking her to go with Winnie; all her energy is concentrated on stopping his ship from sailing. She stares at him dumbly. It is one and the same thing.

'No, Ambrose.'

He shakes his head as if trying to clear some pain out of it and puts his hands up to hold it, or to extract the pain.

Watching him, she says, 'I'll tell you what. I'll go to her when the ship's sailed.'

He drops his hands then and looks at her carefully. His eyes light up with hope. But he says, 'How could I be sure that you'd do that?'

'Because . . . because, you'll help me pack my bag,' she says, her mind racing ahead of her story. And anyway, she thinks it's true, she thinks that this is what she will do, even as they talk about it she sees that it is the right thing; it is no good going on about Janice if she isn't prepared to do something for herself; already she knows she will lose him, so she must make the best of what is left, yes, already she has decided. 'We'll turn the key in together the day that you go . . . and then, then, I'll come down to the ship and see you off. It's so nearly spring, and I haven't seen the sea for so long . . . it'll be something to help me over your leaving.'

'You'd stand out in the cold for too long. I know you, little girl.'

'All right,' she says. 'To please you, I'd let you see me, the last thing, turn away with my suitcase, and you knowing that I was on my way to Winnie's.'

She sees that he believes her. His face is alight with pleasure and she is happy just to have pleased him so much.

'We-ell, if you mean it.'

'I'll tell Winnie when she comes back that I've been thinking it over and I'll be leaving here within the next two weeks. I'll tell her I'll come . . . let's see, as soon as my rent is up. That sounds okay doesn't it?'

'Yes. Very okay,' he says. 'You see that you do that eh?' He gets up, stretching himself, his urgency gone.

What happens next is like the movies. She can see, again, that old Chico and Groucho and Harpo and all would get a real kick

194

out of them. But then, as far as she is concerned, her life has always been a bit like a movie set. She has thought it dull but today it seems a bit of a laugh. That's if you didn't just break up crying.

Janice flaps in again with her eyes like saucers. She doesn't knock, she bangs in as if she is coming through the door. That's one thing that can be said about Paddy's Puzzle though, the doors are solid. When old Paddy Gleeson built the place he put in doors to ward off invaders. It is not easy for the uninvited to get through his doors.

As soon as she steps in she sees the brandy and tea on the bed beside Clara and scoops it up in chocolatey hands. She hasn't even washed before leaving the factory.

'That sister of yours, she's coming down the street. I took off without a by-your-leave and ran all the way.'

'Where is she now?' Clara asks. But she knows, they all know, in that instant. Winnie's footsteps are in the passage. Beneath the window the children sing to the tune of Santa Lucia, 'Arseholes are cheap today/cheaper than yesterday/little boys are half a crown/standing up or bending down.' The voices are thin and sweet; Clara sees that it has stopped raining.

'I dunno. I ran right past her.' Janice's words are plucked from the air and fluttering in her throat.

'Quick . . . Ambrose . . . the stuff . . . you . . . '

'Too late,' moans Janice. 'She's here.'

'Take it Ambrose,' Clara says, shoving the tea in his hands and pushing him into the bathroom. The brandy is still on the bed. She slams the door on him as Winnie bangs at the other door. Doors. In one, out the other, everybody right on cue. She had always loved the flicks, all right.

Winnie walks in past Janice and Clara, her face very shiny and pink, just like it used to be when she was young. She has a dreadful smell clinging to her. She appears to notice it herself as she walks in. The other two look at her feet and one foot has slopped through vomit. It could have been anybody's. Clara thinks of the drunk and now dead captain from a couple of nights ago. Would it have been allowed to lie that long? It occurs to her that this is a reflection of how they live here, that it could have lain a night or two nights and they are all used to it, used to every kind of crap and pollution. She feels ashamed.

'Hello Winnie,' she says. 'You're back early.'

'Yes.' She keeps looking at her shoe. 'Stick it outside. We can hose it down afterwards. You brought some spares, didn't you?'

'They're wet,' she says, and she looks as if she might cry if she let herself, but she isn't going to give in to anybody, especially them. She unlaces her shoes and kicks them outside though and Janice and Clara breathe a sigh of relief as the smell disappears.

'Why are you so early?' Clara knows she is betraying her anxiety but she can't help herself.

She looks at her coldly. 'I couldn't see the man I was supposed to and I didn't want to hang around in the wet. I'm to go back later this afternoon.'

Janice has been sitting on the bed trying to look demure. Clara says: 'This is my friend Janice. She works with me at the factory. My sister, Winnie Hoggard, you know the one I told you about, Janice.'

'How d'you do, Janice,' says Winnie, still in the same cold haughty tone. 'The chocolate factory I take it.' She sniffs the air. The smell of chocolate prevails now, emanating from Janice.

'It's the one next door to Clara's,' says Janice, a shade too quickly. Clara can see that she is terrified of Winnie and for a moment it makes her feel good. At least she isn't the only one.

Winnie goes back to the sink and starts washing her hands, cleaning off the filth from her shoes. 'Oh stop your lies,' she says. 'You've never worked in munitions in your life, Clara.'

'What's it matter what sort of factory it is?' says Janice. She is a bit like a defiant schoolgirl, but she is recovering herself. Clara can see there might be blood on the floor if she and Winnie are let loose at each other. A bit like rats in the drum. 'It's industry,' says Janice.

'Winnie,' Clara says, racking her brains as to how to pacify her and conscious of Ambrose holed up in the bathroom. 'Janice is a good sort. Seeing I was sick she brought over a few things. She brought some stuff over for you to take home to the kids too. I'll bet Jeannie and Caroline haven't seen a whole cake of chocolate in years.'

'They won't either.' Her lips are thin. 'They're stolen goods.'

'We're entitled to a few bits, working there,' says Clara.

'If you worked there. But that's not even true is it Clara, as far as you're concerned?'

'Winnie, you're tying me up in knots.'

The onslaught begins. Throughout it she thinks, dully, that it serves her right. It serves her right for killing her sister's husband. That's what it comes down to.

Winnie's voice is loud and very strong. 'It's nice, isn't it,' she is saying, 'that everyone in . . . in Paddy's Puzzle or whatever this dump is called, has access to your black market tricks. People like you . . . my husband was killed for your sort . . . oh my God.'

They look at each other, and Clara thinks, she knows. She must know.

'Who told you?' she asks, and she is not certain what she is asking her about.

'Oh I didn't need to ask around. Your friends volunteered for you. Your Mrs Hollis across the hall, she said she hoped I'd found the stretcher comfortable. Well I said you'd slept on it, and she said that's what she'd have expected of you, oh you really are a saint, Clara. And how good it was getting extra cocoa this week . . . give and take I think she called it.'

She wipes her hand on a tea towel, looking at it with distaste as she does so. Oh such lily-white hands Winnie, thinks Clara.

'Mrs Hoggard, you don't understand,' says Janice.

'Oh yes. I understand all right. You're a bright pair, aren't you?'

Clara thinks of Albie Tubbs and considers mentioning the subject. Instead they glare at each other.

She moves towards the bathroom door. 'Winnie, where d'you think you're going?' Clara asks, trying to sound as she had the night before, like it really is her place and she can tell Winnie what to do.

'Don't you know?' She pauses with her hand on the doorknob. 'I'm picking up my belongings and getting out of here.'

It is worth one last effort. Clara says, 'We're out of tea. Why don't you go and get us some at the corner shop. Look, it's sunny out there now, and I'll lend you some of my shoes. I'd forgotten we take the same size, had you? We could have a cup of tea and we could talk. I've got some coupons, I'll get them for you.'

'There's plenty of tea. There's more here than I've seen since the war started. I must be thick not to have picked it.' She is turning the door handle.

'You can't go in there.'

'Oh just try and stop me.'

Then she starts to scream. She goes on screaming for quite a long time and Ma Hollis starts beating at the door again. Clara opens it to her, and beneath the noise she hears Ma saying, 'I'm sorry Clara, I'm sorry,' and the smell of her puha cooking with fish heads is pungent and sour, wafting in with all the other smells of Paddy's Puzzle before Clara shuts the door once more. As

Winnie's noise dies down they hear the persistent shuffle of her slippers in the passage way, moving up and down, and then Biddy's voice, and others, join in. They move away and it is quiet outside again. There are just Janice and Winnie and Ambrose and Clara looking at each other.

Ambrose moves gently towards Winnie. 'Take it eea-sy lady, I won't hurt you,' he murmurs.

'Please Win, I can explain everything.'

'Don't bother.' She tears at her suitcase now, pulling Clara's with it from where she had pushed it in her haste before. It falls open, spilling chocolate over the floor. Winnie's face contorts. 'You slut, you evil little bitch. You.' She gathers herself together. 'You prostitute.'

Just like Mrs Mawson. Only the words are slightly different. Funny that.

Ambrose just keeps on looking at her. Clara sees him from out of the corner of her eye. She doesn't look at Winnie.

Ma Hollis listens with her ear to her door. She is troubled and sorry. She has not meant to hurt Clara. When the door across the passage way slams she hesitates briefly then turns and lumbers to the stove. The gas fizzles and splutters out; the pot of glutinous food rolls off the boil as she pushes it to one side. Then she makes her way down the stairs and out onto the street as quickly as her thick and painful ankles will allow.

Winnie's step has been brisk as she left the flat but now, outside, she is uncertain. Clearly she will have to walk if she is to get away from the Puzzle without any further loss to her dignity, and walk as if she knows where she is going. But her sense of direction has been disturbed. From where she stands in the gully, the hilly streets loom up on either side of her, and it is raining lightly again.

Ma Hollis hobbles up alongside her.

'You going then, Mrs Hoggard?' she says. 'I thought you were staying another night.'

'Excuse me,' says Winnie, going to move past her.

'Is there something wrong.'

'If you don't mind, I'd like to get past.'

'Something I said?'

Winnie tries to push her aside which is not the kind of thing you do to Ma Hollis. She grabs Winnie's arm. 'Oh no you don't,' she says.

Winnie is afraid now. 'Please. I just want to get out in the fresh air. That's all. Please.'

'No. No, you're not going anywhere till you've listened to me Mrs La-di-da,' says Ma.

'I've got nothing to say to you,' says Winnie.

Ma drops her arm. 'All right. That's fine. I wouldn't waste my time. We won't none of us bother telling you when she's gone then. Reckon we'll see to her ourselves.' She turns back towards the Puzzle. Winnie waits for a moment, then calls out to her.

'What d'you mean?'

'Doesn't matter.'

'Please.'

They are shouting at each other now, like a couple of fishwives. Heads start to appear at the windows and across the street faces are looking out from the factory as well.

In Clara's room they hear it too. They strain to make out words, but suddenly the voices drop away.

'Keep on walking if that's what you want,' says Ma bitterly to Winnie. 'What's the likes of me got to tell you? So you didn't know how she kept herself? I'll bet she hadn't told you. I can see why too. Nor what was the matter with her. She's got more pride than you think. Not your kind of pride, but you can give me hers any day.'

'Please, what's the matter with my sister?'

Ma Hollis relents then. When Ma takes a shine to someone it's like having a dog that's crazy over you. It only sees the best parts. Ma is like that over Clara. Clara's good and Winnie's bad. Of course it is much more complicated than that, but this is none of Ma's concern. She relents only because Winnie is shaken and near tears, and doesn't now look quite as bad as Ma had seen her in her mind's eye before.

'You been through some bad times too, eh?'

Winnie nods.

'Yes. Most of us have. Easy to forget when things look up. Not that they've done much for me. Except I got Billy. I guess I'm all right. And Clara. Well, she's made a difference. I'll miss her, I can tell you.'

'Miss her?'

'She's not going to get better Missus. Can't you see that?'

'I didn't know,' Winnie whispers. 'I could see she wasn't well, but . . . are you sure?'

'Haven't you ever seen people go with the consumption? T.B. they call it now. Look Missus, we're a rough lot round here but we do for each other. She says she never got round to sorting herself out. I reckon she's got herself sorted out here. She done for us when she could, and now we do for her. That's all.'

Maybe all along Ma knew her better than she knew herself, Clara thinks, hearing it later. She's never known who she is, or what she is, Mumma's or Winnie's, Hamilton or the Junction. Perhaps it is true that now she is, as Ma says, sorted out.

Winnie hasn't had time to think things through like Clara has, though. Later that night she says, 'I still can't understand why you didn't get in touch with us. They might have helped at a sanitorium. They still might.'

'No, not now Winnie. I met Ambrose, and he took care of me. I don't reckon it would have made much difference. I just stayed on.'

'That black man.' Her voice is full of wonder still.

'Yes. That black man.'

'I can't work it out.'

'I knew you wouldn't. But you know, Win, I said to Janice, just the other night, he was for my learning, and it turned out he taught me all I knew. Or ever will now.'

'What about . . . ' Clara knows she is going to say Robin but Winnie sees the look on her face, and says, instead, 'the others?'

'Things always finish. This doesn't.'

'What's he taught you?'

'About love.'

'Love? That's craziness. To talk about love with someone like that, when you could have been getting help. You call that love?' She isn't arguing with her, only with herself.

'Yes Winnie, I reckon it is,' Clara says. 'And I want — this time Win, I want to know all there is to know. All of it.'

After a while Winnie says 'But he says you'll come back to me after he's gone.'

'Yes, I told him that.'

'Well that's something, I suppose. Thank goodness it won't be long. I wish you'd come away with me tomorrow though. You know I've still got hopes.'

Clara doesn't reply.

'He said it would set his mind at rest to know you were with me. He hasn't given up hope. Oh Clara, you mustn't either.'

Hope. She doesn't know what hope is. Well, not what it means to her, anyway.

200

Still later, Winnie says, smiling at herself, 'Would you believe it Clara, I had a proposal of marriage the other day.'

'You did? Who was it?'

'Oh a chap I used to know years ago. You wouldn't remember him. He was a teacher at the Tech. Albie Tubbs his name was.'

'I remember him. Are you going to marry him?'

'Who'd want a name like Mrs Tubbs?'

'It'd be all right. If you liked him. If you loved him.'

She seems amused. 'I reckon I'm a bit old for that.'

'There you are. Nothing stays the same for ever, does it?'

She looks at Clara curiously then and they drop the subject.

Outside the air is fresh and cool. The rain has moved away from the city. Clara hopes the sirens will leave them in peace for another night. A Hudson has droned past but otherwise the dark lies undisturbed. It is all right sitting there with Winnie, but she looks forward to her going in the morning. She needs Ambrose beside her. She has stopped trying to explain to herself or anyone else why she needs him with her.

Sitting here thinking about him, she tries to see him in another place but she can't. This is their place. But of course he will go back to where he came from. As she has told him she will do. But when it comes to the point with her, she wonders. Still, she has promised.

'What are you writing?' asks Winnie idly.

She stalls. 'I was thinking of writing a letter to Mumma,' says Clara, scribbling away.

Winnie brightens. 'She'd like that. I could take it back with me.'

'Would she read it?'

'Oh . . . I don't know,' she admits.

Clara would like to write a letter of love to Mumma. She has often thought of it. Maybe this is as close as she will ever get to it. Besides, the light is failing in Paddy's Puzzle. But then she has been expecting that.

'Win.'

'Yes.'

'Would they throw Mumma's flowers out? Those people?'

'I don't know. Yes. I suppose so. I should have rescued them shouldn't I? The plants?'

They pause. 'I don't expect I would have either,' Clara says at last.

They look blindly at each other across the cold light of the gas flame in Paddy's Puzzle. They think of Mumma, and Clara believes they know at last that they have both inhabited the same warm darkness.

'I wouldn't have had anywhere to put them,' Winnie says.

'No. Neither would I.'

'Has it been all right then Ambrose?'

'It's been all right.'

'Why? What have you got out of it?'

'You ask too many questions.'

'Yes, I know. But what?'

'I got you, Clara Bentley. That's what I got. What about you?'

'Me. Oh, I dunno. A feel for living I guess.'

'You ain't had it before?'

'Mmm. Oh, sometimes maybe. I just never saw all the possibilities before.'

'You seen them now?'

'Oh yes Ambrose. I've seen them near enough.'

She touches the dark plate of his head with her own.

Part Four

WINNIE

CHAPTER THIRTEEN

Jeannie brought Winnie the telegram. There was a late frost and the clouds hadn't lifted. A black frost, as they called it in the Waikato, when the ice lies on the ground all day. It had nipped and blackened the new spring growth. Winnie looked down the garden and thought it would take a while to recover.

She heard the knock at the door, and voices. Then Jeannie came through. She was a spotty girl and although she was always washing her hair it only seemed to get greasier. Winnie guessed she would grow out of it. She loved her so much. But Clara was right, her daughter was going to have a hard time of it.

'The telegram boy said it was bad news Mum,' said Jeannie, frightened.

It was addressed to her, Mrs Winnie Hoggard. She knew before she opened it.

It read, 'Clara died this morning before the ship sailed at noon. It was like a light went out. Ambrose tells you he'll write.' It was signed, Janice.

'She never left,' said Winnie numbly, to no one in particular.

'Left where?' said Jeannie, although Winnie had tried to explain to her some of what happened on her trip to Auckland.

'The Puzzle. She never left Paddy's Puzzle.'

Winnie gave Janice instructions over the phone and arranged to go up the next morning for the funeral. She wondered about putting it in the paper but she couldn't see the point. She rang Miss Cresswell, and then she thought of ringing Robin. She supposed that in time he would have to know but when she had considered it, she decided there was time enough. He might feel he had to do something, go to the funeral, something like that. Or he might be embarrassed about it all. Clara wouldn't have liked that.

Then she had to go and tell Mumma. She and old Mrs Hoggard were playing cards together. Winnie was afraid to tell her. She was so crazy about Clara when she was a little girl, and she had been asking about her lately.

It was strange though. When she did tell her she might not have heard her for all the indication she gave. She and Winnie's mother-in-law went on with their game. 'Did you like dancing?' said Mumma, leaning over and murmuring confidentially to her friend. 'I was very fond of it you know. Very fond.'

Winnie only stayed for the day in Auckland. She didn't like leaving the girls again so soon. It would have been company to take Jeannie but she had exams coming up in a month or so, and she didn't want to take her out of school. She wasn't sure how she could explain Paddy's Puzzle to her either. It seemed better to leave it. In a way she had almost come to terms with the place, for herself, and that was enough. In fact she was almost looking forward to seeing everyone there again. It had been quite a leave-taking the last time she left.

But things had changed, even in ten days. The Puzzle was still there and the smell of chocolate as thick as ever, overwhelming even the worst and vilest stenches in the old rabbit-warren. Janice was tense and anxious and apologised for being in a rush. She had to meet some man called Ron. It was fair enough, she had done more than her share.

As for Ma Hollis, she didn't come to the funeral at all. There had been an accident, though the police were claiming it wasn't. Biddy Chisholm's daughter had been pushed off the top of the Puzzle the night before. They were saying that Billy had pushed her. It was a miracle she wasn't killed, but her head was like pulp and Biddy had been taking on like a banshee ever since. Which was hardly surprising, seeing that the child would never talk properly again and it was said she was dreadfully disfigured.

As for Billy, he just kept shaking his head and laughing and saying that the bloody butcher done it. That's what he had said about the last person to go over the edge too, only it couldn't have been Billy that time. Perhaps it really was an accident, Winnie suggested to Janice before she dashed off. But Janice shook her head bleakly. It would kill Ma if they took Billy away, but you couldn't have a loony like that roaming around. Well could you?

206

In the end there were only six of them at the funeral. Her and Janice; the manager of the chocolate factory; and Charlie Ambler and May Abbott from the Puzzle, May dressed in spotted lavender voile. Winnie and Clara's sister Rita, looking pale and overdressed for the warm day, turned up too. She said Frank was tied up with the calving. And there were the hired pallbearers.

Winnie believed she felt the presence of Ambrose. Perhaps it was just her imagination let loose by his flowers on the coffin, but there was a feeling, someone at her shoulder, a dark and restless shadow. She didn't understand about black men like him, these niggers, and about this one in particular, but she still felt him there.

On the journey back to town she looked out to sea. The Pacific rolled away, darkly blue in the late September sun, and she found herself wondering if Ambrose would make it home. Sooner or later. Clara had seemed sure that he would.

There wasn't much left in her room. Not even a cake of chocolate she could have taken home for the girls. The place had been gone over pretty thoroughly. There were some papers covered with scribble. She nearly left them but then her curiosity got the better of her. They half-filled her big shopping bag.

She walked up to Parnell, sure of her direction this time, and got a tram to the railway station. As she left the Puzzle kids spilled out into the street. An American in uniform was coming towards them and they shrilled, 'Got any souvenirs Yank? Got any gum Yank?'

She thought that she would never go back there again.

In the train she opened her bag and glanced through Clara's papers. She was still trying to read them and sort them into some kind of order when the train pulled into Frankton Junction. Fragments of conversation, letters started and never finished, pieces that seemed to follow on, almost like a diary at times; names written over and over in patterns and variations, Ambrose's written dozens of different ways, then her own and Winnie's, her own and Robin's, her own and Reg's. In this last she supposed that there was some clue to the past, something she had half-guessed and dismissed because it was absurd, or ugly, or both. Someday, when she was stronger, she might confront it. Along with herself. But that was asking too much now. What she did know then, was that she had loved her. She wished she had known so surely when she could have told her but then people are always wishing things like that. Dear Clara. Little sister. In spite of everything. Yes.

As the train rattled south she watched the landscape and the tender greening of the trees beside the wide slow river. On a far bank an old paddle-steamer lay grounded. She thought of her own secret inner life, constrained within her. She thought it might never be released now. Whereas Clara had lived hers out till there was no further to go.

It seemed that her death made more sense and a greater difference than she had believed possible while she was alive.

It was hard to measure the difference though. One evening she was sitting in front of the fire with Caroline. She asked Winnie what her Auntie Clara had really been like. She was, after all, only nine when she had left Hamilton. Winnie said that it was hard to say. 'She was unusual,' she said, but that sounded inadequate, so she added, 'She was named after a film star called Clara Bow. Sometimes I used to think she was a bit like her. I don't know any more.'

'Whose idea was it to call her after a film star?' asked Caroline.

'Mine,' she said, surprised at herself. 'Yes, it was my idea.'